Praise for *The Art of Deception*

"Lets the reader imagine what it would be like if there was another generation of Holmes to set wrongs right."
—*Mystery Scene*

"The novel is written well, the plot intricate, and the solution is not obvious. Fans of Laurie R. King and Charles Finch will find this series a solid TBR (To Be Read)." —*MysteryTribune*

"[A] most entertaining volume, featuring a complicated mystery, a clear knowledge of history, and an undeniable sense of adventure." —*Green Man Review*

Praise for
The Disappearance of Alistair Ainsworth

"Fans of all things Sherlockian will delight in Joanna, so like her father and already training her schoolboy son, Johnny, in the methods that have solved so many cases like this exceptionally tricky one." —*Kirkus Reviews*

"Fans of the original mysteries will get a chuckle out of the antic language, and there is a mercurial Mary Poppins appeal to this not-to-be-trifled-with heroine that will appeal to fans beyond Baker Street." —*Booklist*

"Suspenseful and entertaining, with many twists and turns. . . . This is one of the best Sherlock Holmes series since Laurie R. King's Mary Russell books." —Historical Novel Society

Praise for *A Study in Treason*

"Goldberg matches the style of Conan Doyle's stories and adds the fillip of a female protagonist." —*Kirkus Reviews*

"Avid Sherlockians will be delighted with the many echoes of the original Holmes canon." —*Publishers Weekly*

"There is plenty of pleasure to be found here for lovers of Holmes pastiches." —*Booklist*

"The plot is quick-paced and is sprinkled with unforeseen clues that enhance the overall story. Leonard Goldberg is a great writer and brings to life the legend of Sherlock Holmes." —*RT Book Reviews* (4 stars)

"An extraordinarily entertaining mystery. This is a gift to the fans of Sherlock Holmes." —*The Washington BookReview*

Praise for
The Daughter of Sherlock Holmes

"Fans of Sherlock Holmes will be thrilled to meet his fearless and brilliant daughter, Joanna. Once again the game's afoot, and a new Holmes and Watson unite to solve the unsolvable in this delightful adventure by Leonard Goldberg."

—Tess Gerritsen, *New York Times* bestselling author of *I Know a Secret*

"Cleverly crafted with fascinating characters and a plot that Conan Doyle would be proud of. Sherlock fans looking for a new series need look no further than Goldberg's well-developed and fascinating tale!"

—M. J. Rose, *New York Times* bestselling author

"Adventure, murder, family secrets, and intrigue are abound in this novel, which has incredible characters who are charming, cunning, and smart as a whip. Goldberg has successfully intertwined historical facts with fiction, and has created a must-read novel for fans of historical mystery and of Sherlock Holmes." —*RT Book Reviews*

THE ART OF DECEPTION

A Daughter of Sherlock Holmes Mystery

Leonard Goldberg

MINOTAUR
BOOKS
NEW YORK

Published in the United States by Minotaur Books, an imprint of
St. Martin's Publishing Group

THE ART OF DECEPTION. Copyright © 2020 by Leonard Goldberg.
All rights reserved. Printed in the United States of America.
For information, address St. Martin's Publishing Group,
120 Broadway, New York, NY 10271.

www.minotaurbooks.com

Designed by Omar Chapa

The Library of Congress has cataloged the hardcover edition as follows:

Names: Goldberg, Leonard S., author.
Title: The art of deception : a daughter of Sherlock Holmes
    mystery / Leonard Goldberg.
Description: First edition. | New York : Minotaur Books, 2020. |
Series: The daughter of Sherlock Holmes mysteries ; 4
Identifiers: LCCN 2020001300 | ISBN 9781250224200
    (hardcover) | ISBN 9781250224217 (ebook)
Subjects: GSAFD: Mystery fiction.
Classification: LCC PS3557.O35775 A78 2020 |
    DDC 813/.54—dc23
LC record available at https://lccn.loc.gov/2020001300

ISBN 978-1-250-26981-2 (trade paperback)

Our books may be purchased in bulk for promotional, educational,
or business use. Please contact your local bookseller or the Macmillan
Corporate and Premium Sales Department at 1-800-221-7945, extension
5442, or by email at MacmillanSpecialMarkets@macmillan.com.

First Minotaur Books Trade Paperback Edition: 2021

10 9 8 7 6 5 4 3 2 1

In memory of I.M. and Sheran

Each morn a thousand roses brings.
—"THE RUBAIYAT," OMAR KHAYYAM

Contents

1. The Vandal 1
2. Hawke and Evans 13
3. Felix Dubose 33
4. Johnny 41
5. Albert Dubose 52
6. The Art Historian 58
7. Cholera 69
8. The Countess 78
9. Strange Symptoms 87
10. The Rumor 95
11. The Lockpicks 102
12. Delvecchio 111
13. Scotland Yard 121
14. Wormwood Scrubs 127
15. Two Vandals 137
16. The Exhumation 147
17. The Stewart Gallery 156
18. The Hiding Place 167

19. Dubious Identification ⎯⎯⎯⎯⎯⎯⎯⎯ 183
20. An Unexpected Visitor ⎯⎯⎯⎯⎯⎯⎯⎯ 202
21. A Near Miss ⎯⎯⎯⎯⎯⎯⎯⎯⎯⎯⎯⎯⎯ 216
22. The Wife ⎯⎯⎯⎯⎯⎯⎯⎯⎯⎯⎯⎯⎯⎯ 223
23. An Unseemly Source ⎯⎯⎯⎯⎯⎯⎯⎯⎯ 238
24. A Violent Break-In ⎯⎯⎯⎯⎯⎯⎯⎯⎯⎯ 255
25. Setting a Trap ⎯⎯⎯⎯⎯⎯⎯⎯⎯⎯⎯⎯ 272
26. The National Gallery ⎯⎯⎯⎯⎯⎯⎯⎯⎯ 286
27. The Masterpiece ⎯⎯⎯⎯⎯⎯⎯⎯⎯⎯⎯ 292
28. All the Evidence ⎯⎯⎯⎯⎯⎯⎯⎯⎯⎯⎯ 297

Closure ⎯⎯⎯⎯⎯⎯⎯⎯⎯⎯⎯⎯⎯⎯⎯⎯ 303
Acknowledgments ⎯⎯⎯⎯⎯⎯⎯⎯⎯⎯⎯ 307

What has been done will be done again;

There is nothing new under the sun.

—ECCLESIASTES 1:9

1

The Vandal

December 1916

It was ten days before Christmas when Inspector Lestrade called at 221b Baker Street to wish us, I assumed, the compliments of the season. But I was wholly mistaken, for he brought with him a most difficult case which defied resolution. Little did we realize that the aforementioned crime would produce tentacles which would reach into the darkest of secrets.

Prior to laying out the details of the case, Lestrade warmed his hands before a crackling fire, for a sharp frost had set in and the windows were thick with ice crystals. Only then did he take a long, deep breath as if readying himself for a problematic task. "What appeared to be trivial vandalism has now blossomed into widespread destruction of valuable art throughout the West End of London. These senseless acts have been perpetrated in exclusive galleries and always at night when there were no witnesses to be found. But there are other features which make this business entirely unique."

"Inspector, one must be careful in applying the term *unique* to a given crime, no matter how outlandish it may seem," said my wife, Joanna, who was standing at the window watching snow fall and dust the pavement below. "If you carefully observe any criminal activity, regardless of how exceptional it may appear, you will discover it has been committed before and in most instances solved."

"Even those which resemble the Gordian knot?"

"Particularly those," Joanna replied. "For by definition, the Gordian knot presents an intractable problem, yet it can readily be solved by creative thinking."

"Which is why I have intruded on this most pleasant of holidays," said Lestrade. "But I am afraid this is one knot which even you and the Watsons will have difficulty untangling."

"We shall see." Joanna stepped over to an inlaid shelf that held a Persian slipper which once belonged to her father. It was in the toe of this slipper that Sherlock Holmes kept his supply of rough-cut shag tobacco. Joanna reached in for a well-rolled Turkish cigarette and carefully lighted it with a strike-anywhere match.

"Holmes used the slipper to maintain the freshness of his tobacco," my father reminisced.

"I employ it for the same purpose," said Joanna and started to pace the floor of our parlor, leaving a trail of smoke behind. "And now, Lestrade, if you would be so kind, please describe the details of the crime which brings you out on this frosty morning. Commence with the initial, trivial act."

"But I would think that destruction of the most valuable works of art would be more revealing," Lestrade argued mildly. "For it is here that the vandal seems to concentrate his activities."

"No, no," Joanna insisted. "We must begin at the very beginning of this tangled web if we hope to untangle it."

"Very well, then," Lestrade commenced. "Some ten days ago the perpetrator broke into a pricey gallery in Kensington and proceeded to slash the painting of a handsome woman from the late Renaissance period. The work of art had already been seriously damaged by time and weather, and thus was not considered to be of great value."

"Was it a single cut?" asked Joanna.

"So it would appear," Lestrade replied. "But after slashing, the vandal ripped the painting apart, ruining it completely."

My father and I quickly exchanged knowing glances, for this case seemed similar to one which had occurred years earlier and involved a crazed perpetrator who was apprehended and was currently residing in an institution for the mentally ill.

"Inspector," I interrupted, "your case resembles that of the insane art vandal of some years back."

"So I believed initially," Lestrade went on. "But there are now additional features which suggest otherwise."

"Such as?" I inquired.

"This vandal has now broken into several upper-class homes, only to deface and not steal the works of art."

"How many homes?" Joanna asked at once.

"Two," Lestrade answered. "One of which is the residence of the Earl of Wessex."

Joanna's brow went up. "The Earl of Wessex? The fifth in line of succession to the Crown?"

"The same."

The Crown! Just the mention of it raised the investigation to another level. Lestrade now had our undivided attention and every detail would be pored over with the utmost scrutiny. Joanna abruptly stopped pacing and came over to join us at the warming, three-log fire. "Is the earl in any way connected to the art galleries which have been despoiled?"

"He purchased a painting at Hawke and Evans a week before his home was broken into," Lestrade replied. "This very gallery has been invaded twice by our vandal."

"And the name of the second home you mentioned?"

"An elegant house on Bayswater near Hyde Park that belongs to Mr. Felix Dubose, a well-known jeweler who has stores throughout London."

"Does he have any relationship to the Crown?"

"None whatsoever."

"Or to any of the involved galleries?"

"Again none. The painting in the Dubose home was a gift from his brother who purchased it at a gallery in Paris. The brother personally carried it back to England as a surprise anniversary present."

Joanna said ever so slowly, "That complicates matters."

"Indeed."

Joanna began to pace once more, with her head sunk upon her chest and her hands clasped behind her. It was a sign that her brain was shifting into yet a higher gear. Back and forth she went, trying to connect the pieces of the ill-defined puzzle, but with no apparent success. She stopped briefly to tap on the window which caused some of the ice crystals to fall off, then extinguished her cigarette before coming back to the inspector. "What was the nature of the paintings which were defaced?"

"They were all portraits of women, some young, some old," Lestrade answered. "Most were done by Italian artists from the Renaissance period, a few by French painters named Renoir and Cézanne. I could make no connection between them, nor could the experts at the art galleries. So at this point, all we can say is that the vandal disliked women and went out of his way to deface any of their depictions."

"Hmm," Joanna hummed, obviously not impressed with the inspector's conclusion. "Was there evidence of forced entry at the crime scenes?"

"We inspected the front and rear entrances to the galleries and homes, and found no such indication," Lestrade replied.

"Then, how did the vandal gain entrance?"

"That is to be determined."

"That *must* be determined, for therein may lie a most important key to the crime." Joanna wrinkled her brow, concentrating on the information at hand. She nodded at one thought and shook her head at another, as if one piece of data fit while another did not. Several minutes passed before she spoke again. "I take it no clues were discovered."

"Only a tattered scarf," Lestrade said and reached into his topcoat for a wrapped package. He carefully removed the wrapping to expose a soiled, old scarf which he held out like it was contaminated. "This garment, which we believe belonged to the perpetrator, was found at the scene of the latest act of vandalism."

Joanna asked, "Are you of the opinion that it was left behind unintentionally?"

"So the evidence would suggest," Lestrade responded. "The vandal was going about his work when a security guard on his rounds opened the door to the restoration section of the gallery. The vandal became alarmed and bolted, knocking the guard to the floor in the process. On his way out, the scarf became snagged on a door chain and the vandal, in his hurry, did not stop to retrieve it."

"Was the security guard able to describe the vandal?" Joanna inquired.

"Unfortunately not," Lestrade replied. "The restoration area was quite dim, for the lights were off, and all the guard could see was an ill-defined shadow moving in the darkness."

"Did the security guard give chase?"

"Only after gathering himself, for the fall landed him in a stack of standing paintings and unfinished canvases. By then, the vandal had made good his escape." Lestrade moved the scarf closer to the light of the fire to give us a better view. "As you can see, it is old and worn and appears to contain no worthwhile clues. Nevertheless, I shall show it to one of my sergeants who is quite good at tracking down the source of a given item of clothing."

"An excellent idea," said Joanna. "But it is not the source of the scarf which is important here. Rather, it is the features of the man who wore it."

"Unfortunately there are no clues pointing to its owner." Lestrade raised the scarf even higher and allowed it to unfold itself. "As you will note, there are no tags or written names or initials on the garment. Thus, the identification of the vandal remains a mystery."

"May I?" Joanna requested, reaching out a hand.

"By all means."

Joanna held the scarf up to a nearby lamp and examined every square inch on both sides, first by gross inspection, then with the aid of a magnifying glass. Over and over she went through the same process, paying particular attention to the edges of the scarf and the areas where it appeared most worn. Like a bloodhound that has picked up the scent, she continued her researches, seeming to measure and remeasure with her fingers several stained markings. Finally, she sniffed at the garment and made a face, indicating the presence of a disagreeable odor.

"Coal tar," Joanna remarked.

"Is that of importance?" Lestrade asked.

"Very," Joanna said and gave the scarf back to the inspector.

"But surely that does not reveal the identity of the vandal."

"That remains unknown, but there are a few helpful hints you may find of value." Joanna returned to the Persian slipper for another cigarette and went back to pacing. "You should be searching for a man in his middle years who once had a quite good income, but now has fallen on hard times. He is neat and tidy and cares greatly about appearance. I also note that he suffers from an obvious skin condition that affects his neck and scalp, and requires treatment with coal tar lotion." She stopped pacing to smile at Lestrade and waited while he hurriedly took down notes.

"You gathered all this from the old, worn scarf?" Lestrade asked incredulously.

"There is more," Joanna continued on. "Your vandal is tall and thin, with a height that may well reach six feet."

Lestrade jerked his head up abruptly. "Really, madam! You must certainly be joking."

"I never joke about clues," Joanna replied. "You know my methods. I do not simply see, but observe, and all the information that I have just given you is based entirely on findings within or on the scarf. Shall I elucidate?"

"Please do so."

"The scarf is made of Harris tweed, an expensive, fine weave, so we can reason the vandal was once a man of some means. Yet he continues to wear this worn, tattered garment which indicates he has fallen on hard times. I can deduce he is neat and tidy because he carefully and evenly cuts off any dangling threads, with scissors I suspect, thus attempting to remove evidence that the garment is old and threadbare. It is obvious he suffers from a chronic skin condition, for there is the distinct odor of coal tar, which is a remedy for a number of skin ailments involving the neck and scalp. Since the smell is so strong on his scarf, we can rightly reason that the skin condition affects the back of his neck as well as his scalp."

"How can you be aware that the vandal's scalp is likewise involved?" Lestrade challenged. "He would not wear the scarf on top of his head."

"Again it was a matter of simple observation," Joanna explained. "Stuck firmly in the coal tar lotion on the garment are long strands of hair, to which was affixed large, reddened scales which therefore must originate from the man's scalp. Some of these strands, by the way, are gray in color while others are brown, indicating the vandal is in his middle years."

Even I, who was accustomed to watching Joanna arrive at extraordinary deductions from the smallest clue, had to be impressed with her ability to make so much from so little. But for her to determine the vandal's frame and height from the scarf did seem a stretch too far. I was about to inquire into her line of reasoning, but Lestrade asked the question for me.

"How could you possibly establish the vandal's shape and height with any degree of exactness?" asked he.

"I had to make some basic assumptions, but I think you will find my reasoning sound," said Joanna. "Now, Inspector, please hold the scarf out by its ends while I take accurate measurements." She went to a nearby drawer for a ruler and began measuring. "You will note that the garment is six inches in width, and that in its middle the coal tar stain covers five inches top to bottom. We can assume this neat, tidy man would conceal the entire back of his neck to hide his most unattractive skin condition. Thus, the man's neck runs five inches from its top to its bottom, where the thoracic spine begins. In an individual of average stature, the length would be three to three and a half inches. Since the length of the neck almost always correlates to a person's full measure, we can deduce the owner of the scarf is of greater than average height. Furthermore, we know that in most instances a five-inch neck belongs to a six-foot man, and thus it is reasonable to estimate our vandal is six feet tall."

"Remarkable," Lestrade commented, shaking his head in wonderment. "How do you come by such information?"

"I make it my business to know what others do not," Joanna said nonchalantly, though for a moment she seemed pleased at the evident admiration. "The clues were sitting there, waiting to be discerned."

"But how then do you know he was thin?" Lestrade asked, again jotting down the data. "Tall people can also be obese."

"Which this individual was not," Joanna attested. "My measurements also revealed that the width of the coal tar stain was only three inches. A neck that is five inches in length and only three inches in width at its rear must obviously be possessed by a tall, thin man."

"So noted," Lestrade agreed. "But I am curious as to whether this man's rash might be more generalized and not confined to the neck and scalp. This, too, could aid in his identification."

"I should leave that up to Dr. Watson and his considerable experience in the practice of medicine," said Joanna.

"A most excellent question, Inspector," my father replied. "And I suspect the answer is yes. You see, the skin condition Joanna so ably described fits well with the diagnosis of psoriasis, which is characterized by red, scaly lesions that may be present on the extremities and torso as well."

"And at times it is associated with a most deforming type of arthritis that involves the small joints of the hands," I added. "It may also affect the fingernails, causing them to become heaped up and crusted over."

"So, Inspector," Joanna summarized, "you are searching for a tall, thin man with red, scaly lesions on his neck and scalp and perhaps elsewhere on his body. He is in his middle years, with long, gray hair, and carries the distinct odor of coal tar wherever he goes. His attire and shoes are most likely worn and no doubt out of fashion, for he has now come on hard times."

"These are most helpful clues," Lestrade told us, with a nod of gratitude. "We shall see if there is an individual with these characteristics who is associated with the vandalized galleries or has been seen in their vicinity. The presence of a deforming arthritis in his hands would be noticed by most."

"Do not count on our vandal having severe arthritis of the hands," Joanna suggested. "Such an individual could not grasp a knife and proceed to slash a painting on thick canvas, nor tear it apart."

"So noted," Lestrade said again, as he jotted down a final entry. "Your observations will be put to good use, but I am afraid they will not lead to rapid resolution which is so important at this point in time. The art galleries, which depend on Christmas sales for much of their yearly profits, are being greatly harmed by these crimes. People tend to stay away from businesses that have been vandalized, and this is particularly so for art galleries, where shoppers unjustly fear that paintings may have been damaged or somehow altered, yet still put on display. Add to this the newspapers telling of how recently purchased paintings have been traced to and torn apart in private homes, and you can understand why sales at virtually all galleries have dropped off precipitously. Some are even said to be facing bankruptcy. Thus, time is of the essence in putting a stop to this vandalism."

"The pressure on Scotland Yard to solve this case must be enormous," my father ventured.

"And growing by the day, Dr. Watson," Lestrade said, and taking a deep breath, gazed over to Joanna. "I wonder if you and the Watsons would be good enough to lend assistance in this most important case. This being the holiday season, I know you must have other obligations, but your help in bringing this matter to a close would be greatly appreciated."

"We should be happy to do so," Joanna agreed without hesitation. "Where was the very last act of vandalism committed?"

"At the Hawke and Evans gallery," Lestrade replied. "It was here that the most extensive damage was done. A total of five paintings were defaced."

"Then that is the place we shall begin," Joanna said. "I take it the crime scene is still intact?"

"It has been cordoned off and the gallery closed."

"Please see that it stays that way," Joanna requested. "If it is convenient, Inspector, we shall meet you there within the hour."

Lestrade departed our rooms with a step that was far livelier than the one he entered with. My father followed the inspector out with his gaze, then came back to us. He waited to hear the sound of the front door closing before he spoke. "This is certainly not the most interesting of cases, but then senseless vandalism seldom is."

"There is more to this than meets the eye," Joanna said mysteriously. "It is not simple vandalism."

"Based on what?" I asked.

"Everything Lestrade has told us," Joanna answered. "There is a plan afoot here and there is a method to the man's apparent madness."

"Do you believe it will reveal itself at Hawke and Evans?" my father asked.

"There and other places where the acts of vandalism occurred."

"What makes you so certain the vandal will leave other clues behind?"

"Because he is careless and obviously new at the game," Joanna replied. "An experienced criminal, particularly one on hard times, would never depart without his valued scarf."

"But it snagged on a door chain."

"Pshaw, Watson! One good pull and it would have immediately freed itself."

"The failure to do so also tells of his carelessness," I opined.

"That and the fact he overlooked something on his first visit to Hawke and Evans, and had to return a second time."

"But to what end?"

"That is what must be determined, for it is the key to resolution," Joanna stated. "All seemingly senseless crimes, if carefully observed, will be found to have a common denominator which will connect all loose threads into a recognizable pattern, and that is what we must search for here. Show me the common denominator and I will show you the vandal."

2

Hawke and Evans

On our arrival at Hawke and Evans, Joanna did not hurry to the crime scene, as was her usual custom, but rather took a slow, deliberate walk down a footpath that ran alongside the art gallery. The path held no noticeable clues, for it was covered with the early morning snowfall, yet Joanna stepped off every foot of it, staying close to the two-story, sandstone building itself. Just ahead was the side entrance that rested within a small alcove and was thus free of snow.

"Note the footprints by the door," Joanna observed, as she knelt down to examine the muddy impressions with a magnifying glass. "They are most instructive."

I moved in for a closer view and could only see a jumble of footprints, many superimposed upon one another, with none standing out as a whole. "It would appear that a sizable number of men assembled here for some reason."

"There were only three when you count the distinct toes of the shoes," Joanna informed. "One was a working man as evidenced by the square toe of his boots and the roughness of their soles. The other two members wore pointed shoes of different sizes, indicating they belonged to a higher economic class."

"But why were they stepping over one another?"

"Because they were here at different times," replied Joanna. "There is no other plausible explanation."

She gave the muddy imprints a final look and, carefully avoiding them, moved to the heavy, brass door lock that had been recently shined. Again using her magnifying glass, she meticulously examined it, paying particular attention to the keyhole itself. "I can detect tiny nicks, some no larger than a pinprick."

"From a key perhaps?" my father suggested.

Joanna smiled at the answer, then twisted the knob, but the door did not give. "Yes, my dear Watson, it was a key of sorts."

My father considered the clues further before saying, "In all likelihood, the door was opened by the owner or a trusted employee, for they alone would have such a key."

Joanna waved away the explanation. "The tiny nicks were made by a lockpick who accompanied the vandal. He was the individual wearing the boots belonging to a working man. The vandal had on shoes with pointed toes."

"And the third man wearing pointed shoes?"

"Undoubtedly Lestrade or one of his men who trudged over the evidence and may have mucked up important clues in the process."

"Surely this combination of happenings is no more than an educated guess," said I.

"It is based on several very sound assumptions that are backed up by clear-cut observations," Joanna replied. "First, you will note there is a lamppost near the front of the gallery. Only a fool, which our vandal is not, would attempt to break in through a well-lighted entrance where he could be easily noticed. Thus, he would plan to enter via a side door that is situated on a darkened alleyway. But here he encounters a lock of the best type. He cannot smash the door down, for this activity would cause a great ruckus that would be heard by all in the vicinity. So our vandal has to hire an expert lockpick to do the deed for him."

"But our vandal is a man of limited means," I argued.

"Lockpicks come cheap, particularly those who pick and run," Joanna explained. "So, here is the crime at the very beginning, as I see it. The vandal and his hired lockpick sneak down the alleyway in the dark of night. Snow is falling, so their footprints will be covered should some passerby happen to glance down the footpath. In the alcove, the light is poor which causes the lockpick to miss the keyhole as he tries to insert the pick. This accounts for the tiny nicks that can only be seen with a magnifying glass. The position of the working man's shoes tells us this is where he leaned over to pick the lock. Once the door is opened, the lockpick is paid no more than a crown or two, then quickly departs so the vandal can get on with his work. Lestrade came to the scene later and tramples on the footprints of our vandal and his lockpick. This scenario accounts for all the clues left behind."

"Your observations and conclusions are very astute, Joanna, but I do not see how it brings us any closer to the vandal," said my father.

"It is the lockpick which should draw your attention, Watson." With a final look at the door lock, Joanna led the way down the footpath to the front of the art gallery. Only then did I notice the nearby lamppost that would have illuminated the gallery to such an extent that a break-in could have been witnessed from half a block away. And across the street were dwellings above the stores and shops, the occupants of which would have surely heard any disturbance in the late night. Thus, all of Joanna's conclusions seemed spot-on, but

I still wondered how a lockpick might lead us to the vandal. Lockpicks were commonplace in London and could disappear into the shadows before an eye could blink.

Our attention was abruptly drawn to the crisp sound of a ringing bell. Just down the footpath a jolly Father Christmas, with a flowing white beard and dressed in bright red attire, was attempting to attract shoppers into nearby stores, most of whose entrances were adorned with strings of glittering lights. By contrast, the expansive frontage of Hawke and Evans was far more reserved, with only boughs of holly trimming its wide window, behind which stood a striking painting of Jesus ascending into heaven. As we entered, we had to lower our heads to avoid the hanging mistletoe in the doorway.

The interior of the gallery was richly appointed and clearly spoke of refined wealth. Its floor was constructed of burnished wood and its walls paneled in mahogany that provided an ideal backdrop for the splendid hanging paintings. Above, a pearly white ceiling was lined with exquisitely carved crown molding. Despite the opulence and captivating display, not a single customer was to be seen.

At the rear of the spacious gallery, Inspector Lestrade was waiting for us near a row of hanging paintings that were replete with dazzling colors and religious icons. None were defaced, but then none featured the portraits of women. At Lestrade's side was a tall, well-built man, in his middle years, with silver gray hair and sharp, aristocratic features. His perfectly fitted suit was dark, with pinstripes, and highlighted by a bright red tie and an equally bright boutonniere. His gray attire could not hide the worry on the face of Simon Hawke, the owner of the gallery.

Joanna nodded ever so briefly at the introductions, and instead focused her attention on a large painting that showed the interior of a massive cathedral, with a stained-glass image of Jesus Christ looming over the altar. "From the Italian Renaissance period, I would guess."

"You are correct, madam," Hawke agreed. "This particular work is by Francesco Albani, a quite good artist of that period."

"But certainly not a Michelangelo or Leonardo da Vinci."

"Nor a Raphael for that matter, but then again, who is? Nevertheless, Albani's paintings are still highly sought after."

Joanna glanced about at other, nearby works of art before commenting, "They all seem so similar with their religious connotations, with some being signed and others not."

"They are all from the same period, madam," Hawke informed, and began to point. "This one is by Carlo Cignani, and that by Pietro da Cortona who is much better known for his depictions in *The Rape of the Sabine Women*. All are signed in one way or another, for that was how the artist could prove the work was truly his."

"May I inquire as to their price?"

"The lesser ones would begin at a thousand pounds, madam."

Joanna smiled thinly to my father and I as we grasped the reason behind her line of questioning. The intruder was interested in vandalizing and nothing more, for it would have been a simple matter to snatch and roll up a number of valuable paintings and quickly sell them on the London black market, where such merchandise could be purchased for a quarter of its worth and then never seen again. So here was a vandal of limited means, who once enjoyed a comfortable income, yet he ignores the golden opportunity to return to his previous status. It all appeared to be the work of a crazed vandal, but I kept remembering Joanna's statement that there was a method and meaning to these destructive acts.

Simon Hawke broke the silence by asking, "Do you

believe these valuable paintings are in any way connected to the break-ins?"

"Were any of the gallery's paintings missing?" Joanna inquired.

"None," Hawke replied at once. "We immediately performed a thorough inventory and every piece was accounted for."

"Then your other paintings have no connection to the break-ins," said Joanna. "Which leads us to the question of how the vandal gained entrance to your gallery. I take it there are only two doors. Correct?"

Hawke nodded. "One is to the front, the other to a side alleyway, neither of which has been tampered with."

"Oh, the lock on the side door has been tampered with, for that is where our vandal entered."

"Impossible!" Hawke raised his voice at the notion. "That door is secured by a Chubb detector lock which is unopenable unless one has the key."

"How many keys to the door exist?"

"Two," Hawke replied and reached for a gold chain on his waistcoat that held a large key on its end. "I have one; the other belonged to my former partner, Andrew Evans, who died from consumption several years ago."

"Did you retrieve his key?"

"I—I saw no need," Hawke stammered. "Shall I inquire to his widow about the key?"

"As you have stated, there is no need," Joanna answered. "Were this key to fall into the wrong hands, they would not wait years to use it, nor would they employ it for the sole purpose of apparent vandalism. And most importantly, our vandal entered by having the lock picked and thus had no requirement for a key."

"I fear you are on the wrong track here," Hawke disagreed. "As I just mentioned, that door, like the one on the front, is secured by an impenetrable Chubb detector lock. Any attempt to pick it causes the lock to immediately seize up."

"What one man has invented, another can circumvent." Joanna carefully laid out the evidence showing that the lock had indeed been picked, with particular emphasis on the tiny nicks and pinpoint markings around the keyhole. "It was not quickly picked and may have required hours to undo this formidable lock. Allow me to give you a brief history on the best of Chubb locks, which applies in this instance."

All present gathered in to hear this most interesting story, for it no doubt could account for the entire series of break-ins by the vandal.

"You are correct, Mr. Hawke, in your statement that the Chubb detector lock will seize up if incorrectly picked," Joanna began. "It was not just unbreakable, but designed to alert the owner if someone attempted to open it. So impenetrable was their lock that the Chubb company held a contest to determine if the lock could be picked, with a reward of a hundred pounds to the individual who was successful. According to my father's unpublished monograph on the subject, no one succeeded until a young American came along and performed this task. But it required multiple attempts and nearly an hour to open it. The Chubb people then improved the lock further. But the lesson here was learned. A highly skilled lockpick can open any lock."

"Did Sherlock Holmes mention how this American was able to perform such a difficult task?" asked Lestrade.

"Not in detail," Joanna replied. "He only stated that the man who was successful intentionally tripped the detector mechanism, which caused the lock to seize up. He then picked the lock in the opposite direction to reset the detector. He repeated this maneuver over and over until he learned the lock's inner mechanisms so well he could devise a method to overcome it."

"Ingenious," Lestrade remarked.

"Quite," Joanna agreed. "And now that we have established his mode of entrance, let us examine the vandal's work."

"To the restoration area, then," said Hawke.

We followed him down a long staircase that led to the expansive basement of the gallery. Several dozen paintings were strewn about, many in frames, others on their stretchers and leaning against the wall like folding chairs. Standing alone were two obviously vandalized works of art. Both were torn apart, with half of a woman's face still recognizable on one. Off to the side and under a bright light, a young man was diligently at work on a large painting that showed a teenaged lad peeling fresh fruit. The restorer was quite short—no more than five feet two—with a kind, yet serious face and the physique of a well-trained athlete. As we quietly moved in closer, the strong odor of turpentine reached our nostrils.

"What is the purpose of the solvent?" asked Joanna.

"It is used to remove old varnish that diminishes the colors," Hawke explained, then went into detail. "Artists often apply varnish to their paintings to protect them from dust, light, and weather. Unfortunately, with time, the varnish takes on a yellowish hue which dulls the colors and can significantly lessen the value of the work. The best of restorers have their own formula for solvents to remove the varnish, but even they must use it carefully to avoid damaging the original coloration."

Joanna studied the restoration at length before saying, "The fruit in the painting is so lifelike one can almost feel it."

Hawke nodded at Joanna's assessment. "Which exemplifies the magnificent skill of Caravaggio, madam. The painting before us is entitled *Boy Peeling Fruit* and is considered by some to be his very best work. It has been said that the fruit painted by Caravaggio was so real one could taste it and smell it as well as see it."

"Does it have a price?" asked Joanna.

"Caravaggios are so valued and rare they never come to auction," Hawke answered. "But if one did, its asking price would be beyond extraordinary."

Joanna gave my father and me a knowing glance, for once again the vandal showed no interest in precious art, not even one as priceless as a Caravaggio. She came back to Hawke and said, "I take it your restorer is one of the highest quality."

Hawke nodded once more, his eyes never leaving the restorer's hand as he used a damp cotton swab to gently rub away the dark yellow discoloration caused by aged varnish. Now we had a clear view of the fruit the boy was peeling. It appeared to be a delicious pear which was beautifully shaded in brown. Hawke was correct. One could almost taste it.

Joanna watched the restorer reach for and wet another cotton swab, then quietly commented, "From his Mediterranean complexion, I would think your restorer is Italian."

"He is."

"Southern Italy, then."

"He was born in Naples, but spent his formative years in Florence."

"Where he no doubt learned his trade."

Hawke nodded a third time. "His name is Giuseppe Delvecchio and he comes to us via the Uffizi where he studied under the master Zinetti."

Joanna and I exchanged warm smiles, for on our honeymoon in Italy we visited the renowned Uffizi Gallery which housed some of the world's greatest art. In our estimation, it clearly surpassed the Louvre. One could easily spend a week there and never tire of viewing the works of Leonardo da Vinci, Michelangelo, Botticelli, and Raphael, just to name a few.

"Are all the restorers so young?" I asked.

"Some of the very best are," Hawke replied, before tip-toeing up to Delvecchio and introducing us.

The restorer discarded a wet, discolored swab in a slow, easy motion, giving the indication he was not to be hurried. He used another swab to remove the stains from his fingers, then bowed gracefully to Joanna. "Ah, the daughter of Sherlock Holmes."

"The very same," she said.

"Then you must use all of your talents to catch this *persona pazzi* before he does more damage."

"Why do you believe this person to be crazy?" asked Joanna who was fluent in German, and knew bits and pieces of Italian. "Have you experienced this sort of vandalism before?"

"It occurs in Italy as well," Delvecchio replied. "But it is usually done with paint or lipstick, and never by slashing. This is someone who truly hates works of art and wishes they no longer be seen by anyone."

"Or perhaps he hates only women," I ventured.

"That is true so far, but who is to know what this madman will do in the future?" Delvecchio moved over to the damaged painting that now showed only half of a woman's face. "As you can see cutting is not enough for this idiot. He has to tear the canvas apart for good measure."

"Can it be repaired?" Joanna inquired.

Delvecchio gave the painting a long, studied look before saying, "It will take a great amount of time, for the work has been retouched on multiple occasions. Thus, not much of the original remains."

That detail seemed to pique Joanna's interest. "Would the vandal know that it had been retouched over and over, thereby debasing and bastardizing its intrinsic value?"

"That would be most unlikely, madam, for one cannot de-

tect new restorations to the work by eyesight alone." Delvecchio switched off the lights and caused the room to darken.
Next he reached for a handheld ultraviolet lamp and shined
its light on the half of the painting that remained intact. "You
will note that there are many areas of black blotches which
indicate retouching. From my earlier studies, I estimated that
over seventy-five percent of the painting had new colors applied at one time or another."

"Yet Hawke and Evans still purchased it, so the painting
must have retained its value," Joanna noted.

"Oh no, madam, this painting belongs to the Crown and
we have been commissioned to do the restoration," Delvecchio explained.

Joanna's eyes narrowed noticeably. "To the best of your
knowledge how many other vandalized paintings were ever
the property of the Crown?"

"Only the one at the home of the Earl of Wessex," Delvecchio replied. "It was given to the earl as a gift, so I was told."

Joanna sighed briefly, signaling her disappointment at the
failure to make connection between the vandal and the royal
family. She glanced around at the large number of paintings
waiting to be attended to by Delvecchio. "You have a considerable backlog of work ahead of you."

"It will require months and months to clear this lot,
madam, for I am the only restorer on the premises." Delvecchio gestured to several damaged paintings on the nearby
wall. "In addition, I must attempt to restore the slashed portraits from the other art galleries. These very same works
were retouched here only months ago, but now the restorations will be much more difficult."

Joanna's eyes narrowed suddenly. "Were all the defaced
portraits at the other galleries previously retouched at Hawke
and Evans?"

"So it would seem, madam," Delvecchio replied, giving the vandalized works of art a final look. "I am afraid Mr. Hawke will eventually have to bring in more restorers to assist me."

"There is currently a great demand for skilled restorers in the art world, for they are in such short supply," Hawke interjected. "We were most fortunate to obtain the services of Mr. Delvecchio."

"But surely there were restorers here at Hawke and Evans before Mr. Delvecchio," Joanna remarked. "For an art gallery of this caliber, I would have assumed you had arranged for a transition that brought in new hires as the older ones departed."

"But sadly that was not the case, for the sudden departure of our former restoration experts was totally unexpected," Hawke said, then went on to describe the tale in detail.

It was indeed a most sad story as yet another criminal activity had engulfed Hawke and Evans a year earlier. The gallery's two premier restorers, one named Harry Edmunds, the other James Blackstone, had secretly used their unique skills to produce spot-on forgeries that were sold on the London black market. Copies of Renoirs and Manets were done so wonderfully well that they commanded fees of a hundred pounds or more, and were purchased the moment they appeared on the market. Some of the very best forgeries began to be shown in the homes of aristocrats, while others found their way to auction houses, where experts were called in to authenticate the paintings. They quickly determined that the works were forgeries when they discovered undeniable evidence of recent production, as well as flaws in the pigments used. Furthermore, the experts knew the locations of the original paintings, which were being held in museums and private collections outside of London.

Hawke concluded by turning to Inspector Lestrade, saying, "Scotland Yard was called in and the good inspector here devised a splendid trap on the black market for the forgers and it worked to perfection. Harry Edmunds is now residing in Wormwood Scrubs where he will spend the next five years of his life. His compatriot, James Blackstone, was never apprehended, although he was clearly implicated. Some believe he fled to Australia, for there was evidence indicating he had done so."

"Were his bank accounts looked into?" Joanna asked.

"It was our first order of business," Lestrade joined in. "James Blackstone had deposits of over a thousand pounds at both Lloyds and the Bank of England, which were princely sums for a man with a yearly income of less than a hundred pounds. We have kept a close eye on these accounts, and there has not been a single attempt to withdraw or transfer any of those funds. This is quite strange for a man who has disappeared and remains so, and who can never be employed again with this scandal attached to him. Nevertheless, as Mr. Hawke mentioned, there is evidence he set sail for Australia, and he may be waiting for more time to pass before reaching for his ill-gotten gains."

"Have the Australian authorities been alerted?"

"On several occasions, but without result," Lestrade replied. "But keep in mind, an individual can easily vanish in that vast country."

"Particularly so in what they refer to as *the bush*," my father said.

"And even more so in their outback," Lestrade added.

"I am surprised this crime was never covered by the newspapers," Joanna remarked. "I do not recall having read of it."

"We begged the inspector to remain close-lipped and not disclose these forgeries, for had they become known our gallery would have been ruined forever," Hawke said, giving

Lestrade a sincere nod of gratitude. "No one would have ever purchased a painting from us, and for good reason. The very last thing a reputable art gallery wants is to have its name associated with forgery. With such a crime hanging over our heads, every painting would become suspect. And of course the Crown, for whom we do considerable restoration work, would be obliged to withdraw from any further affiliation with Hawke and Evans. Word of this impending disaster never leaked, thanks to the inspector."

"Well done, Lestrade," Joanna lauded, but with a sly smile to my father and me. We were very much aware that the inspector would go to great ends to inform the newspapers and magazines of any crime solved by Scotland Yard. These publications would in turn heap great praise on the Yard and those involved, thus covering for their abysmal failure rate when it came to crime solving. I can only begin to imagine the immense pressure placed on Lestrade by higher-ups to keep his investigation secret in every way. Otherwise, every detail of the forgeries would have been publicly disclosed.

Joanna returned her attention to the figures depicted in the defaced paintings. She studied the faces and religious icons at length before asking, "Did the vandal concentrate his efforts on symbols of Christianity?"

"So it would appear," Delvecchio replied. "It was the Madonna he seemed most interested in disfiguring."

"Was the slash made in the sign of the cross?"

"No, madam. It was random and made only to disfigure."

Joanna cautiously used the tip of a finger to lift up the torn edge of the painting, so she could peek behind it. Its backing had taken on a brownish hue with age and had no markings upon it. "Were the backings of the five ruined pieces also slashed?"

"No, madam. They remained pristine in every instance."

The loud hum of an electric fan abruptly filled the air and for the moment drowned out further conversation. A hot draft from an overhead duct blew down on us and quickly warmed the basement further. The duct itself penetrated through a thick brick wall that closed off the far end of the room.

"It will shortly quiet down," Hawke said, then waited patiently as the noise of the fan began to dissipate. "We had a central heating unit installed, which helps protect our paintings, particularly those undergoing restoration. Mr. Delvecchio insisted on it, for without it he could not guarantee his work."

"Is the room temperature that important?" my father inquired.

"It is not so much the temperature, Dr. Watson, but rather the humidity and cleanliness of the air," Hawke replied. "Our restorer can explain it best."

"When it comes to paintings, dryness protects while humidity destroys," Delvecchio elucidated. "That is why the figures painted on the walls of the Egyptian pyramids have survived for thousands of years. The dry desert air protects them, you see. Prior to my arrival, Mr. Hawke used a coal-burning stove and fireplace to heat the area. It was not very effective and, in addition, it polluted the air with dust particles. The new system is far superior in every regard."

"And far more expensive," Hawke noted, and pointed to the brick enclosure. "The installers surrounded the furnace with bricks on all sides to limit the escape of heat and particles produced. We had primarily walled off the fireplace for the same reason."

"And to eliminate the bad smell," Delvecchio added.

Hawke groaned under his breath at the remembrance. "Apparently several large rats or squirrels had found their way into the chimney where they became trapped and died, leaving a most unpleasant odor behind. When the fireplace was closed off, the heat no longer escaped and the odor never recurred."

Joanna carefully placed a wetted fingertip on the brick enclosure in several places above and below her shoulders. "The bricks are warm, but not hot, which indicates they are serving their purpose well. This also of course permits the heat to be more evenly distributed."

"Just as the installers predicted," Hawke said, but then a quizzical look crossed his face. "Are the warmed bricks in any way related to the acts of violence?"

"I think not," Joanna replied, but she eyed the enclosure again, side to side, ceiling to floor, as if measuring it. "The furnace within must be quite large."

"So large it had to be disassembled before it could be moved into the building."

Joanna nodded, apparently satisfied with the explanation. She then strolled over to the three remaining defaced paintings and studied them at length. I saw nothing that distinguished them from the other ruined portraits. The slashes went across the Virgin Mary's face, splitting the canvas into two. In one painting the religious icons were badly damaged, while in the others the icons remained unharmed. If there was another signature to the vandal's work, I could not detect it. Now Joanna was repeating the same inspection she had performed on the other canvases. She gently inserted a finger between the cut edges and pulled one side open. Then she peered in, at first with the naked eye, then with a magnifying glass.

"Are there any clues present?" Hawke asked anxiously.

"Only those telling us that we are dealing with a very deliberate vandal," replied Joanna, and turned to Delvecchio. "I take it the backings of these paintings have not been replaced?"

"No, madam. There was no need, for they remained pristine and unscarred."

"Ah, so you had mentioned," Joanna said, as if reminding herself. "Well then, we won't intrude further on your valuable time. But I would suggest, Mr. Hawke, that you change the lock on the door in the alleyway to a newer and perhaps improved model."

Hawke's brow wrinkled with concern. "Do you expect the vandal to return here yet again?"

"I do."

"Based on what?"

"The singular fact that he was interrupted while here last," Joanna replied. "I am afraid our vandal has unfinished work at Hawke and Evans."

"Then we shall prepare for him with surprises even he could not anticipate," Hawke vowed.

"Do not underestimate this vandal, for he is most clever," Joanna cautioned.

"May I remind you, madam, that there are only two entrances into this gallery and I can assure you both will be closely guarded."

"And I assure you, sir, that our vandal will be much aware of this very same fact."

Joanna's warning gave little comfort to Simon Hawke, but it was the truth and the owner needed to be forewarned. It was clear to all that a rapid resolution was not to be had in this case, and on that rather pessimistic note we departed the gallery.

Outside, we gathered in a circle and pulled up our collars against the chilled wind and falling snow. Christmas shoppers were now out in force, entering and leaving the shops up and down the fashionable avenue. But none even approached Hawke and Evans, and none would until this dreadful case was solved.

We held our silence as a group of carolers, all splendidly dressed in Victorian attire, passed by us on the footpath singing the sweet "God Rest Ye Merry Gentlemen." More than a few of the shoppers, with wrapped gifts in hand, gathered around the young carolers and happily joined in the most pleasant Christmas song. Their merriment did little to raise my spirits, for I feared we remained in the dark as to the who and why of the baffling case before us. Inspector Lestrade seemed to share my opinion.

"I am afraid we have come up empty," he said, shivering against the cold. "I saw no new clues."

"There are a few which could prove helpful," Joanna suggested.

"Such as, madam?"

"The lockpick."

"But there are hundreds of lockpicks in London," Lestrade countered. "And most of them are quite good."

"But not good enough to penetrate a Chubb detector lock," Joanna went on. "Such a feat would require a master lockpick who towers above the others. How many can fit into that category, Inspector? I will wager very few."

Lestrade gave the matter thought as he tapped a finger against his chin. He then considered the question further, now moving his lips while he counted. "Three come to mind, madam. There is Samuel Marr who we can eliminate, for he is currently serving a sentence at Pentonville."

"But he was caught!" Joanna challenged.

"Only because one of his crew ratted on him," Lestrade explained. "The other two worthy of consideration are Joseph Blevins and Archie Griffin, both sharp as a knife and always one step ahead of Scotland Yard."

"Who is the more needy of the two?"

"Blevins, for he is said to be going blind."

And thus he would be the less costly of the pair, I thought to myself, remembering that our vandal was a man of limited means. But would a blind man still be picking locks? Of course he would. Picking a lock depends on feel and not sight.

"Then it is he who you must start with," Joanna said.

"Neither will confess, madam, for it is not in their best interest to do so," Lestrade pointed out. "A confession would send them to prison and both know it. There is no getting around that."

"Oh, but there is, Inspector," said Joanna. "Bring the pair in for questioning that is to be done at Scotland Yard, which will emphasize the gravity of the situation. Place each in a separate room and tell them you know of their involvement in the crime at Hawke and Evans, mentioning an eyewitness who will remain nameless. If they describe the man who hired them, they will be set free with a warning. If they refuse, they will be charged and can expect the worst."

Lestrade nodded slowly. "They would certainly have no allegiance to the vandal, and would wish only to save their own skin."

"Precisely," Joanna agreed, clearly warming to the plan. "You might also inform each that failure to identify the vandal will add significantly to their sentences."

"You do of course realize that in all likelihood they will not know the vandal's true name."

"But they will know his face and that is what we require at this point in time."

"Let us hope one of these fish bite."

"Use the correct bait and he will."

We hurried to the warmth of our waiting four-wheeler and remained silent as we rode back to 221b Baker Street where we hoped to indulge in one of Miss Hudson's sumptuous brunches. The snow was falling heavily now and a very white Christmas seemed assured, but the joy of the season would certainly not visit the art galleries in the West End. My mind returned to the Hawke and Evans gallery where so little was learned. I could think of nothing that would lead us in one direction or another, and attempting to track down the vandal via the lockpick he hired seemed a long shot indeed.

"What bothers you so, John?" Joanna asked, breaking into my thoughts. "And before you inquire, I determined you are bothered because of the tightening of your jaw and the stern expression on your face. You appear to be a man trying to solve an unsolvable riddle."

"I see so few clues in this case. All we have at our disposal are slashed paintings and a picked lock, which leaves us quite in the dark."

"Ah, but there is more."

"Such as?"

"The backings of the five slashed paintings."

"You consider them to be important?"

"Exceedingly so."

"Is there any point to which you would wish to draw my attention?"

"To the curious nature of the backings."

"But the restorer Delvecchio said they were pristine and unscarred."

"That was the curious nature," Joanna remarked and turned to watch the snow fall.

3

Felix Dubose

With Lestrade having made the arrangements, we visited the home of the renowned jeweler Felix Dubose later that afternoon. It was a most handsome structure that was located on Bayswater Road and overlooked the northern edge of Hyde Park. Mr. Dubose, who was portly and balding and well into his middle years, received us in an elegant, spacious parlor which spoke of both wealth and taste. The furnishings were fine French antique upholstered in blue silk, whilst the walls were decorated with impressive paintings of landscapes and children with angelic faces. Only the slashed canvas showed a woman's portrait. But Joanna's attention was riveted on a mahogany door off to the far side that had a most unusual feature. It had a small, round porthole, much like those seen on ocean liners.

Dubose followed her line of gaze and commented, "That strange door came with the house that I purchased some years ago from an admiral in the Royal Navy. There was a small room behind it that the admiral used to store his military memorabilia. I had no use for it, but my wife thought it would be a fine place to display her collection of antique Staffordshire figurines and sterling silver miniatures. If you wish to have a look, please feel free to do so."

Joanna, as well as my father and I, had to remove our hats to move in close and peer through the porthole at the magnificent collection. There were hundreds of colorful figurines and polished silver miniatures lining every shelf in the well-lighted room. It must have taken Dubose's wife years and years to acquire all the striking pieces that glowed in the bright light.

"Stunning," Joanna remarked.

"I believe the vandal also found it so," said Dubose.

Joanna tried the door and window; the former was locked shut, the latter opened easily. "Did he actually enter the room?"

"That was not possible, for the door is secured by a Bramah lock."

"Are the other doors in your house protected by Bramahs?" Joanna asked.

"All," Dubose replied.

"Well, sir, he found his way in through one of those sturdy locks."

"Yes, yes," Dubose said unhappily. "In our phone call, Lestrade mentioned that one of our outer locks was in all likelihood picked." He reached into his waistcoat and extracted an odd-appearing key that resembled a hollowed-out tube with deep notches on its end. "This key cannot be duplicated, so obviously the lock had to be picked. But fortunately he did not bother with the door to my wife's collection. Yet he was interested, for he opened the porthole and stuck his head through it."

"Based on what evidence?" Joanna asked.

"He left an unpleasant odor on the edges of the porthole," Dubose responded. "It was quite similar to that of tar."

"Coal tar, to be precise," said Joanna. "The same aroma was detected at another of his crime scenes."

"It is used to treat various skin conditions," my father explained. "In this instance, it affected his neck and scalp."

"I hope it is not contagious?" Dubose asked concernedly.

"It is not," my father assured.

"Nevertheless, I had the entire porthole thoroughly scrubbed," Dubose said. "I thought it best to err on the side of caution."

"Quite so," my father agreed.

Dubose nervously tapped a finger against the mahogany door, while his eyes stayed focused on its shined brass fittings. "Perhaps I should have all the locks changed."

"There is no need, for the vandal will not return," Joanna advised as she strolled over to the slashed painting. "And now let us turn our attention to the purpose of our visit. We were told you received the portrait as an anniversary gift from your brother. I need to know every detail, from the moment he purchased it to the moment it was placed in your hands."

"There are no mysterious circumstances here," Dubose began. "My brother was in Paris on a business trip when he saw the striking painting by the French impressionist Cézanne. It depicted an old woman holding a rosary that was beautifully done. He paid an extraordinary price for it, carried it back to London personally, and presented it to my wife and me on our twenty-fifth anniversary. Why this vandal chose to deface such a lovely painting is beyond me."

"How was the painting transported to London?" Joanna inquired.

"By ferry, with the assistance of Bikram, his manservant who assists my brother in every way, for my dear brother is paralyzed from the waist down, compliments of an Afghan bullet, and is now confined to a wheelchair."

My father's eyes widened in surprise. "Your brother fought in the Second Afghan War?"

"He did indeed, Dr. Watson," Dubose replied. "Dear Albert was wounded near the very end of it at the Battle of Kandahar."

"I, too, served in that dreadful war," my father reminisced. "Do you recall which regiment he was assigned to?"

"That I do not know."

"Might it be possible for me to speak with him on this matter?"

"I am certain he would be most pleased to do so, but unfortunately he is currently hospitalized undergoing treatment for a stubborn bedsore."

"Perhaps once he recovers, then."

"Or better still, give him a day or two to regain his strength and visit him at St. Bartholomew's," Dubose suggested. "I can assure you he would welcome a visit of someone from his soldiering days. If you like, I could inform him of your upcoming visit."

"Please do."

Joanna was meticulously examining the slash that cut into the painting and bisected the woman's face, but she was obviously listening to the conversation as well. "Is your brother also involved in the jewelry business?"

"He is indeed, madam, and I simply could not manage without him, for it is he who determines the quality of the diamonds we sell," Dubose replied. "His expertise is such that other jewelers in London often seek his opinion when they encounter a particularly rare or unusual diamond."

Joanna cautiously lifted up a torn edge of the Cézanne and peered behind it at its backing. "So I take it he knows his four Cs quite well."

"Oh, he is well aware of the four—color, clarity, cut, and carat—but his true talent resides in grading the cut, for that determines the gem's brilliance."

"Does he himself do the cuts?"

"Oh no, madam, but I suspect he could if he wished."

Joanna used her magnifying glass to inspect the frame and back of the painting and, apparently satisfied, turned away from it. "Tell me about Bikram, your brother's manservant."

"He is an exceptionally tall, well-built Sikh, with dark skin and a pleasing manner," Dubose described. "Bikram has been at my brother's side for over thirty years and is loyal beyond words. I am certain he would give his life for my brother without the slightest hesitation."

"One last question about the Cézanne painting," Joanna requested. "Did the painting ever leave the sight of Bikram or your brother?"

"Not to my knowledge," Dubose replied. "But it might be best for you to ask Albert."

"And so we shall," said Joanna, and strolled over to a nearby painting that depicted ballerinas. It was eye-catchingly beautiful and had not been vandalized. "This, too, appears to be the work of a French impressionist."

"The artist is Edgar Degas who is known and celebrated for his lovely ballerinas." Dubose moved in closer to straighten the slightly tilted painting, then blew at a speck of dust on its frame. "Fortunately, the vandal either overlooked or showed no interest in Degas's work."

"He did not overlook the painting, but chose not to slash it, for the ballerinas are turned away with their heads down and do not show faces that the vandal is so intent on defacing."

"I do pray this criminal can be apprehended before he does even more damage."

"As does the entire West End of London."

"Is there any hope?"

"Only a glimmer," said Joanna, and gave the defaced

woman holding the rosary a final look before thanking Felix
Dubose for his time and assistance.

We departed the home via the tradesman's entrance
which Joanna correctly predicted had been used by the vandal. The Bramah lock was old and rusted, but on its surface
were scratches and markings recently made by the lockpick.
Any footprints that may have been left by the vandal and his
accomplice were long gone, however.

"The number of small dints and scrapes suggest the guilty
lockpick is Joseph Blevins who is losing his sight," Joanna
noted. "He would need to depend on feel alone in the darkness even if a torch was available."

"And he would be the least expensive," I added.

"That, too."

Following Joanna's instructions, we stayed off the footpath on the side of the home and took measured steps across
a well-manicured garden. She reasoned the intruders would
not use the paved footpath upon which their heels might click
and thus alert the household of their presence. The soft grass
of the lawn would mute any sounds made by their approach.

"Here!" Joanna stopped abruptly and pointed down to a
large bed of flowers. Those in the middle were flattened and
crushed, those on the sides still standing. "They came and left
this way."

"Would not two men hurrying along trample a wider
area of the flower bed?" I asked.

"Not if they were in single file," Joanna said. "Remember, Blevins is nearly blind. He would have to be led in the
darkness, most likely from behind the vandal."

"Your observations are very keen, Joanna," my father
praised. "But I fear they do not bring us any closer to this
despicable vandal."

"Perhaps," Joanna responded. "But I make it a habit never

to discard findings, no matter how trivial they may appear. In the future, you see, they might turn out to be quite useful, so I shall docket this information for now and store it along with the other data we have uncovered thus far."

We strolled on and passed a window that looked into a large, brightly lighted kitchen where servants were scurrying to and fro. On a long wooden table lay a splendid goose that was being dressed for the oven by a hatted chef. A hidden vent allowed appetizing aromas to escape into the early evening air.

"It is obvious that Mr. Dubose is a man of considerable wealth," said I.

"All of which he would happily give up in return for his dear brother's paralysis to disappear," my father noted.

"Which brings us to your upcoming visit with Albert Dubose at St. Bartholomew's," Joanna interjected. "This visit could be most important, Watson, for it may lead to resolution of the case before us."

"How so?" my father asked, clearly puzzled. "How in the world would the time we spent in Afghanistan relate to this spree of vandalism?"

"It is not your soldiering days that I am interested in, but the Cézanne painting Albert Dubose gave to his brother," Joanna went on. "You see, it is the odd, missing piece here. All of the defaced paintings had been in or passed through the galleries in the West End of London. Thus, the vandal had to know these galleries or the works of art they possessed. That is the common denominator that should point to the culprit. But this notion falls apart with the slashing of the Cézanne painting at the home of Felix Dubose. That painting was purchased in Paris and to his knowledge was never seen or in any way connected to the West End galleries."

My father nodded ever so slowly. "Which presents quite a dilemma."

"A stubborn dilemma unless we can prove that the Cézanne painting somehow passed through a London gallery prior to being purchased."

"Should I ask him directly?"

"That would not be wise, particularly if there is some reason he wishes all to believe the painting was truly purchased in Paris rather than London."

"Why would he do that?"

"Perhaps to impress his brother, for a Cézanne painting bought in Paris, where the artist once lived, would make the gift even more treasured. Mind you, I am not saying he did, only raising an unlikely possibility, and all unlikely possibilities must be eliminated for us to find the truth."

"But surely he will wish to talk mainly of our service in Afghanistan."

"And so you should. During your visit with Albert Dubose, you will naturally show a deep interest in his days during the Second Afghan War. Then be good enough to demonstrate a similar interest in the Cézanne painting and, using your knowledge of Paris, have him account for every moment the canvas was in his hands. Gently persuade him to inform you on the details of the journey, from the purchasing to the transport to the giving of the gift, all the while searching for an event, however trivial, that will connect the Cézanne to the art galleries of West London."

"Which will clearly establish the common denominator."

"Precisely," said Joanna, and signaled to a passing four-wheeler.

4

Johnny

"We are at a disadvantage," said Joanna as we gathered around a flickering fire. Outside, the weather had turned cruel, with a most heavy snowfall and an arctic wind that howled down Baker Street in powerful gusts. Even the three logs in the fireplace had difficulty overcoming the chilled air in our parlor. "The vandal has knowledge that we lack and without which this case cannot be brought to resolution."

"You do not appear to be convinced that our vandal is simply a crazed individual who searches out portraits of women," my father surmised. "Which of course is the opinion of Scotland Yard."

"That conclusion does not fit the facts, Watson." Joanna reached for a metal poker and stoked the logs, causing them to blaze up anew. "An unbalanced person could certainly know of paintings in various art galleries, either by advertisements or by actually visiting the establishments. But he would not be aware of their restoration sections, such as was the site of vandalism at Hawke and Evans. These areas are closed off and restricted, and a casual visitor would never be allowed in.

Then your crazed individual would have to somehow gain knowledge of the Dubose home and the Cézanne painting in its parlor. But it is the technique of his vandalism that draws my attention. You will recall he carefully slices into the canvas to make certain its backing remains pristine and free of any cuts or scratches. What do you make of that?"

"Perhaps he used a razor which would not penetrate deeply," I suggested. "This is particularly so if the sharp point alone did the damage."

"The slashes are too wide for a thin razor," Joanna countered. "At the end of the cuts, the width is broad and somewhat uneven, indicating a large, sturdy knife was used. In other words, I am of the opinion that he intentionally did not go deep, as would be expected if his singular goal was the destruction of the painting."

"But why not go deep?" I asked at once.

"Think back, John, to each of the defaced portraits, and recall how they were torn in a most unusual fashion," Joanna prompted.

"The edge was lifted and appeared to be partially folded back."

"To what end?"

The answer came in an instant. Both my father and I cried out together, "He was looking for something!"

"But what?" Joanna answered back. "And here is where we require an expert in the works of the great artists. We need someone who is an acknowledged authority in the paintings from the Italian Renaissance as well as those of the French impressionists. He should be able to speak of either Raphael or Renoir without skipping a beat."

"What would you expect to learn from him?" I asked.

"If my assumptions are correct, and I believe they are, there is something of great value hidden beneath the canvas,"

Joanna replied. "But here is where I stumble, for the list is long."

"Another painting?" I ventured.

"Possibly, but how would the vandal know this?" Joanna lighted a Turkish cigarette and began pacing, no doubt assembling the possibilities in her mind. At times she muttered to herself, nodding at one thought and shaking her head at another. "There is quite a list of items which might be hidden behind a valuable painting. You mentioned it might be a second painting, but consider the fact that these works of art may well have been framed and reframed on a number of occasions, and anything concealed behind the canvas would have certainly been seen. Moreover, what does the portrait of a woman have to do with the hidden item? Is it a marker or a telltale sign? Here, an expert in the history of art could prove most helpful."

"I would cast my vote for it being yet another painting," my father asserted. "It would surely explain why the vandal made his cut in such a superficial fashion."

"But why a painting, Watson?" Joanna argued mildly. "Could it not be an ancient historical document of immense value, such as a copy of the Magna Carta, which would be worth untold millions? Or perhaps it holds old currency. The King Edward the Third florin is the most valuable coin in the world. Only three are known to be in existence and all would easily fit behind a canvas. So, at this point we have an extensive list of possibilities, and we have no way of ranking them in order of probability."

"How could an art historian be of help in this matter?" I asked.

"He could tell us how often this type of vandalism has occurred in the past and describe all the circumstances that surrounded those events," Joanna replied. "Please recall what

I mentioned to Lestrade earlier in this case. There are no truly unique crimes—all have been committed before."

"Are you saying we are dealing with a copycat crime?"

"That possibility has crossed my mind."

"But where should we look for a noted art historian?" I asked.

"In an old case of Sherlock Holmes's." My father arose and went to a large shelf that held the files of the great detective's cases. While rummaging through a box marked with the date 1885, he told us of a most unusual case involving an art theft in Belgravia.

"A very valuable Rembrandt was stolen from a mansion near Buckingham Palace. Scotland Yard had made little progress in its recovery and asked for Holmes's assistance. Of course my friend had been involved in similar situations over the years, and had extensive experience when it came to art theft. In most instances the painting found its way to the black market where it landed in the hands of an individual who specialized in the sale of such ill-gotten merchandise. However, when dealing with the works of the great masters, such as Raphael or Rembrandt, the old rules did not apply. They rarely came onto the legitimate market, and the black market would show little interest, for the buyer could never display the famous work. If he was foolish enough to do so, word would quickly spread and reach the ears of Scotland Yard."

"Perhaps it could be ransomed," I suggested.

"That would be a reasonable option, but no such note was received," my father went on. "So that was the problem facing Sherlock Holmes. Now, as you may recall, my colleague had a profound knowledge of chemistry, anatomy, and sensational literature when it dealt with crime and horror. Yet he knew little of art and cared even less about it, but his insight into London's black market surpassed all others. Holmes was convinced the Rembrandt would turn up on the black market where a single buyer awaited its arrival."

"Everything was prearranged!" Joanna exclaimed.

"Yes, but by and for whom?" my father asked. "This information would remain highly confidential, with only the thief and the buyer being aware of the dealing in which a hundred thousand pounds or more would change hands. Every avenue we tried in an effort to track down those involved proved fruitless. So, it was at this point we called upon Edwin Alan Rowe, a noted art historian who taught at Cambridge and sat on the board of their renowned Fitzwilliam Museum. He was particularly well acquainted with the work of the Dutch masters."

"Perfect for a Rembrandt!" I thought aloud.

"And, as you will shortly learn, he had a nose for crime as well," my father continued on. "When presented with the case, he agreed completely with Holmes. The theft and sale had been arranged beforehand in an unwritten contract. And of even more importance, he had heard of a Chinese real estate magnate named Kee Chow, who desperately desired a Rembrandt and had offered museums and even a few private collectors an extraordinary amount of money for one of the Dutch master's work. He was refused by all. Nonetheless, it was known that his quest remained unabated. Thus, in all likelihood, it was Kee Chow who was the prearranged buyer. With that information in hand, Holmes began to track down the seller."

"But why would this Kee Chow pay an absurd amount of money for a painting he could never display?" I asked.

"It could not be shown in Europe or America for obvious reasons, but that presented much less of a problem in Peking or Shanghai," my father responded. "In the Orient, Western rules and laws often do not apply and, when they do, are quite lax. Holmes of course was aware of this."

"How was my father able to single out the seller?" Joanna inquired.

"By simple deduction," my father replied. "Holmes knew that virtually all of the stolen, highly priced items on the West End of London were handled by Roger Bellamy, the most notorious and successful of black-marketers. Holmes was also aware that such a valuable transaction could not include a middleman. The Rembrandt would have to be hand-delivered to Kee Chow in China where experts could validate its authenticity. With the assistance of Scotland Yard, the passenger lists on all ocean liners leaving England for China were carefully examined. Bellamy and his wife were scheduled to depart in a fortnight on RMS *Aquitania*. Shortly after boarding, the Bellamys' belongings were searched and the Rembrandt was discovered nicely tucked away in the wife's crinoline petticoat."

"Bravo!" said I.

"Now you see the value of having Edwin Alan Rowe involved," my father stated. "He is now long retired, but remains active as a consultant to the National Gallery. I saw him last year at a charity gala where we had a jolly good time reminiscing over the case of the stolen Rembrandt."

"Do you by chance have his phone number?" Joanna asked.

"As a matter of fact, I do." My father reached into a file box for a card attached to a thick folder. "I was to contact him for a luncheon date, but foolishly neglected to do so."

"Please be good enough to call him," Joanna requested.

"It is rather late," said I, glancing at my watch. "Perhaps we should wait until morning."

"Nonsense," my father said, walking over to the phone.

"As I mentioned earlier, the man has a nose for crime and would be happy to receive my call and involve himself in our case."

My father dialed Edwin Alan Rowe's number and spoke with the historian's wife whom he had been introduced to at the charity ball. After exchanging amenities, I heard my father say, "Taking a bit of a tour, is he? . . . I see. So he will avoid Eton and return to London by the weekend. . . . I shall call him then. . . . And it was a pleasure speaking with you as well, Margaret."

My father placed the phone down. "Rowe should be back in London on Thursday. He was scheduled to make a stop on tour at Eton, but will bypass it, for there has apparently been an outbreak of cholera in that vicinity."

Joanna's jaw dropped as her face suddenly lost color.

"What is it?" I asked her concernedly.

"Cholera again," Joanna said, her words coming out in a whisper.

In an instant I made the harrowing connection. Cholera was the disease that killed Joanna's former husband, the distinguished surgeon John Blalock. And now there was an outbreak of the deadly disease in Eton, where Joanna's son Johnny attended school.

"Are they certain it is cholera?" I asked.

"There is no mistaking that disease," my father replied. "Those who have seen cholera never forget it."

"As have I," Joanna said, for the most part having regained her composure. "Watson, please call your contacts and determine the extent of this outbreak."

Three separate phone calls were needed—two to specialists in London, one to Eton—before my father had acquired enough information to make an accurate assessment. As he placed the receiver down, the worry was obvious on his face.

"The outbreak is quite real and spreading, with the first cases being diagnosed late last night," he reported in a most serious voice. "It is believed that a Spanish ship discharged its waste along the coast near Southampton and contaminated an oyster bed with the cholera organism. The infected shellfish were transported to Eton and the nearby area. To date there have been over a dozen cases and more are expected. The outbreak should shortly be brought under control, thanks in large measure to modern sanitation that keeps our water supply well separated from the sewage systems. Nevertheless," my father went on, "a group of students from Eton are known to be among the ill."

I hurried to Joanna's side and tried to offer some comfort. "Surely the school would have notified you if Johnny was ill."

"Perhaps," Joanna agreed weakly. "But will they guarantee me that he will not be affected? Remember Watson's words. The disease is still spreading."

She dashed to the telephone and made an operator-assisted call to the headmaster at Eton. She asked him direct questions and relayed his answers to us.

"Is my son John Blalock affected?"

"He is well," Joanna repeated the answer.

"Are any of his roommates or classmates ill?"

"Several are. How many are several?"

"Four. Where are they being treated?"

"In their rooms, for the hospitals are presently over-crowded." Joanna paused, her tone of voice now becoming clinical. "What measures are being taken to protect the uninfected from the infected?

"Curtain between the beds and careful disposal of waste," she reiterated, as her expression hardened. "That is not good enough, Headmaster, for it leaves my son at real risk. I shall arrive in a matter of hours. Please inform my son and have him prepared to depart Eton."

Joanna slowly put the phone down and said, "Curtains are virtually no protection at all. All it takes is one misplaced hand and the inadequate disposal of waste, and the disease spreads."

"Perhaps Johnny did not partake of the contaminated oysters," my father hoped. "That would lessen his chance of being afflicted."

"Oysters and other shellfish are among his favorites, and thus he most likely did ingest those contaminated oysters," Joanna noted. "If that is the case, I want him here in our rooms on Baker Street where we can treat him effectively. And the sooner he is brought home the better."

"But you cannot possibly reach him tonight," said my father. "Coach and car travel are out of the question in this dreadful weather, and there are no trains at this late hour."

"But every minute counts," Joanna warned. "Once the disease strikes, one must make all efforts to replenish the fluid loss. Otherwise, the end result can be horrific, as I sadly learned when my former husband was so afflicted."

"Let us pray young Johnny does not come down with cholera, but should he be ill on your arrival, begin treatment immediately," my father advised. "All replenishment can be given by mouth, using the standard solution."

Joanna nodded knowingly. "Saline solution with adequate amounts of glucose added."

"And do not depend on the patient's thirst to guide you," my father cautioned. "Remember the disease begins with explosive diarrhea and a patient can lose as much as five quarts of fluid each day. So, to the best of your ability, estimate the output and attempt to replace it at once. Equip yourself with a large bucket and rubber gloves before entering the infected area. And always keep in mind that this vicious microorganism can be transmitted by incidental hand-to-mouth contact."

"I am quite familiar with that mode of transmission, for that is how the disease came to me from my former husband."

"Then you know the symptoms well."

"All too well," said Joanna and rose from her chair. "I shall now go gather my things, for I plan to be on the first train out of Paddington tomorrow morning."

"I would be more than glad to accompany you and lend any assistance that may be required," I offered.

"Thank you, John, but I am afraid you would only be in the way," Joanna replied. "You see, the living quarters for the boys at Eton are quite crowded, with all the beds lying side by side in a large, single room. The only privacy would be a curtain between the beds, and those are now no doubt in short supply."

"It would be most difficult for both of us to squeeze between the beds, if Johnny is ill," said I, with a nod. "And of course crowding increases the chance of further transmission."

"Exactly," Joanna concurred. "You should stay behind and, with Watson, follow up on the available clues we now have at our disposal."

"But I fear my mind will be elsewhere."

"Then you must occupy yourself with the art vandal and leave the worrying to me," Joanna said, with a wry smile that quickly faded. "I shall call you from Eton to inform you of the latest."

I watched Joanna retire to our room and waited for her to close the door behind her, then spoke to my father in a concerned voice. "How serious is this outbreak?"

"Quite," my father replied, his tone matching mine. "It

is not yet under control and spreading at a rapid rate. Apparently the shipment of contaminated oysters went to more than a few restaurants and markets in the area, and all those possibly infected must somehow be tracked down."

"Which may well be impossible when it comes to markets where strangers often come and buy the various foods without leaving behind any identification."

"The same holds true for most restaurants, and thus the authorities must depend on newspapers, posters, and word of mouth to warn the public."

"Yet by now, the disease has shown itself in those infected, for as I recall the incubation period is quite short."

"It usually runs twenty-four to thirty-six hours, but it may be prolonged to as many as four days, depending on a variety of factors, including which subgroup of the cholera organism is responsible. According to the experts I spoke with, their incubation period is unpredictable, and so is their viciousness."

"Do we know which subtype is present in the Eton outbreak?"

"The bacteriologist will have to determine that feature. But whatever the subtype, it appears to be one which is particularly nasty."

"Based on what?"

"The fact that there have already been two deaths associated with it."

5

Albert Dubose

Approaching the hospital room of Albert Dubose the following morning, we were greeted by the noxious smell of rotting tissue. We had been forewarned by the specialist caring for the patient, but the unpleasant odor was so strong that it could not be masked by a heavy dose of deodorant that was also in the air. The poor man was suffering from a bedsore which had now reached the necrotic stage. These sores, also referred to as decubitus ulcers, are localized injuries to the skin and underlying tissue caused by sustained pressure to the area, usually over a bony prominence. They are not uncommon in paralyzed individuals who are confined to wheelchairs. In Mr. Dubose, the bedsore was located on his buttock and was resistant to all forms of treatment. As a last resort, his physician was now treating the open wound with maggots.

"It is an archaic type of therapy that has been passed down through the ages, but it can work remarkably well," my father explained. "It is a quite simple procedure in which live larvae of maggots are inserted into a dressing that is firmly placed upon the open wound. The breeding maggots feed only on the dead tissue and this thoroughly debrides the ulcer and allows for healing."

"How long does this treatment last?" I asked.

"Two to three days usually suffices."

On entering the small room, we were warmly received by Albert Dubose who was propped up and lying on his side in a rather large bed. "Ah, Dr. Watson and his son, I presume."

"Indeed we are," replied my father.

"Welcome then, and please forgive the unpleasant surroundings that at this moment are so unavoidable." Even under the sheets we could discern that Dubose was a short, thin man, with obviously shriveled legs. His face was narrow and pale, with a carefully trimmed black beard and goatee. As he attempted to prop himself up further, he called over to his manservant, "Bikram, lend a hand if you will."

The tall, well-built Sikh hurried over and effortlessly lifted his master from the mattress, then gently rested him down. The manservant was close to six feet in height, with quite broad shoulders and dark skin that was highlighted by the white turban and uniform he wore.

"Thank you," Dubose said, and remained lying on his side so as not to put pressure on his bandaged bedsore. "Allow me to introduce my trusted aide, Bikram. He came to my assistance at the Battle of Kandahar, and without his courage and devotion I can assure you I would not be alive today."

Bikram showed no response to his master's praise. He continued to stand tall and motionless, like a stone statue in the corner of a museum. But his eyes never left Albert Dubose.

"So, Watson," Dubose went on, "my brother tells me you too soldiered in Afghanistan."

"I did indeed," my father replied. "I was an assistant surgeon attached to the Fifth Northumberland Fusiliers, and was ordered to report to my regiment which at the time was stationed in India. But before I could join them, the Second Afghan War had broken out. On landing in Bombay, I discovered that my corps had advanced through the passes and was already deep in enemy territory. I of course followed and succeeded in reaching Kandahar, where I found my regiment." My father paused as his mind appeared to go back decades in time. "Shortly after my arrival in Kandahar, I was removed from my brigade and attached to the Berkshires, with whom I served at the tragic Battle of Maiwand. That campaign brought honors and glory to many, but for me it held nothing but pain and misfortune."

"Although not involved, I recall it well," Dubose reminisced. "The battle was mismanaged and a total disaster, with some of the brigades losing over half of their men."

My father nodded slowly. "The Berkshire regiment itself lost nearly three hundred. It was there that I was struck by a jezail bullet which shattered bone and grazed the subclavian artery. I survived only because my orderly Murray threw me across a pack horse and succeeded in bringing me safely back to the British line."

Dubose nodded in return. "You had your Murray, I my Bikram."

"It required months and months for me to convalesce, but my health was never the same and to this very day I am still reminded of the jezail bullet."

"And I paid an even dearer price at the Battle of Kandahar. It was there, where my corps, the Ninety-Second Highlander, was storming the village of Gundi Mulla Sahibdad, that an Afghan bullet pierced my spine and left me paralyzed from the waist down. Were it not for Bikram, who fought at my side and carried me to safety, my dried bones would still be baking in the Afghan desert."

"Such a terrible price," my father lamented.

"Of which I am reminded on a daily basis," Dubose said, then waved a hand as if dismissing the memory. "But enough of old war stories. Let us talk of the vandalized Cézanne that I suspect is the true purpose of your visit."

"Did your brother so inform you?" asked my father.

Dubose smiled thinly. "He believes you came to reminisce over our soldiering days, for he, like most jewelers, tends to see things at their face value. I prefer to delve a bit deeper, and when one puts the Watsons and the daughter of Sherlock Holmes together with a series of vandalized art, one reaches a different conclusion."

"You are most perceptive, but I must admit I am always interested in hearing and sharing stories from that war of long ago."

"As am I," Dubose said, and gently shifted his position. "Now tell me how I can be of help."

"We are tracking all of the vandalized paintings, from the moment they were purchased to the day of the defacing," said my father. "We are in hopes this will provide clues that will lead to the apprehension of the villain."

"Mine was a straightforward transaction," Dubose reported. "I stopped at an art gallery in the Marais section of Paris to browse about when I spotted the Cézanne. It was exceedingly lovely and even more expensive, but I simply had to have it."

"Do you recall the name of the gallery?"

"It carries the name Galerie Galbert and it is somewhat of an artistic powerhouse, with galleries in Italy, Switzerland, and Greece."

"Do they have a branch in London?"

"Not to my knowledge."

"Pray continue."

"After purchasing the Cézanne, we returned to our hotel on the Champs-Élysées, from which we departed the following day."

"I take it you returned by ferry?"

"We did, and a rough journey it was, for the weather over the weekend had become storm-like, with high waves that pounded us relentlessly. I have a brake on my wheelchair which I applied, but it still required Bikram's strong arms to keep me from bouncing about."

"Was the painting placed in storage aboard the ferry?"

"Heavens, no!" Dubose replied at once. "We anticipated some turbulence, and one can readily imagine the damage it might do to a fragile painting. For that reason, the Cézanne was always in Bikram's hands or on my lap. We were met at the dock by a motor car and driven home."

"Do you reside at your brother's home?"

"He wishes me to do so, but it would be most inconvenient, for a man in a wheelchair requires somewhat special accommodations. The doors must be widened, cabinets and shelves lowered so they can be within reach, and of course there must be no stairs or steps. My home in Notting Hill is so outfitted and, with the assistance of Bikram, I get along quite nicely."

"Since it was to be a surprise gift, I suspect you kept it well hidden in the event your brother paid you an unexpected visit."

"Exactly so, Watson. The Cézanne was covered and placed on the top shelf of a locked closet, where it remained until the day it was given to my brother."

A dead-end, I thought dispiritedly. Despite my father's careful questioning, we had discovered no clues that would connect the Cézanne to the other vandalized paintings. My father and I exchanged subtle glances, indicating it was time to depart. But it was at that moment that a final question came to my father's mind. "Was the Cézanne wrapped as a gift?"

"Of course, for removing the wrapping adds immeasurably to the delight of receiving a gift," Dubose answered, and looked to his aide. "Who did the wrapping for us, Bikram?"

"The art gallery that repaired the frame, sir," Bikram replied.

"Yes, yes," Dubose recalled immediately. "Several of the screws on the frame had become disjointed, so we thought it best that it be fixed by an expert."

"Was the expert at an art gallery?" my father asked at once.

"Naturally," Dubose said. "Who else would you trust with a Cézanne?"

"And the name of this art gallery?"

Dubose looked once more to Bikram who answered, "The very fine gallery of Hawke and Evans, where it remained for an entire day so the necessary repairs and reconditioning of the frame could be done in a most excellent manner."

With that information in hand, we bade Albert Dubose good-bye, with wishes for a speedy recovery, and with the very same thought in both our minds.

Joanna now had her common denominator.

6

The Art Historian

On our arrival home we found Joanna and her son waiting for us in the parlor, chatting over cups of tea. Johnny appeared to be well, but his face was a bit drawn and fatigued, no doubt from the long day that had begun at dawn.

"Ah, Johnny," my father greeted the boy warmly. "How nice to see you again."

The lad hurried over to shake my father's and my hand, saying, "It is always a pleasure being in your company." He moved in closer to us and sniffed at our clothes once, then twice, and asked, "Have you two been in contact with a carcass?"

The grandson of Sherlock Holmes, I thought to myself. He not only carries the great detective's looks, but his brain and nose as well. "Would you care to guess what we encountered?" I asked. "Was it animal or human?"

"The odor is the same for both," Johnny replied. "But since my dear mother told me you were visiting a hospital this morning, I would place a wager on the source being a very ill or dead human."

"It emanates from a patient who is quite alive," my father replied. "But before we delve into those details, I must inquire on the status of the cholera outbreak at Eton."

"I am afraid it continues to spread," Joanna answered. "There have been five more cases reported, two of whom are Johnny's classmates. I am surprised London's newspapers have not reported more on the particulars of this dreaded outbreak."

"I suspect their articles have been somewhat sketchy on numbers, so as not to unduly alarm the public," my father surmised. "Even the editorials play down the extent of the outbreak and assure it will shortly be brought under control."

"Surely this is the case," said I. "The safe water supply and modern sanitation facilities should limit the number of those afflicted."

"It will, but not before considerable harm is done," my father went on. "As one editorial so wisely pointed out, cholera is not a disease of the past, but one lying in wait, and given the right set of circumstances, will strike with deadly effect."

"But highly unlikely in England," I ventured.

"And highly unlikely in Italy and Spain, yet in the past year alone outbreaks have occurred in Naples and in a fishing village south of Barcelona." My father gave further thought to the dreadful infection before grazing over to Joanna and asking, "Are they certain the disease was brought to England by a Spanish ship?"

Joanna nodded. "Which is believed to have become contaminated during a brief stopover in Morocco."

"Well, let us hope that Eton is both the beginning and the end of this outbreak, so we can devote our full energies to the art vandal," said my father.

"That reminds me," Joanna interjected. "The art historian Edwin Alan Rowe called, having returned from his tour earlier than expected. He of course has heard of the art vandal and is quite eager to lend his assistance in solving this case. I took the liberty of setting a meeting with him this afternoon at the National Gallery."

Johnny's lidded eyes opened noticeably. "May I inquire as to the details of this case, Mother?"

Joanna sighed to herself, knowing there was no way to get around the lad's inquisitive mind. She studied his face briefly, no doubt having the same thought I had earlier. He looked so much like a young Sherlock Holmes, with his long, narrow face, heavily lidded eyes, and jutted chin. "I shall give you a brief summary, but you should hold your questions until I am done."

"Of course, Mother."

Joanna outlined the case of the art vandal, describing the defacing of the paintings and the various places where the vandalism occurred. She emphasized the point that most of the destructive acts happened in art galleries, and only a few in private homes. In conclusion, she added, "Scotland Yard believes this is the work of a crazed individual. Are you of the same opinion?"

Johnny gave the matter his fullest attention before asking, "Do the private homes invaded belong to the owners of the art galleries?"

"They do not," Joanna replied. "They are separate and distinct."

"Then how could this vandal possibly know that the paintings were in these homes?"

"That is the key question."

A thin smile came to Johnny's face. "Mother, I am afraid you are not dealing with a crazed person, but rather a clever one who has a purpose."

"Which is?"

"To learn that, you will have to catch the villain."

"We may well be a step nearer to this vandal," my father chimed in. "For my son and I have now connected the Cézanne to a local art gallery."

"How so?" Joanna asked at once.

"Albert Dubose informed us," my father continued on. "He did indeed purchase the Cézanne from a Parisian gallery and brought it back to London under the careful eye of both he and his manservant, Bikram. The only time the painting left their possession was when Bikram took it to a prominent London gallery to have its frame repaired and reconditioned. Would you care to guess the name of the gallery?"

"Hawke and Evans," Joanna breathed.

"Hawke and Evans indeed."

"And that is where we can place our villain," Joanna said in a rush. "Think of the various occurrences which lead to that conclusion. The Hawke and Evans gallery was broken into twice, not once, and this is more than any other gallery. Furthermore, both of the paintings in the private homes had also been retouched by hands at a single London gallery, namely Hawke and Evans."

"We also know that, according to Delvecchio, the slashed paintings in the other galleries were previously retouched by the restorers at Hawke and Evans," my father added.

"That, too," Joanna agreed.

"But who at Hawke and Evans might be responsible?" I asked.

"Any of them, past or present, for none should be placed above suspicion," Joanna replied.

"But our main suspect—the individual with the obvious dermatitis involving the scalp and neck—does not work at Hawke and Evans," I countered. "Lestrade told us by phone that he carefully questioned Simon Hawke in this regard and the owner emphatically stated that no one in his employ matches that description."

"Which complicates matters," Joanna conceded. "Yet the man with the noticeable dermatitis is most certainly our vandal. But how he fits in at the gallery remains beyond our grasp."

"Could he be a hired hand?" I wondered.

"Unlikely, but possible," Joanna said before glancing at her watch. "Oh goodness! We must hurry or we shall be late for our meeting with Edwin Alan Rowe."

"May I come along, Mother?" Johnny requested.

"I think it best that you rest, for you have had a very long day already. I believe a nap would be quite in order."

"But you must promise to tell me of any important knowledge the art historian imparts to you."

"You have my word," Joanna assured and hurried to the coatrack. "Now we must be off, but on our way out I shall ask Miss Hudson to prepare one of her most sumptuous lunches for you."

"Please do not, Mother, for at the moment I have little appetite," Johnny begged off. "Perhaps it is the fatigue that accompanies a tiresome journey and the excitement of the day which dampens my desire for lunch. After a brief respite, however, my appetite should return and I will ring for Miss Hudson whose lunches are unsurpassed and to which I always look forward."

We grabbed our hats and coats and hurried down the stairs, all believing that the fatigue and excitement of the day had indeed dampened Johnny's usual keen interest in Miss Hudson's wonderfully prepared lunches. But in retrospect, we should have known better, for his symptoms were the prodrome of something far more serious to come.

★ ★ ★

On entering the National Gallery, we spotted Edwin Alan Rowe at the place we were appointed to meet. Tall and slender, with long gray hair and hawklike features, he was studying van Gogh's famous painting *Sunflowers* and seemed most interested in the lowest section of the canvas. Out of the corner of his eye he must have seen us, for he waved us over and, after rapid introductions, regaled us with the story that lay behind the remarkable work of art.

"Van Gogh actually painted five *Sunflowers,* of which the National Gallery has one, whilst the others are spread all over the world," Rowe informed. "What makes the paintings so unique is that they are all done in three shades of yellow and nothing else."

"You seemed to be focusing your attention on the lower portion of the canvas," I inquired. "Is there a reason?"

"I was studying his signature on the painting which of course is Vincent, his first name," Rowe replied. "As you may know, there have been numerous attempts to forge *Sunflowers,* most of which were not that good. But there was one in particular that was well done and duped some of Europe's so-called experts. We were asked to authenticate it, and determined it was a forgery based on van Gogh's signature. You see, to age a painting, forgers use a special baking technique that produces small cracks and wrinkles in the canvas, and these of course are signs of aging. Our forger performed this task admirably, but for some reason the paint applied to produce the name *Vincent* remained relatively recent. Thus I always tip my hat to van Gogh's first name." Rowe studied the lower section of *Sunflowers* once again, then gave it a final nod. "But you are not here to learn of van Gogh, but to delve into the mystery of the art vandal. So, with that in mind, let us retire to a more private setting."

We followed him up to the second level and into a small,

cramped office with barely enough room for a desk and three chairs. On the walls were photographs of men who at one time or another had occupied the upper echelon of the National Gallery. A thick mahogany door muted any sounds coming from the corridor.

"I of course have read the newspaper accounts of the art vandal, but know little else," Rowe began. "So please be good enough to furnish all the details and any clues you may have at your disposal."

Joanna provided Rowe with a concise, yet comprehensive summary, with particular emphasis on the nature and sites of the West End vandalism. She concluded by informing the historian of the connection of the destructive acts to the Hawke and Evans gallery.

Rowe steepled his fingers and peered at us over them. "Hawke and Evans, you say?"

"So the arrows seem to point," Joanna replied.

"Which raises the possibility of the said gallery collecting insurance on the damaged paintings, for Hawke and Evans is known to be hanging on the edge of financial insolvency."

"As a result of the recent vandalism?" asked Joanna.

"Oh, no," Rowe went on. "Their financial difficulties started with the death of Andrew Evans who was the founding partner and the driving force behind the gallery. Hawke was allowed in because he married Evans's sister, and subsequently paid a large sum to have his name placed first on the signage. It was at this time that Evans's health was failing and he wanted the extra money to provide security for his wife. In any event, it was Evans who had the eye for the art and the business acumen that is so necessary for an art gallery to thrive. When Evans passed away, the downfall of Hawke and Evans began."

"But why bother to slash paintings in other galleries?" Joanna pondered.

"As a cover," Rowe answered. "If you destroy others, it takes attention away from yours. Nevertheless, I have my doubts that this is the purpose behind the vandalism. There are too many galleries involved. One or two would be acceptable. Five would be an unnecessary exaggeration."

"And the vandalism at private homes surely does not fit with that notion," said Joanna.

"That, too," Rowe concurred. "Which brings us to the possibility that the damage was done to stir up the restoration business for the art gallery. Restoration is most profitable, for although labor intensive, it requires little space and even less materials. It is not uncommon for extensive restoration to involve months of work which can cost a hundred pounds or more. In unscrupulous galleries, the time needed to complete the work is prolonged and the cost inflated. But this possibility is unlikely for a reason."

"The damage is far too extensive," Joanna noted.

"Precisely," Rowe agreed. "Widely slashed canvases are most difficult to restore and when they are, the mending is quite noticeable unless done by a master restorer, of which there are few. The vast majority of vandals used either paint or lipstick to deface paintings, and those can be removed with solvents before the retouching is undertaken. So, with these facts in mind, I believe we can exclude insurance and restoration as causes. There must be another that fits better."

"There is," said Joanna. "But I neglected an important clue which points to the most likely reason. I did this purposely so that you would give us the broad range of possibilities, and not focus on a single answer."

"And that clue is?"

"The vandal made a vertical slash on all the canvases and then lifted and folded one edge."

"He is searching!" Rowe cried out.

"But for what?"

"A number of possibilities, but the most likely one is there is another painting that was hidden beneath the slashed portrait." Rowe rubbed his hands together, clearly warming to the new subject. "Concealing one painting beneath another is an age-old device used by thieves and smugglers to hide and transport the work of art from country to country to a waiting buyer. Think about it for a moment. How often is a painting taken down and removed to ascertain if something of value lies behind it? Virtually never is the answer."

"Unless one knows it is there," Joanna interjected.

"And that raises a difficult question," Rowe said quickly. "Allow me to give you an example. Several of the paintings slashed date back to the Italian Renaissance and have remained in their frames since that time. How could the vandal possibly know that yet another painting was hidden behind the original?"

"Could he have read about it in some obscure document?" I suggested.

Rowe's eyes brightened. "An excellent idea, and one that connects to similar cases I have dealt with over the years. Mind you, these are long shots, but they would be a best fit. In one instance, a master forger on his deathbed gave his son an old letter that spoke of a hidden painting behind a painting. The son retrieved it, but was apprehended while trying to sell it on the black market. The second case was more challenging and required a court order to unravel. Here, the information was passed from brother to brother in a last will and testament. And the third case will surely draw your interest. The thief, who was also an art historian, had come across an ancient scroll while on a sabbatical leave in Italy. The scroll mentioned such a concealment, but the name of the concealed painting was written in code. The code spoke of a gallant warrior protecting the secret masterpiece, and that turned out to be *Saint George Slaying the Dragon* by Carlo Crivelli. With the message deciphered, my colleague devised a plan to remove the Crivelli painting, which revealed a masterpiece by none other than the great Michelangelo da Caravaggio."

"The Michelangelo who adorned the ceiling of the Sistine Chapel?" I asked.

"No, no," Rowe replied promptly. "That was Michelangelo Buonarroti. The hidden masterpiece was done by Michelangelo da Caravaggio, who was every bit as talented as Buonarroti. Some actually consider Caravaggio the superior of the two."

"Was your colleague successful?" Joanna inquired.

Rowe shook his head, with a quick smile. "Fortunately my colleague was a better historian than thief."

"Are you suggesting our vandal read some ancient scroll?" Joanna asked in disbelief.

"That is most unlikely unless he is well versed in the Italian language and a scholar in Italian art from long ago," Rowe replied. "More likely, assuming there is hidden art, I would think your vandal learned the secret from another thief, and he was told that the site of the hidden art centers around the portrait of a woman. Perhaps the words or message would state that the painting is concealed behind the lady or that a lady's face cloaks it. This blends in nicely with the vandal slashing open portraits of women."

"Given all the possibilities, which would be your best assessment?" Joanna requested.

"Your vandal is someone who knows art and knows his way around art galleries. He in all likelihood learned of this information by word of mouth from an art thief or perhaps through a forger. By all accounts he is clever and has attempted to disguise his true purpose with the outward appearance of vandalism. If he has accomplished his goal, there will be no further acts of vandalism. If he has not, expect more until he finds the hidden painting."

On that note, we thanked Edwin Alan Rowe for his time and advice, and left the National Gallery, walking out into the bright, crisp sunshine that glowed down on the monuments in Trafalgar Square.

"What do you propose we do next?" my father asked Joanna.

"We retrace every step the vandal took, and search for the hidden clue that will lead to the resolution of this case."

My father waited for a group of tourists to pass before asking, "Where shall we begin?"

"With Hawke and Evans, for that is where the clue lies and the vandal resides."

7

Cholera

Something was wrong!

Whether it was maternal instinct or the fact she was a light sleeper, the sound of footsteps scurrying to the lavatory caused Joanna to bolt from our bed and dash into the parlor, with me only a step behind.

My father was already there, standing in the center of the room and grim-faced as he announced, "I am afraid that cholera has come to 221b Baker Street."

Joanna's face paled whilst she struggled to collect herself. "Are—are you certain?"

"It is by far the most likely diagnosis," my father replied. "When explosive diarrhea occurs in the midst of a cholera outbreak, that disease must be considered first and foremost."

"But there are certainly other possibilities," Joanna said, hoping against hope.

"There are," my father answered without conviction. "At times, infection with *Salmonella* or *Shigella* can produce similar symptoms, but they almost always occur when there are others afflicted with the same disorder."

"So," Joanna muttered softly, "for the third time in my life I am encountering this dreadful disease which has cost me so dearly."

"But even in its most vicious form, the mortality rate is less than five percent, and when appropriately treated that rate is lessened by half."

"That is what they told me when the diagnosis was made in my former husband." Joanna paused to take a long, deep breath as a look of melancholy came to her face. "Three days later he was dead, so you will understand when I say that supposed mortality rates mean little to me."

"But the circumstances in John Blalock's death were quite different."

"Death is still death, Watson."

Joanna never discussed her former husband's disease with me, but my father knew the details all too well, for he was on staff at St. Bartholomew's where John Blalock died. The distinguished surgeon apparently perished because he had a silent, underlying kidney disease that lapsed into fatal renal failure brought on by the severe dehydration that can accompany cholera. I wondered if Blalock's kidney problem was congenital in nature and, if so, had he passed the disorder on to his son Johnny. I could not help but wonder if this terrifying possibility had also crossed Joanna's mind.

The silence in the room was broken by the sound of running water. We waited patiently for Johnny to appear, but the door remained closed.

"As I recall, fluid replenishment is the single most important treatment for cholera," Joanna said, now gathering her clinical wits.

"It is," my father agreed. "And it must be done with vigor, with every milliliter lost being replenished."

"So the loss has to be accurately measured, which is impossible to do when the discharge is into a toilet bowl."

"We can estimate," I proposed.

"Not good enough," Joanna said at once. Her eyes rapidly scanned the room, from the unlighted fireplace to the bookshelves to the individual pieces of furniture. In a quick motion, she brought her gaze back to an old chair with a straw seat that had seen better days. She hurried over to it and tested the firmness of the knitted straw-like material. "It needs to be replaced."

"I will get to it eventually," my father promised.

"It is fortunate you have not done so, for we shall put it to good use." Joanna reached for a sturdy knife she used to pin important messages to a bulletin board, and carved out a six-by-six-inch square from the center of the straw seat. "We shall place a bucket beneath it and Johnny can use it as a bedside commode. This setup will allow us to obtain an accurate measurement of his output."

"We will require a good-sized bucket, for in cases of cholera gravis patients can lose an enormous amount of fluid, at times exceeding a quart an hour," my father noted. "And when he leaves the bathroom shortly, we should have a quart of liquid ready for him to slowly consume. I have the recipe written down in one of my files."

"I know it all too well," Joanna said and hurried to a nearby cupboard, from which she extracted bags of sugar and salt. "And we have plenty of the ingredients on hand."

"Excellent," my father approved, but then added a solemn caution. "We must hope that he is not affected with the nausea and vomiting that may accompany the disease."

"Did he complain of these symptoms?" Joanna asked worriedly.

"He did not, but then again he was in a rush to relieve himself."

A cry came from the lavatory, followed by another.

"I had better attend to Johnny," my father said, racing for the bathroom and closing the door behind him.

Joanna remained stoic for a moment, then flew into my arms and whispered in a trembling voice, "I am so frightened, John, for I find myself in the midst of events I cannot control. All of my wit and cleverness are of no use to me at this dreadful moment."

"We shall make certain he recovers," I comforted.

"From your words to God's ear."

For the first time in our marriage, Joanna showed helplessness and vulnerability which she could neither control nor hide. But then again, I reminded myself, her most precious possession, her son Johnny, was at real risk and just the thought of losing him was more than she could endure.

"I am so fortunate to have you at my side," Joanna breathed, as her lips brushed my cheek.

"And I, you," said I, holding her close and knowing I could never love another as much as I loved my dear Joanna.

We parted as the door to the lavatory opened and my father reappeared. "He is fine."

Joanna quickly regained her composure before asking, "What was the cause of his discomfort?"

"A bit of intestinal spasm," my father reported. "It has passed."

"Let us pray it does not recur," said Joanna, relieved at the diagnosis. "How long will the diarrhea persist, Watson?"

"Usually two to three days, but sometimes longer if the dose of the cholera bacteria is large."

"Does the same hold true for the other diagnoses you mentioned?"

"I am afraid so. Thus, the length of time of the symptoms does not distinguish between these infectious disorders."

"So time is of no help."

"None whatsoever," said my father. "But they can be separated by having the bacteriology laboratory culture the lad's stool specimen. If it is indeed cholera, the bacteria will grow out on a culture plate within twenty-four hours."

"That test should be set up at St. Bartholomew's as soon as possible."

"I will see to it."

The three of us busied ourselves preparing the sugar-salt solutions that were to be used to rehydrate Johnny. Joanna placed several quart-sized bottles containing the liquid on our windowsill, so that the chilly outside air would cool the sugar-salt solutions and make them easier to swallow. I was reaching for yet another bottle to fill, when the door to the lavatory opened wide. Johnny stepped out into the parlor on shaky legs and slowly made his way to a chair by the fireplace.

Sitting down heavily, he complained in a weak voice, "The runs are dreadful."

Joanna came to his side and was about to reach out for Johnny's hand, but decided not to, for such contact could spread the disease to her. With patience, she explained every aspect of the disorder to him and how it was to be treated. She emphasized the absolute need for the fluid lost to be accurately measured and replaced ounce for ounce with oral liquids. "We will set up a bedside commode so we will know your exact losses and this will determine how much you have to drink in order to avoid becoming dehydrated."

"How long will this awful business last, Mother?" Johnny asked through parched lips.

"A few days, so it is imperative that you follow our instructions to the letter."

Johnny nodded weakly. "I shall do my best."

"Your symptoms will occur intermittently," my father told the lad. "It is during the calm periods that you must replenish yourself. Drink slowly, giving each mouthful a chance to reach your stomach and be absorbed into your system. Do not attempt to force large amounts down all at once, for this can result in regurgitation."

"I do not believe I could ingest large quantities of fluids quickly, even if ordered to do so."

"Are you having any nausea and vomiting?" my father asked concernedly.

"No, sir," Johnny replied and rubbed at his stomach. "I do feel a bit queasy now and then, however."

"Not to worry," said my father. "That is to be expected."

"I am sorry to be of such bother," Johnny apologized.

"Nonsense," my father insisted. "You will never be a bother to us."

A faint smile came to Johnny's face, but it quickly faded. In a fraction of a second he jumped to his feet, but he was weak and wavered from side to side. Joanna hurriedly reached up and grabbed her son's hand which steadied him and allowed him to regain his footing. Only then did he dash for the lavatory. But on his way he picked up a bottle of replenishing liquid to take with him. Even in his worst moments, I thought, that marvelous brain of his continued to work.

Joanna sighed sadly and, rising from her chair, walked over to the Persian slipper that held her Turkish cigarettes.

"Do not smoke!" my father cried out.

Joanna rapidly withdrew her hand. "Will the cigarette smoke adversely affect Johnny?"

"Not Johnny, but you," warned my father. "You see, you just touched your son's hand that is no doubt loaded with the cholera bacteria. Your hand will transfer the bacteria to the cigarette, and when you bring that cigarette to your mouth it will carry with it heaven knows how many of those vicious microorganisms. And we will then have a second case of cholera in these rooms."

"Thank you for being the wise and good physician, Watson," Joanna acknowledged gratefully.

"Not at all," my father said and reminded us that, although the initial cases of the disease occurred as a result of ingesting contaminated food, the disease can spread in the general population as a result of hand-to-mouth contact. "So we have to institute the following preventative measures. First, after Johnny finishes with his current bout of diarrhea, we must thoroughly scrub down the bathroom and anything else he may have touched, and restrict the lad to his bedroom and bedside commode. Next, we should stock up on rubber gloves and use them whenever we have contact with Johnny or any item he may have touched. Even then, it is wise to wash your hands with soap and water after any such contact. We are to have no visitors and Miss Hudson is not to be allowed in these rooms. Mail and messages and dishes of food can be left outside the door. We shall inform her that Johnny has severe bronchitis and it may well be contagious."

So we set out to scrub down each and every room at 221b Baker Street, paying particular attention to anything Johnny touched or otherwise came in contact with. Once we had thoroughly cleaned the parlor, we waited until Johnny exited the bathroom, then washed down every surface of the toilet and basin, as well as every inch of the floor and walls within arm's reach. It required several hours for us to complete these tasks and by then sunlight was streaming in through the window that overlooked the snow-covered street.

As we sat around the fireplace for a well-deserved rest, the phone rang. We debated briefly whether to answer it, for we were in no mood to do so, but then again it may be related to the outbreak of cholera and some new aspect of the disease.

Joanna reached for the phone and spoke at length with Inspector Lestrade. Her expression remained neutral as she agreed to something or other at a designated place. She then insisted on his presence there and received his consent before placing the phone down.

"Lestrade has arranged for us to meet with the Earl of Wessex later this morning," Joanna informed us. "I was about to ask the inspector to delay the meeting, but was told the earl would shortly leave for his country estate. Thus, I agreed to a meeting at noon."

"But surely you will wish to remain here to care for Johnny," said I.

"And so I shall, for you will go in my stead," Joanna went on. "We must learn all the details of the break-in and every aspect of the painting that was slashed. Delve deeply into the painting itself, namely the artist, the time period of his work, and how the earl came by it. And most importantly, how and why the painting found its way to Hawke and Evans for restoration."

"What shall I hope to uncover?"

"Another important yet undisclosed clue."

I hesitated to agree to the meeting, for my place was here with my family. "But what if I am needed to assist in Johnny's care?"

"Watson and I can deal with any problems which arise," Joanna said. "Furthermore, we need someone to deliver the stool specimen to the bacteriology laboratory at St. Bartholomew's. Please be good enough to drop off the specimen on your way to meet with the earl."

"You can of course reach me by phone at the earl's house if you require my presence."

"We shall inform you if such a need arises."

As I retired to change from my bedclothes, I could not help but notice the firm resolve in Joanna's face, but I also saw the sadness and worry in her eyes, and I knew I would carry the pangs of guilt with every step I took away from 221b Baker Street.

8

The Countess

The Earl of Wessex, with Lestrade at his side, received me in
the elegant drawing room of his mansion that was located in
the affluent neighborhood of Belgravia. Lord Granville was
quite short and slight of frame, with inquisitive brown eyes
and a gentle face that held no pretense. After the introductions, he greeted me with a warm handshake, but seemed
disappointed not to see Joanna.

"I had hoped to meet the famous daughter of Sherlock
Holmes," said he. "Is she indisposed?"

"No, my lord," I replied. "She unfortunately was called
away on a most urgent matter."

"Relating to the art vandal?"

"So it would seem," I lied easily.

"Is there then hope for a rapid resolution?"

"Only a glimmer," I said and turned my attention to the
defaced painting.

"Ah, to the painting which is the purpose of your visit."
Following my gaze, the earl walked over to the slashed portrait and shook his head sadly. "It is a precious work of art

whose value goes far beyond its market price. You see, it was a wedding gift from Queen Victoria herself."

"Was it from the Royal Collection?"

"One does not make such inquiries," the earl replied in a guarded tone. "But why do you ask?"

"I have been told that the Royal Collection in fact belongs to the people, and that the Crown is only its guardian and protector."

"And so Victoria was," the earl said, with a thin smile. "But then again, a queen can do as she wishes without there being a murmur of complaint. The Crown does have certain privileges."

Particularly when those privileges remain secret and away from public scrutiny, I thought, but held my tongue.

At that moment, a massive, heavy-boned mastiff ambled into the room and sat on his haunches not more than ten feet away. To his side was a large, beautifully adorned Christmas tree, with a silver star atop and nicely wrapped gifts beneath it. The hound ignored the tree and gifts and seemed only interested in the visitors, upon whom he kept his eyes fixed.

"Nelson is a most serious dog and is aroused by any change in the household," said the earl.

"Was he here the night of the break-in?" I asked at once.

"Unfortunately not, Dr. Watson, for he was spending the night at the veterinarian's," the earl replied. "Had he been present, I can assure you the vandal would have been in for a most unpleasant evening."

"I take it there are no other dogs within your home?"

"None, for Nelson does not enjoy canine companionship."

My attention returned to the defaced portrait that had been bisected with a long, vertical slash. Although an edge had been folded back, one could see the woman portrayed had a lovely face and short blond hair. Most striking was her deep purple velvet dress that had orange decorations on its shoulders. It, too, was slashed into unequal halves. "Can it be restored?"

"With some effort, I was told."

"Who will do the restoration?"

"No doubt Hawke and Evans, for that is who my wife will choose. You see, she is a true patron of the arts and makes such decisions for us."

I moved in closer to the painting and with a finger delicately moved a cut edge to the side, which gave me a clear view of its backing. As with the other vandalized portraits, the backing was pristine and had no slashes or deep scratches.

"What do you search for?" asked the earl.

"Markings that may have been left by the vandal, my lord."

"Were there any?"

"None to the naked eye."

I stepped back to again admire the glorious colors and painter's eye for exquisite detail. "Who was the artist of this fine work?"

"Paolo Veronese," said a feminine voice from behind me.

I turned and watched the approach of a most attractive woman of medium height, with sharp features and raven black hair that flowed down to her shoulders. But it was her doe-like eyes that caught and held one's attention. They were deep blue, the color of a calm mountain lake, and seemed to be looking both at and into you. Before joining us, she paused for a moment to warm her hands in front of a blazing fire which gave off the sweet aroma of burning applewood.

"May I present my wife, Lady Katherine," introduced the earl.

"And you, sir, are Dr. Watson, the chronicler of your

wife's most excellent adventures," said she, adorned in a riding outfit, complete with cap, red jacket, and white trousers tucked into well-shined boots.

"I am, my lady," I greeted, with a half bow that she acknowledged with a quarter of a nod. "My wife and father could not be in attendance, for they have been called away on an urgent matter and so I find myself here alone."

"You are nevertheless most welcome," Lady Katherine said warmly. "Now let us return to your question. The artist you asked about is Paolo Veronese, an Italian Renaissance painter whose true name was Paolo Caliari, but who gained the nickname Veronese because he was based in Verona where he acquired his fame. He was a most excellent painter and the portrait before you is entitled *La Bella Nani*. It was considered one of his best works and dates back to the year 1560."

"Dr. Watson had inquired if the portrait was originally part of the Royal Collection," the earl interjected. "I had no answer."

The countess shrugged indifferently. "I doubt that very much, but who is to know? If it did come from the collection housed at Windsor it would hardly be missed, for it would have been buried away in one of the world's greatest assemblages of art, which includes the works of Leonardo da Vinci, Michelangelo, Raphael, and Rembrandt. Although difficult to believe, there are over five hundred sketches and drawings by Leonardo da Vinci alone that are currently stored at Windsor. So, as talented as Veronese was, he could not begin to stand up to the others."

She reached for her riding cap and tossed it over to Nelson who quickly caught it with his lips, then trotted to a leather-backed chair and deposited it there. "You see, I have had the rare opportunity to review the Royal Collection, and the incredible sketches by da Vinci simply took my breath away, as did the glorious Titians and Caravaggios that have never been publicly displayed. I sit on an advisory committee and am on excellent terms with the curators at Windsor, and it was in this capacity that I directed certain restorations to Evans and Hawke before Andrew's untimely death."

"Do you continue to recommend that particular gallery for the royal restorations?" asked I.

"Not as vigorously as I once did."

It was now clear to me that it was Lady Katherine and not her husband who would hold the most knowledge about the painting and its projected restoration. Fortunately she seemed quite eager to share this information.

"But it is beyond me why anyone would vandalize such a gorgeous work of art," Lady Katherine went on. "It is akin to attacking a defenseless child who cannot speak."

"But hopefully it can be restored," I consoled.

"It *will* be restored," Lady Katherine said determinedly.

"By Hawke and Evans, I presume."

"By Evans and Hawke," she corrected as her face hardened.

"I am not sure I follow you, my lady."

The countess took a deep breath and her expression softened, but her lips remained tight. "The firm was founded by my dear cousin Andrew Evans, who had a most keen eye for art and knew his way around the business world as well. It was he who brought the gallery to prominence and it was he who brought in Simon Hawke to be a partner. Simon was junior to Andrew in every way and I believe he deeply resented it. When poor Andrew came down with consumption, Simon took over the management and the downfall of the gallery began." She abruptly flicked her wrist, as if waving away the memory. "So much for the past."

But I was determined to learn more about Simon Hawke

and his gallery that was connected in so many ways to the art vandalism. I decided to tantalize her with a fact we had uncovered earlier. "We were told that Hawke had to pay a heavy price for the name change of the gallery."

"Ten thousand pounds." Lady Katherine spat out the words. "For the gallery and all its contents, which was a most low valuation by anyone's estimate. But Andrew was dying and wanted to make sure his family would be looked after, knowing full well he could never depend on Simon Hawke. Simon of course took advantage of the situation and changed the gallery's name before dear Andrew was cold in his grave. And that is when the downhill slide began."

"We heard tell that the gallery is on the brink of financial insolvency."

"Which is not surprising due to Simon's mismanagement."

"And his gambling debts and the upkeep of his young mistress," the earl added.

"That, too," Lady Katherine agreed. "But it is his mismanagement that continues to boggle the mind. Allow me to give you one example. The gallery had the opportunity to obtain *The Baptism of Christ* by del Verrocchio who was believed to be da Vinci's mentor. Da Vinci's mentor!" she repeated with gusto. "Here was the artist who taught the famous Leonardo."

"Did they ever collaborate?" I asked.

"A most interesting question, for which the answer is yes," the countess replied. "It is believed that Leonardo actually painted an angel in the corner of del Verrocchio's *The Baptism of Christ*. Now, how in the world can you resist a work of art so closely tied to the great da Vinci? How? In any event, my cousin Andrew realized its incredible worth and was in negotiation with the owner when he was overcome with consumption. Andrew implored Simon Hawke to purchase the painting, but Simon refused because of its high price and need for extensive restoration. Instead, the Crown bought it and restored it, and this glorious painting will shortly be on display at the National Gallery. That is all one needs to know about Simon Hawke and his failing business."

"And the acts of vandalism certainly do not help his gallery," I noted.

Lady Katherine's eyes narrowed sharply. "You and the daughter of Sherlock Holmes should be aware that more than a few of the defaced works of art were among those Simon Hawke regretted purchasing."

"But the slashed paintings we saw were there for restoration and not for sale," I recalled.

"Some were, but others belonged to Simon and were for the most part gathering dust." The countess turned to Lestrade and said, "It would be a simple matter to determine if the damaged paintings owned by the gallery were insured or perhaps overly insured."

"Several were insured, but for less than five hundred pounds," Lestrade answered. "And those can be restored, which will significantly lower the amount the insurance company will pay out. Thus, insurance seems an unlikely motive for the destructive acts."

"Any port in a storm," Lady Katherine recited.

"You seem to have an unfavorable view of Simon Hawke," Lestrade said bluntly.

"I am not alone in that opinion."

"Countess, I should say that dislike does not make one a criminal," Lestrade pointed out.

"It doesn't make one innocent, either."

Lady Katherine had more than dislike for Simon Hawke, I thought immediately. It bordered on real hatred and I wondered if it was based on happenings other than Hawke's poor treatment of Andrew Evans. Was there a secret relationship between the two? Was she a scorned woman? Or was there a promised vow made but not kept? I wished Joanna was here, for she was quite clever at discerning the underlying reasons for feminine bitterness. In addition, it would be most interesting to watch Joanna and Lady Katherine match wits, although I had no doubt who would end up the winner.

I returned my attention to the painting *La Bella Nani* and said, "The colors in this work are so dazzling."

"That is because it was recently restored," the countess explained. "It had been protected over the years with a thick varnish that unfortunately yellowed with time and dulled the colors. The excellent restorer who performed the work is no longer at Hawke's gallery, having gone wrong and been convicted of forgery. I am not certain who we shall turn to now for yet another restoration."

"Simon Hawke has employed another talented restorer who trained at the Uffizi," I said.

"Who gave you that information?" Lady Katherine asked.

"Simon Hawke."

"Let the buyer beware."

Another dagger thrown at the heart of Simon Hawke, I thought immediately. What could be the deep-seated reason behind her intense dislike of the gallery owner? I once again considered the possibilities. A secret affair? A broken vow? An investment that went sour? At this point it was speculation and guesses. All that was certain was that here was yet another connection which led directly to Simon Hawke.

For some reason, Nelson the mastiff decided to let forth a loud bark as he jumped to his feet.

"Nelson," the earl rebuked mildly.

The mastiff growled and barked even louder again.

Lady Katherine gave the dog a sharp look and said firmly, "Stop it!"

Nelson quieted immediately and hung his head, as if in shame.

"Down," the countess commanded in a softer voice.

The mastiff dropped his haunches and laid down on the floor in a most placid manner, his huge brown eyes peering at his mistress and awaiting her next order.

I nodded to Lestrade, indicating our visit should come to an end, then returned to the royal couple. "Thank you both for your helpful information and suggestions."

With Nelson escorting us to the door, the inspector and I departed the Belgravia mansion and walked out into a gray day, with darkening clouds and a chilled wind that threatened yet more unpleasant weather.

"Nothing much there, eh?" said Lestrade, turning up the collar of his topcoat.

"A little, perhaps," I replied, deciding to downplay the obvious fact that it was Lady Katherine who ruled the household, who was an expert in the world of Italian Renaissance art and restoration, and who would know all the hidden secrets of Simon Hawke. It was she, and not the earl, who Joanna should both talk with and investigate. Something deep within told me that Lady Katherine, the Countess of Wessex, held the key to unraveling the mystery of the art vandal.

9

Strange Symptoms

I returned to 221b Baker Street and found the mood lighter than when I departed. Johnny's explosive outbursts had diminished, giving us some hope that the dreaded disease was remitting. But my father warned that such apparent remissions were often temporary and could be again followed by violent discharge. We tried to remain optimistic as we gathered around a three-log fire in our comfortable overstuffed chairs and ignored the wind and rain outside that seemed to be gaining force.

Joanna was pouring tea when a loud knock sounded on the door to Johnny's bedroom. We stopped our chatter and pricked our ears, for such a rap was usually accompanied by a disturbing report.

"The replenishing liquid is becoming most difficult to swallow," Johnny called out.

My father quickly looked to the bedroom. "Have you become nauseated?"

"A bit, sir."

"Are you throwing up?"

"I just have the nausea, sir, which I believe is caused by the high sugar content of the liquid."

"The sugar is important, for it represents your only source of nutrition which is required for your recovery."

In a low voice, Joanna suggested, "Perhaps we should lower the sugar concentration to make the fluid more palatable."

My father nodded his approval.

"Johnny, listen carefully," Joanna instructed loudly. "I want you to empty the bottle by a third, then replace it with water from the basin. This will lessen the sugar content and make the taste more agreeable. I would like you to do this with all the remaining bottles."

"Yes, Mother," Johnny replied and we heard the sound of water running.

Joanna came back to my father and said, "Of course when we decrease the sugar we also diminish the salt content which is critically important for hydration. Thus I propose we reconstitute our mixture to contain the same amount of salt, but half as much sugar. I would rather sacrifice calories than salt, for it is dehydration which kills in cholera, not nutrient deprivation."

The worry on Joanna's face and in her voice was obvious, for every aspect of the disease brought back a nightmarish memory. I injected a note of optimism by saying, "Perhaps the zenith of the disorder has passed."

Joanna turned to the bedroom door and called out, "Should we attend to your bucket?"

"Not as yet, Mother."

The three of us nodded to one another, for it was another good sign that indicated the lad's discharge was lessening. But a moment later we heard distressing sounds coming through the door to Johnny's bedroom and our confidence dipped.

"This is to be expected," my father said, unconcerned. "There will be ups and downs for a while yet, so do not become discouraged, for this is the usual course of cholera."

"But I still worry," Joanna admitted. "And will not rest until my son is well."

"That is understandable," said my father. "But if good fortune is with us, our Johnny will be on the road to recovery before the laboratory confirms the diagnosis of cholera." He glanced over to me and asked, "Were there any difficulties in arranging for the culture to be done by the bacteriologists at St. Bartholomew's?"

"None," I replied. "Although I thought it best they be warned that the infecting microorganism might be *Vibrio cholera*."

"I trust that you did not reveal that Johnny was the source," my father inquired.

I shook my head. "I told them it came from a colleague at Eton who did not have confidence in the local laboratory."

"Good show," my father approved. "No need to alarm the entire city of London, for the true source would have certainly become a topic of conversation at St. Bartholomew's and quickly spread outside its walls."

"I took the liberty of giving them our phone number, so they could call in the results, then hurried to the meeting with the Earl of Wessex, for I was behind time."

Joanna went back to pouring tea, with milk added beforehand, her mind now focusing on the mystery of the art vandal. "Was Lestrade there?"

"He was," I replied. "But I must say he did not seem overly eager to participate in the questioning."

"It was not his participation, but his presence that was of importance," said Joanna. "Even the royalty takes notice when Scotland Yard is actively involved, and they are more likely to pay attention and answer honestly."

"I believe their answers were indeed honest and then some, particularly so for the Countess of Wessex, who was quite forthright and provided information I think you will find most interesting."

"Was there a reason you directed your questioning to the countess?" asked Joanna.

"It was through no effort of mine," I responded. "For you see she rules the roost at the Wessex home."

Joanna's eyebrows went up. "In a stern voice?"

"By exhibition," I answered. "She simply took over the conversation in a smooth and easy fashion which indicated she was accustomed to such a role. And then there was the manner in which their dog responded to her commands, but not the earl's."

Joanna raised her brow again, higher this time. "There was a dog on the premises?"

I nodded. "A bloody huge mastiff, with a mouth and jaw large enough to take on a wolf and win."

"Was the hound in the home the night of the break-in?"

"Unfortunately not, for he was housed at the veterinarian's that evening."

Joanna sighed her disappointment. "Most unfortunate indeed."

The three of us exchanged knowing glances as we recalled the curious incident of the dog in the night that was mentioned by Sherlock Holmes in the case of *Silver Blaze*. The dog did nothing and did not bark at the intruder, indicating it knew the individual. Had the huge mastiff done the same, our list of suspects would have been narrowed down substantially.

"But what was most remarkable about the countess was

her vast knowledge of paintings from the Italian Renaissance period. The names of the famous and not-so-famous artists seemed to roll off her lips, and she easily recited their first names and the dates of their work. She apparently is a true patron of the arts and is quite close to the royal family."

"We know that the earl is fifth in line to the throne, so some degree of closeness is to be expected," Joanna said.

"Oh, it is more than that," I continued on. "For she is one of the select few allowed to view the Royal Collection at Windsor, and I suspect she has visited there on a goodly number of occasions. You see, she has viewed the hundreds of Leonardo da Vinci's sketches, as well as the works by Raphael, Michelangelo, and Caravaggio, and no doubt many others. This of course would require multiple visits to Windsor, and only those close to the Crown would be allowed to do so. The countess also sits on an advisory committee and on occasion has a say in the restoration of famous paintings."

Joanna leaned forward quickly, her interest piqued. "What kind of say?"

"Ah, here all becomes delightfully interconnected, for she has directed some of the restorations to the gallery of Evans and Hawke."

"You mean Hawke and Evans," Joanna corrected.

"No, my dear. Evans's name should be placed first and therein lies a story that is certain to grab and hold your attention."

In detail I described the sad saga of Andrew Evans who founded the gallery and guided it to prominence, then allowed Simon Hawke to become a partner, and shortly thereafter developed severe consumption and was taken advantage of by Hawke whilst Evans lay on his deathbed. "But the most tragic part of the story was that both would have become wealthy had Hawke only followed the advice of Evans. There was a famous painting entitled *The Baptism of Christ* that came on the market for an extraordinary price. Evans knew its true value, for the painting was by del Verrocchio who was Leonardo da Vinci's mentor. It is believed the mentor asked Leonardo to paint an angel in the corner of the work and the young pupil obliged him. A dying Evans begged Hawke to purchase it, for its value far exceeded its asking price. Hawke refused, Evans died, and the painting was soon after purchased by the Crown who had it so beautifully restored that it will shortly be on display at the National Gallery. It was upon Evans's death that the title of the gallery was reversed. I was somewhat surprised that Evans's name was not removed altogether."

Joanna smiled thinly. "Not so surprising when you consider the fact that it was Evans who had the sterling reputation, and that Hawke would wish to continue to take advantage of his dead partner's good name."

"This Simon Hawke is quite a piece of work," my father opined.

"And now comes the tantalizing connection," I went on. "It was abundantly clear that the Countess of Wessex has a deep, visceral hatred of Simon Hawke, for the partner Andrew Evans who Hawke treated so poorly was the countess's dear cousin."

"How dear?" Joanna asked promptly.

"Quite, for she spoke of him in a most loving voice."

"Were they close cousins?"

"I did not inquire."

"We must determine that," said Joanna. "For that sort of hatred begins with a deep, painful wound."

"Are you suggesting a romantic assignation gone bad?"

"A woman scorned has a mean voice," Joanna noted. "But there are other possibilities as well. A family feud can engender an unabating hatred that is passed down through the generations. Or perhaps the countess and her husband invested heavily in the gallery, only to watch their money disappear before their very eyes."

"The latter would fit if the investment was made during Andrew Evans's tenure when the gallery was thriving," I thought aloud. "According to the earl, the business is near to financial insolvency due to Hawke's incompetence and extravagant lifestyle."

Joanna arose from her seat and reached for a Turkish cigarette, then began pacing the floor of the parlor. She did so in silence, assembling the facts and deliberating on their possible interconnections. Abruptly she stopped and said, "There is more here than meets the eye."

"Are you thinking of Simon Hawke?" I asked.

"The Countess of Wessex," Joanna answered. "She must be questioned again, with particular reference to the restorations."

"Yes, yes," I said in a rush. "She mentioned the restorations currently being done at Hawke and Evans, and subtly questioned the quality of their workmanship. She seemed to have some concerns about Delvecchio, the young restorer who trained at the Uffizi."

Joanna smiled humorously. "She appears to be remarkably well informed on a gallery she despises and has no apparent connection to."

"And, according to her husband, their defaced painting will be restored there."

"Which is another contradiction. Why trust your valuable painting to a restorer whose ability you question? And why to a gallery you dislike so intensely?"

"She must be questioned again."

"Eventually, but first we should look into the two restorers who worked for Hawke and Evans before Delvecchio arrived on the scene."

"But one of the forgers has disappeared in Australia."

"How convenient."

"And the other is currently imprisoned at Wormwood Scrubs."

"Then he is the one we must question, for I require information that he alone can provide."

There was a loud rap on the door to Johnny's bedroom, and a moment later he cried out, "Mother! Mother! I can't move my legs!"

We rushed to the bedroom, with Joanna leading the way.

10

The Rumor

Johnny was curled up on the edge of his bed, grasping his knees and holding them firmly against his chest. The grimace on his face and the moaning sound he made told of his terrible discomfort.

"They won't move, Mother!" he complained bitterly, his agony heartbreaking. "The pain is more than I can bear."

My father hurried to the bedside and carefully examined the lad's legs with gentle palpitation. "Cramps! Severe muscle cramps brought on by the loss of nutrients," he diagnosed.

"Should he ingest more of the salty brew?" I suggested.

"Definitely not," my father replied. "For some strange reason, additional salt intake only worsens the condition."

"Is there any treatment?" Joanna asked anxiously.

"Pickle juice," my father answered.

"What!"

"Pickle juice," my father repeated. "It's an old remedy, but it works quite nicely. The juice seems to contain the nutrients which Johnny is now deficient in."

"Where can I find this pickle juice?" Joanna inquired.

"In Miss Hudson's pantry, for she oddly considers pickles to be a delicacy of some sort. Tell her you need it for one of your experiments, which she will believe without question." My father slowly stretched out Johnny's legs and began a deep massage to the large muscles, first to the gastrocnemius, then to the quadriceps. The agony gradually left Johnny's face.

"Thank you ever so much, Dr. Watson," the lad said, breathing a sigh of relief.

"You are most welcome," my father replied. "Now, you should walk about in your bedroom while your mother goes to fetch Miss Hudson's pickle juice. It has a disagreeable, sour taste, but its therapeutic effect cannot be denied. You must drink it to prevent further attacks."

"I shall manage, sir."

"I know you will, my boy. And be sure to swallow the pickle juice in small gulps, for otherwise it may back up on you."

"Tiny swallows, then."

"Exactly so," my father said and, after patting the lad's shoulder, led the way out of the bedroom. He then washed his hands with an antiseptic solution and advised us to do the same, in the event we had touched anything contagious in Johnny's room.

After drying her hands, Joanna hurriedly rang for Miss Hudson, then retreated to the long table where she carried out her experiments. In quick order she cleared an area before lighting a Bunsen burner, atop which she placed an Erlenmeyer flask filled with water.

"What sort of experiment do you plan?" asked I.

"None," Joanna said. "I am boiling water so I can brew fresh black tea for us. But it will also be useful in impressing Miss Hudson that I am deeply involved in my work, and thus she won't ask too many questions regarding her pickle juice."

As if on cue, Miss Hudson rapped gently on our door and quietly entered.

"Ah, Miss Hudson," Joanna greeted our landlady. "We are in need of pickle juice."

"How much?" Miss Hudson inquired.

"As much as you can spare."

"May I ask its purpose?"

"Of course. I wish to determine how long the odor of pickles will remain after staining various materials."

Miss Hudson's eyes brightened at the sight of the lighted Bunsen burner. "A clue to a mystery, then."

"Quite."

"Do you prefer sweet or dill?"

"Both."

Miss Hudson scurried out and returned minutes later with two large jars of pickle juice. Before Joanna's freshly brewed black tea was ready to serve, Johnny was sipping the vile liquid and, according to my father, tolerating it remarkably well.

"Well, then," my father said, returning to the fireside and wearily dropping into his comfortable chair. "Let us hope that is the last of today's excitement."

"Will the terrible muscle cramps recur?" Joanna asked.

"Probably not, but if they do it will be in a milder form," my father answered. "Once the lacking nutrients are replaced, the cramps will be gone for good."

"Excellent," said Joanna. "And thank you for your superb care."

"It was my pleasure to be of help."

The phone suddenly rang and we all instantly wondered what news it might bring. It was now early evening and only essential or dire revelations would be delivered at such a later hour. My father rushed to the phone saying, "It may be the laboratory. Sometimes they perform a Gram stain on the specimen and can preliminarily identify the infecting bacteria."

It was not the laboratory, but Edwin Alan Rowe who was calling.

"Hello, Edwin," my father greeted the art historian warmly. "Oh, not at all. I always look forward to hearing from you."

Joanna and I tried to interpret the phone conversation by piecing together the unconnected words and phrases we heard. The terms *masterpiece* and *black market* came up over and over. My father motioned to us for pen and paper which we rapidly supplied. He scribbled one note after another, often asking Rowe to repeat or clarify. Finally the lengthy conversation came to an end and my father hurried back to us, gleefully rubbing his hands together. "Oh, how the plot thickens!"

"Start at the very beginning, Watson," Joanna urged. "Provide us with every word and every detail."

"Our colleague Edwin Alan Rowe knows how to sniff out criminal behavior and he has demonstrated this talent yet again," my father commenced. "He of course has contacts in the not-so-reputable section of the art world, which includes London's black market. Rowe has learned there is a strong rumor circulating that a masterpiece of incalculable value will shortly be put up for sale."

"Did Rowe use the word *shortly*?" Joanna interrupted.

"Several times," my father replied. "He could not determine the nature of the artwork, other than it was a masterpiece which of course indicates it is a painting by one of the great masters."

"Could it be a sculpture, for those, too, can be considered masterpieces?" asked Joanna. "If that were the case, we would be following the wrong lead here."

"I so inquired, but was told that sculptures have little value on the black market, for they are far too large and bulky and thus difficult to move and even more difficult to sell. For example, only a museum or institute would be interested in a Rodin, and would only purchase it after its origin and authenticity were established. With this in mind, Rowe is certain we are dealing with a well-known masterpiece that relates to a painting. But here is where a problem arises." My father referred to his notes briefly before continuing. "When a true masterpiece is about to come onto the black market, it is a sure sign that it was recently stolen. Yet no such theft has been reported, which is usually the scenario when a heist of this magnitude occurs. There has not been even a whisper of such an event in the world of art, which is quite odd in itself."

Joanna gave the contradictory information thought before asking, "That may well hold true for thefts from museums and institutes, but what if the stolen painting is from a private collection whose owner wishes to avoid unwanted publicity?"

"According to Rowe, even in those circumstances word leaks out to the inner crowd who keep a sharp eye out, for such masterpieces are few and far between," said my father. "Yet Rowe remains convinced it is a stolen painting by one of the great masters, and I believe we should value his informed opinion."

"Indeed," Joanna agreed. "And the fact that the rumor is being circulated indicates there is no prearranged buyer for the work of art, in that such arrangements demand and require absolute confidentiality."

"Plus there would be no need to advertise the availability of the masterpiece by rumor, since a sale would already be assured," I added.

"That, too," Joanna concurred. "More than likely the seller is testing the waters to ascertain the price he could demand."

"But he would surely have to mention the name of the artist, for it is that and not the title of the painting which would drive the asking price to the heavens," I opined.

"Perhaps," Joanna said. "On the other hand, the thief may be playing it quite cleverly and only wishes to see who will nibble at the rumored bait. In this fashion, he can assemble a list of potential buyers who are connected to the enormously wealthy, who in turn would be willing to pay a huge sum for the masterpiece. Then he would release the name of the great master which would drive the price even higher."

"Are you saying there would be an auction?" I asked.

"Probably not, for that would draw too much attention," Joanna responded. "If I were the thief, I would insist on a onetime, make-your-best-offer arrangement. That simplifies matters and avoids unwanted complications that could unravel everything and land our thief in prison."

"What unwanted complications?"

"A false buyer slipped into the black market by Scotland Yard."

"You make him sound most clever."

"He is when it comes to the black market which tells us that he has experience in that dark world."

"Could he be using a middleman?" my father pondered.

"I think not," Joanna replied. "Why employ an intermediary when there is no need? Our thief knows full well there is no one in the black market who he can truly trust, so why take the chance? In addition, the buyer will have questions about the masterpiece that a middleman could not possibly answer. Again, why complicate matters when there is no need?"

My father reached for his cherrywood pipe and slowly packed it with Arcadia Mixture, as he arranged his thoughts before speaking. "So we have a very clever fellow who knows his way around the black market. All well and good, but is it a wise idea to let a rumor float about in that dark, sinister world where one misstep can cost you everything, including your life? Would it not be wise to move ahead without delay?"

"I find myself in agreement with my father," said I. "It would seem best to do an immediate cash-and-carry sale, with our thief collecting a large bundle of cash before disappearing into the shadows."

"All excellent assessments," Joanna chimed in. "But I fear your conclusions are neglecting an obvious obstacle the thief is facing."

"Which is?"

"He does not yet possess the masterpiece and that is why he delays," Joanna answered. "Recall Rowe's exact words that the masterpiece will *shortly* be on the market. This statement would indicate that the thief does not yet have the painting, but expects to have it in hand and available for sale soon."

"So the delay works to our advantage," said I.

"Only to the smallest extent."

"Why so?"

"For two reasons," Joanna replied, glancing over at the boiling water in the Erlenmeyer flask and rising from her seat. "First, he knows what he is searching for, and we do not."

"And the second reason?"

"He knows where the masterpiece is hidden, and every slashed portrait brings him closer to it."

11

The Lockpicks

The next morning, with Johnny on the mend under my father's careful eye, Joanna and I arrived at Scotland Yard where Inspector Lestrade awaited us. He had at last rounded up two of London's very best lockpicks and brought them in for questioning. Both Joseph Blevins and Archie Griffin adamantly proclaimed their innocence and each had a solid alibi to back up his whereabouts on the night of the Dubose break-in.

"Solid alibis, you say?" Joanna asked skeptically.

"Quite so, madam," Lestrade answered. "Archie Griffin was participating in a darts match at the Rose and Lamb, and four other members of his team vouched for his presence there until just before midnight, whereupon his son accompanied him home to the arms of a loving wife. The other lockpick, Joseph Blevins, the near blind one, was home all evening with his wife who swears to his presence, for he never goes out at night because of his inability to see, which is made worse by the darkness."

"I take it you challenged the wives."

"I did, but they stuck firmly to their stories," Lestrade replied. "I am afraid you have dug a dry hole, as our American colleagues would say."

"I think not."

"Then which of the two do you believe guilty?"

"Both."

An odd expression crossed Lestrade's face. "I beg your pardon!"

"You will shortly see my reasoning," said Joanna. "Let us begin with the near-blind lockpick."

"Even if he is guilty, his vision is such that he can barely distinguish light from dark, and will be of little assistance in describing the vandal."

"Blind people often sharpen their other senses which could prove of value here. You should not underestimate them, Lestrade."

We followed the inspector into a small room that was windowless and bare except for a wooden table and three chairs, one of which was occupied by a gaunt, hollow-cheeked man, with unkempt hair and a beard that had not seen a razor for many a day. But his most remarkable feature was his hands that had long, delicate fingers, like those one might expect to find on a violinist.

"Joseph Blevins," Lestrade introduced, "you are about to be questioned by a lady who often assists Scotland Yard. You are to answer her inquiries as if they were asked by a police officer. Any false statements will be held against you."

"I have never been interrogated by a lady before," said Blevins, staring past us into a sightless world. "Perhaps we should have a cup of tea for starters."

"Tea later perhaps, but only after you have answered the questions posed to you by the daughter of Sherlock Holmes," Joanna retorted.

The name of the great detective and his closeness to the questioner must have struck a nerve, for Blevins's mouth dropped open to expose dreadful dental hygiene, with only a few rotten teeth remaining. He attempted to gather himself, but still spoke in a weak voice. "It does not matter who you are, for I am innocent."

"I have an eyewitness who states otherwise," Joanna challenged.

Blevins smiled mischievously. "How could there be an eyewitness when the night was pitch black?"

Joanna smiled back. "I did not say the crime occurred at night. How could you know this if you weren't there?"

Blevins squirmed in his chair before an answer came to him. "The inspector asked me about my whereabouts on a particular night, so that is when the break-in must have occurred."

"Good," Joanna approved. "There is a brain behind your bony forehead, but let us see how you maneuver around my next question. You may wish to think before answering."

Blevins's nearly sightless eyes widened, now further on guard.

"Did you not feel regret when you stomped on that lovely flower bed alongside the Dubose home?" Joanna asked. "Certainly you must have sensed it."

"How could you know it was me?"

"The eyewitness."

"But it was the dark of night."

"Here I am afraid your sightlessness proved to be an even greater disadvantage," Joanna elucidated. "For in your journey alongside the house, you and your hirer passed by the window of a well-lighted kitchen. The light shined out into the garden, allowing both of you to be seen by the help as you trampled the flower bed."

Blevins was about to come to his own defense, but then thought better of it and remained silent.

"I suggest you give it up and stop wasting our time," Joanna demanded. "Tell us all and the good inspector might decide to be lenient, for otherwise you are facing up to ten years at Pentonville, where you will probably not live long enough to serve out your sentence."

"Ten years for only picking a lock?" Blevins asked desperately.

"Oh, there is more to your crime than simply picking the door that allowed entrance into the Dubose home, for you performed the same task at Hawke and Evans," Joanna went on. "It was during the latter crime that a security guard was assaulted and injured."

"But I did not go downstairs where the assault occurred," Blevins pleaded.

Well, well, I thought to myself, so the lockpick actually entered the art gallery, along with the vandal. But why? What purpose could he serve? The same question had apparently come to Joanna's mind.

"Once you were inside the gallery, I take it there were other locks to be picked," Joanna probed.

"Two," Blevins answered. "One that led down a flight of stairs, the other to a small room off to the side of the main gallery."

"Do you know what was behind the door to the second, smaller room?"

"An office of some sort."

"How could you possibly know that?"

"Because the man who hired me instructed me to remain by the office door until he returned from downstairs."

"Do you have any idea what he did in the office?"

"I cannot be sure, for all I heard were large pages being turned, one after another."

"Pray tell how do you know the pages being turned were large?"

"They make a different sound than do the smaller ones."

Joanna nodded, seemingly pleased with the new information. "Can you describe the man who hired you?"

Blevins considered the matter briefly before saying, "He was tall, close to six feet, for I had to reach up to his shoulder while he guided me. The creaking sound of his footsteps on the wooden floor—compared to mine—would indicate he was somewhat heavier than me. His clothes were old, particularly the shoulder of his coat that felt threadbare. And most annoying, he had the deep smell of coal tar embedded in his coat. So strong was it that it seeped into my own clothes as well."

"Very good," Joanna said, pushing her chair back.

"Madam, before you leave, please speak with the inspector about leniency," Blevins beseeched.

"I shall do my best."

We departed and walked quickly down a deserted corridor to a quiet alcove that was well away from the room where the questioning took place. Only then did Lestrade speak in a somewhat annoyed voice.

"You should have told me about the eyewitness," he growled.

"There was no eyewitness," Joanna explained. "I invented him to induce Mr. Joseph Blevins to confess to the crime. There was a lighted window in the kitchen that overlooked the garden and there was a trampled flower bed just outside the window. So I mixed in those two observations with my imaginary eyewitness and came up with a rather convincing story, wouldn't you say?"

"Madam, you never cease to amaze me," Lestrade said sincerely. "However, your fabricated scheme has left me with quite a problem, for I must now write a report that details how the confession was obtained from Mr. Blevins. I cannot do this without including your imaginary eyewitness, which of course is no eyewitness at all."

"Then you are obliged not to write such a report, and thus be most lenient with the nearly sightless Joseph Blevins who I suspect will never again be a threat to society."

"Are you suggesting we allow Joseph Blevins to go free?"

"I am suggesting you let justice and common sense supersede the written law."

"After all, Inspector, it is Christmastime," I chimed in.

Lestrade sighed resignedly. "Shall we be allowing the second lockpick, who you say is also guilty, to go free as well?"

"Only after he has provided us with the information we require," replied Joanna.

We entered a small room quite similar to the one we had used to question Joseph Blevins. But the individual sitting behind a wooden table was altogether different than the emaciated Blevins. Archie Griffin was a large, well-built man, broad across the shoulders and middle-aged, with neatly combed gray hair. His clothes were presentable, with a colorful sports coat and white shirt that had its collar unbuttoned.

Lestrade again made the introductions, but on this occasion noted that Joanna was the daughter of Sherlock Holmes. If that fact moved Archie Griffin, he did not show it.

Joanna went directly to the point. "We know you are involved, Mr. Griffin, so do not waste our time denying it. There is evidence against you, but it is less than overwhelming and for that reason we can offer you a most lenient way to escape punishment. Tell us all and you walk out with a warning. If, on the other hand, you deceive us or omit details we deem to be important, you will be marched out of Scotland Yard in handcuffs, without saying good-bye to your wife and family."

"I want a written statement to that effect," Griffin insisted.

"Absurd demands will not advance your cause," said Joanna. "If you must, speak in a third-person fashion."

"Which will not be a confession and cannot be construed as such."

"Obviously."

Griffin cleared his throat, as if preparing for a formal presentation. "Let us say a friend of mine was approached by an unnamed person to pick the lock of an art gallery. It is a pricey place, so the lock will be difficult."

"Was he informed that it was a Chubb detector lock?"

"Now that you mention it, I believe he was."

"Would your friend be required to enter the gallery once the lock was picked?"

"That was an absolute requirement, as I recall, and that would make the job a bit dicier," Griffin replied. "Pick and run is far more simple and less likely to end with a bad result."

"Which translates into being discovered."

"Exactly, for such galleries often employ security guards that patrol throughout the night. In any event, my friend, who was going through a prolonged slow period, showed some interest initially but it quickly faded when he learned the hirer was willing to pay only a single pound for the job. With that, my friend said good-bye and took his leave."

"But only after telling the prospective buyer of a colleague who was down on his luck and would be willing to perform such work at a discounted price."

"Quite so."

"Be careful with your next answer," Joanna warned. "Did this down-on-his-luck colleague have a particular handicap?"

"I was told he had a problem with his sight."

"And finally, did your friend give a description of the hirer?"

"I cannot help you there, for they met in darkness in an alleyway next to a pub. According to my friend, the prospective hirer wore a thick scarf that covered his neck and lower face."

"Did it carry an odor?"

"Coal tar, disgusting coal tar."

With an approving nod, Joanna said, "Inspector Lestrade will see to your release shortly."

Lestrade accompanied us to the front entrance of Scotland Yard and hailed a four-wheeler for us. Opening the door of the coach, he asked, "How did you know that both of the lockpicks were involved?"

"There were a number of clues indicating we were dealing with a nearly sightless individual," Joanna replied. "These included the multiple scratches around the keyhole and the trampled flower bed indicating at least two individuals had walked over it in single file, as if one were leading the other. And then there was the cost of an experienced lockpick. The blind one would be far less expensive for obvious reasons and that would be an important consideration for our vandal who had fallen on hard times."

"And the involvement of Archie Griffin?"

"The vandal would attempt to hire the best at first, and turn to the lesser talent when he had no other choice."

As we rode away, I could not help but believe the man with the terrible dermatitis was the key player who was involved in every aspect of the criminal ongoings. For he was the vandal who knew the paintings and their locations, who hired the lockpicks and directed their activities, and who slashed the portraits to peer inside. And it was no doubt he who would place the hidden masterpiece on the black market and sell it to the highest bidder. Yet we were no closer to his identity than we were on day one.

"We have to put a face on the vandal," I thought aloud.

"Agreed," said Joanna.

"But where do we look next?"

"On the first floor of Hawke and Evans, for there is where it lies."

"What is the basis for that conclusion?"

"The sound of turning pages the blind lockpick heard," Joanna said, and leaning back on the headrest, she closed her eyes and drifted off.

12

Delvecchio

Big Ben was striking ten when our four-wheeler reached the front entrance of Hawke and Evans. As we stepped out, we noticed two constables exiting from the alleyway alongside the art gallery. They must have recognized Joanna, for both tipped their hats to her.

"Good morning, Officers," Joanna greeted and, pointing to the alleyway, asked, "Is there some problem which brings you here this morning?"

"A minor disturbance, madam," the taller of the constables replied. "Late last night, a security guard within the gallery thought he heard a knock on the side door. In order to investigate, he went to a barred window and shined his light into the alleyway. There was nothing to be seen, so he continued on his nightly rounds and gave it no further concern."

"He must have had some worry, for he reported the incident," said Joanna.

"Not to us, but to Mr. Hawke who then called us, for he wishes to take no chance that his gallery will be vandalized yet again."

"I take it you investigated the side door."

"We did indeed, and found nothing of interest."

"In that case we will detain you no further."

"Very good, madam."

Joanna watched the constables stroll away and, when they were well out of hearing distance, said, "Let us have a quick look."

We walked carefully down the alleyway and searched for anything out of order, but there were no signs that someone had come and gone or caused mischief in the narrow passageway. The door and its lock showed no evidence of damage or forced entry. But it was the barred window that drew Joanna's attention. I saw nothing of interest other than the thick iron bars that were heavily rusted.

"You will note that the small window is a good fifteen feet away from the side door."

"And?" asked I.

"And there is no way the security guard's torch could have illuminated that door," Joanna answered.

"But surely the vandal would not have knocked to announce his presence."

"He would have if he wished to determine if there was a guard on duty."

I had to smile at Joanna's conclusion which both the constables and I overlooked. "The light shining through the window would have been a sure sign."

"Which could have been seen at a distance, should the guard have decided to crack open the door and peer out."

"So it would seem our vandal is determined to break into the gallery yet again."

"Which tells us he firmly believes that this is where the masterpiece he so desperately wants is hidden."

We hurried along to the front entrance and entered a deserted art gallery. There was not a single person to be seen, despite the Christmas season and the throngs of shoppers on the street. A slender, middle-aged clerk stepped out of the shadows to greet us as potential customers, but upon recognizing us and knowing our purpose she quickly retreated.

In a small office at the rear of the display room, we found Simon Hawke holding up a painting to the light for careful inspection.

"Lovely, isn't it?" he remarked and placed the canvas on a stand beside his desk. "It is entitled *Crucifixion* for obvious reasons."

The painting showed Christ on the cross, with his wounds spurting blood that was being collected by small, angelic figures hovering above. People gathered at the bottom of the cross, including the Virgin Mary, were clearly in mourning.

"It was painted by Bernardo Daddi, an early Italian Renaissance artist of some note," Hawke went on. "Unfortunately, his work has never been of great value, and this particular work has been devalued because of the badly faded angels collecting the blood of Christ. With appropriate restoration, it would become more desirable."

"So the painting is here for a restoration?" Joanna asked.

Hawke nodded, his eyes still on the canvas. "But we are so far behind, it may well take months before Delvecchio can give it his attention."

Joanna moved in for a closer look. "I see the Virgin Mary at the bottom of the painting is also noticeably faded."

Hawke nodded again. "She, too, will need retouching."

Joanna inquired, "Was this painting in the gallery the night the vandal broke in?"

"It was, awaiting restoration," Hawke replied. "Why do you ask?"

"Because for some reason the vandal decided not to

deface the feminine figure of the Virgin Mary," Joanna noted and gave the matter more thought as she restudied the painting. "Perhaps because it was not a true portrait."

"Perhaps."

"Are the areas to be restored recorded in detail?"

"Oh, yes. We note and list every defect, including fading, scratches, creases, and so on. The cataloging is done in the presence of the owner and the restorer, with me standing as a witness. The document avoids any dispute once the restoration is complete."

"Done in duplicate, I would think."

"Most certainly, with one belonging to the owner, the other remaining here." Hawke reached over to his desk for a large, metal ring folder, with a sturdy cardboard cover. He opened it and pointed to a front page that lay atop a stack of others. "On the *Crucifixion,* for example, we meticulously described the color and fading of the flying angelic figures."

"Who actually writes the description?"

"The restorer, for he knows the words and terms that fit best."

Joanna examined the page, paying particular scrutiny to the signatures. Then she turned to the next underlying document and the one after. "Do all these documents pertain to paintings awaiting restoration?"

"Some refer to those waiting, but most are records of those completed over the past few years."

"Each nicely documented," Joanna noted, and gestured to another similar, metal ring folder that lay close by. "Does that also record restorations done by Hawke and Evans?"

"No, madam. That folder holds the receipts for paintings I have sold to other galleries who have a client for such work," Hawke replied. "The price is clearly noted, for on occasion the purchasing gallery may wish to return the painting if their client reneges. With such a receipt in hand, there can be no dispute as to the amount paid."

"Quite wise," Joanna said, and quickly flipped through the pages which were much smaller than the restoration documents. "Such details are always of importance."

"Do you believe the receipts may somehow relate to the acts of vandalism?" asked Hawke.

"Only if you can give me a reason why a returned painting might be the target of a vandal."

"I am afraid I cannot."

"Nor can I, but all gathered information may later turn out to be significant on a case such as this," said Joanna and looked at the door. "And now, Mr. Hawke, if you would be so kind, please accompany us to the restoration section, for I have a few questions for Mr. Delvecchio."

Simon Hawke led the way down the stairs, after signaling to the female clerk that he would be absent momentarily. The restoration area was brightly lighted and quite warm due to the nearby central heat furnace that was hidden behind a brick wall. The restorer, Giuseppe Delvecchio, was seated in front of a painting that had the hallmarks of works done by French impressionists. It depicted well-dressed children playing in a park near a calm, blue lake that had boats upon it. We watched Delvecchio wrap a bit of cotton around a wooden dowel, then wet it with solvent and gently swirl it against the canvas. As a layer of varnish was removed, a child's head appeared. Another dip and swirl brought out the little girl's golden hair.

"It appears to be a Renoir," I commented.

"But it is not, although its owner insists it is the work of Pierre-Auguste Renoir," Delvecchio replied. "Most likely it was painted by Frédéric Bazille, who was a fellow student and greatly admired Renoir's style."

"Did you so inform the owner?"

"I did, but he was convinced it was an authentic, unsigned Renoir, and I saw no benefit to argue the point." Delvecchio rose from his chair to stretch his back and asked, "Are you interested in Renoir?"

"To a limited extent," I replied, as rehearsed on our ride to the gallery. "It is Paolo Veronese who arouses my curiosity."

"Is there one particular work of his that you admire?"

"*La Bella Nani.*"

"Ah, I see you have been to visit the Countess of Wessex."

"I have."

"She considers Veronese among the greats, but not all share that opinion."

"Do you?"

"No," Delvecchio said at once. "How can you worship the work of an artist who paints a large woman with a head that is far too small for her body?"

"It did seem a little off."

"Yet that oddity is considered one of his very best works."

"I hope you did not express that opinion to her," Hawke interjected.

"I may be crazy, but I am not a fool," Delvecchio said, with a mischievous smile.

Joanna asked, "Did she bring the painting into the gallery?"

"No, madam," Delvecchio answered. "She insisted I visit her home. Apparently Scotland Yard wished the painting to remain in place."

"To keep the crime scene intact."

"So I was told."

"Did you find her to be as well informed as I did?" I asked.

"The countess is very knowledgeable, particularly in the paintings from the Italian Renaissance," Delvecchio replied. "But why she places Caravaggio above Raphael is beyond me."

"With Veronese being well below both."

"All would agree to that assessment."

"I take it she nonetheless wished for you to restore the Veronese painting."

"That was her wish, but only after thoroughly investigating my credentials." Delvecchio huffed. "She actually made a long-distance call to the Uffizi in my presence."

"Was she satisfied?" I asked.

"Women like the countess are never satisfied."

"I say!" Hawke said indignantly.

"I withdraw the remark, although it is true," Delvecchio said. "She must be in control of everything, including her husband and the dog."

One could not but like the restorer, for like most Italians he was outspoken and forthright, but with no meanness and a pleasant spirit.

"But I must say I got along well with the husband who knows nothing about art," Delvecchio continued on. "And I even managed to befriend their mastiff Nelson."

"While I was there, the hound eyed me rather warily," I recalled.

"Did you give him a dog biscuit?"

"I did not."

"You should have, for to a dog nothing is more important than food, and the person who provides it automatically becomes a friend."

"So you knew beforehand that the countess had a dog."

"I had no such information," Delvecchio said. "It was only good fortune, for I always carry one for my own sweet greyhound, Mimi."

Joanna gestured to a water dish on the floor near the wall. "Do you bring the dog to work? Or more importantly, does she ever spend the night here?"

A most intriguing question, I thought immediately, for the greyhound would have barked at a nighttime intruder and frightened him away. Unless of course the dog was *familiar* with that individual.

"I am not permitted to bring my dog because when I did he barked incessantly," Delvecchio said in a sad voice.

"The barking went on and on," Hawke added. "And was most disturbing, for it could be heard in the gallery above."

"It was so unusual for Mimi to behave this way, for at home she is quiet as a lamb." Delvecchio pointed to the thick wall that enclosed the central heating furnace. "She barked and even clawed at the wall, as if she had picked up the scent of a rabbit or some other prey."

"A pest control expert was called in and seemed convinced that a squirrel or some other rodent had become trapped in the chimney behind the wall that had been bricked off to prevent the loss of heat, so I had to pay a mason to brick off the top of the chimney as well," Hawke stated unhappily. "All of the masonry came at added expense, which the gallery could ill afford, with our business so depressed. And I fear that it will continue to be so unless the despicable vandal is caught."

"We now have a partial description of him," I encouraged.

"So I have been told," Hawke said. "Inspector Lestrade inquired about a person associated with the gallery who had a red, quite noticeable rash about his neck and back of his head. No such individual has ever been employed here."

"Did the restorer who was a forger and supposedly fled to Australia have an obvious skin condition?" asked Joanna.

"James Blackstone certainly did not, nor did Harry

Edmunds, although the latter did suffer from terrible dandruff," Hawke remembered.

"Describe in detail Edmunds's dandruff," Joanna said at once.

"It was quite severe, in that he would shed large white flakes that ended up on his shoulders," Hawke recounted. "He wore a very tight beret to minimize this most unattractive shedding."

"Did he apply a coal tar lotion in an effort to control the dandruff?" Joanna asked.

Hawke shrugged. "He used all sorts of remedies, but none worked well. Nevertheless, because of their peculiar odors, we insisted he use the lotion at home and not in the gallery. We were concerned the odors might seep into the canvases he worked on, perhaps by touch, which of course would be disastrous."

"He is our vandal!" I said excitedly.

"But he does not have the noticeable rash that Inspector Lestrade described," Hawke countered.

Joanna waved away the contradiction. "Edmunds's dermatitis was located on his scalp which he kept hidden with his tight beret. And the large dandruff flakes you depicted were in fact small plaques of psoriasis that were embedded in the scarf the vandal unintentionally left behind." She considered the matter further and asked, "Did Edmunds wear a scarf around his neck while at work?"

"Never," Hawke answered. "But he always had the collar of his coat up to mimic the French artists he so admired."

"Which concealed the lesions on his neck," Joanna said, as all the pieces fell into place. "I believe Harry Edmunds is the vandal we are seeking. By chance, is Mr. Edmunds quite tall and rather thin? Does that fit his description?"

"It does indeed."

"Then he is beyond a doubt our vandal," Joanna reiterated.

"That is impossible, for Harry Edmunds is currently imprisoned at Wormwood Scrubs where he is serving a five-year sentence," Hawke argued. "You must admit, madam, that undeniable fact renders your conclusion quite impossible, does it not?"

"Only if you assume that Harry Edmunds remains locked up behind the walls of the prison," said Joanna and searched for a nearby phone.

13

Scotland Yard

"Dead!" Joanna exclaimed in disbelief.

"Quite, according to the governor of the facility," said Lestrade.

We were seated in the inspector's office at Scotland Yard, listening to his every word. Moments earlier he had completed a phone call to the governor at one of His Majesty's most secure prisons, which was located in the Hammersmith district of London.

"Was he killed by another inmate?" asked Joanna.

"No, but rather in an explosion," Lestrade replied.

"An explosion in a secure prison?" Joanna questioned. "Please explain how that could have occurred."

"Wormwood Scrubs is one of England's most progressive prisons, where deserving inmates are given the opportunity to learn a trade, so they might be gainfully employed upon their release," Lestrade elucidated. "In one of their workshops the ability to repair and restore furniture is taught, but always under careful supervision so that tools and other such instruments, which can become weapons, do not go missing.

Apparently Harry Edmunds was mixing up a solvent to be used for removing old varnish when the accidental explosion happened."

Joanna nodded slowly. "He used a similar solvent to remove old varnish from paintings, so he would be quite experienced in doing the same to furniture."

"That was their thinking, madam. The prison officials were aware of his talent, and even allowed him to teach others how to go about restoring and refinishing. Edmunds was apparently in the midst of preparing a batch of solvent when another prisoner, who was smoking a cigarette, came too close to the mixture and caused a fiery explosion that killed Harry Edmunds."

"I take it the body was badly burned."

"To a crisp."

"Yet positive identification was still possible?"

"I asked Governor Bradshaw the very same question and he assured me there was not the slightest doubt as to the identity of the body. First, there were several inmates who witnessed Edmunds mixing up the solvent just prior to the explosion. Next, the measurement and weight of the corpse were the same as those recorded for Edmunds upon his entrance to the jail." Lestrade paused to review his notes from the phone call. "In addition, a ring and pocket watch engraved with his initials were found on Edmunds's body. And finally, a careful check of the entire population at the prison revealed only one missing inmate, and that individual was Harry Edmunds."

"The witnesses and the ring and the engraved watch found on the body are highly suggestive, yet not proof that the body belonged to Harry Edmunds," Joanna thought aloud. "But the fact he was missing from the prison roll is much more difficult to get around."

"All put together, the prison officials feel confident they have enough evidence to make a positive identification," said Lestrade. "And the coroner who examined the body was of the same opinion."

Joanna reached for a cigarette in her purse and, after lighting it, began to pace the floor in Lestrade's office. She circled a standing lamp with a brass base twice before speaking. "I am still not convinced that Harry Edmunds is dead."

"But the prison has proof that says he is."

"And we have proof that says he isn't, for every piece of evidence clearly indicates that Harry Edmunds is our vandal."

"At an official inquest, do you believe your proof would supersede the judgment of a coroner who actually examined the body?"

"You raise a good point," Joanna acceded. "But tell me, when did Harry Edmunds's death occur?"

"Three weeks ago," Lestrade replied. "So unless a burned corpse was able to pass in and out of Wormwood Scrubs as often as it wished, which of course it couldn't, then it is impossible for Edmunds to have perpetrated the acts of vandalism that have been plaguing us for the last two weeks."

"Another good point," Joanna admitted, as she continued to pace. "But my father once said that if you eliminate all other factors, then the one which remains must be the truth. It is a cardinal rule of deduction and it applies here. Thus, we must eliminate Harry Edmunds's death for him to be the vandal."

"Which means you will have to disregard the coroner's ruling," said Lestrade.

Joanna waved away the inspector's argument. "Coroners for most prisons are not the sharpest knives in the drawer. Chances are he was told the name of the deceased and given the evidence which surrounded his death. He no doubt took the path of least resistance, which required the least amount of thinking. Let me assure you if this matter was under investigation for an insurance claim, the company would have surely sent in their own medical examiners to either confirm or deny the insured person had died."

"Do you propose that we bring in another, perhaps more expert, examiner?" Lestrade asked.

"We have one sitting in front of you," Joanna replied.

"Oh yes, Dr. Watson, of course," Lestrade recalled.

"Who would not be swayed by the findings of others," Joanna stated firmly.

"Are you suggesting the body be exhumed?"

"We may have no other choice."

"That will require a great deal of paperwork, for it cannot be done without a court order."

"Inspector, it would be in your best interest to expedite the exhumation, for the longer the permission to do so takes, the greater the chance our vandal will find the masterpiece and disappear forever."

"If things go well, the permit will be issued in a day's time," Lestrade estimated.

"Then please begin the process immediately," said Joanna. "By the way, where is Edmunds buried?"

"In a potter's field, for his wife claimed she was too impoverished to afford a proper funeral."

Joanna stopped pacing and gave Lestrade a lengthy look. "Too impoverished, you say?"

"So I was told."

"Did you check her finances, in particular a bank account and the money it might contain?"

"None were uncovered."

"Did you bother to look at her style of living to see if it matches that of a poor woman?"

A quizzical expression crossed Lestrade's face. "To what end?"

"To determine if she is lying."

"Why would a poor widow lie on such a matter?"

"To give a reason why she could not provide a funeral for her husband," Joanna answered. "While the real reason was she knew the man being buried wasn't her husband."

"That is a bit of a stretch," said Lestrade.

"But it fits, if my hypothesis is true," Joanna asserted, and turned to me. "John, what questions should be asked prior to the exhumation?"

"Hold on!" Lestrade interrupted. "You do realize you will be dealing with a charred corpse that is burned beyond all recognition."

"The flesh may be gone, but the skeleton remains intact, and that is where the unique findings may lie," I explained. "You see, bones often leave behind an undeniable signature."

Lestrade suddenly showed great interest and searched for a notepad and pen. "Please be good enough to give me some examples, for future reference should the need arise."

"Very well," I agreed. "I shall begin with the head and work my way down. If you find any of the anatomical terms confusing, do not hesitate to interrupt."

"Do your best to use words that the court will understand," Lestrade requested. "Such clarification may be important when I present the argument for exhumation."

"I shall keep that in mind. Now starting with the skull, the examiner should look for congenital abnormalities, such as micrognathia, which is an underdeveloped jaw and gives the appearance of a person with a small, recessed chin."

"Which would be easily recognized in a photograph or on actually viewing such an individual," Lestrade noted, as he wrote.

"That is the point, Lestrade," I said. "One must take the skeletal finding and apply it to a given appearance. In this regard, the teeth embedded in the jaw are an even better example. If the person you are trying to identify had a full set of teeth and the skull has none, you immediately know you are dealing with two individuals and not a single personage."

"A dentist would be an important witness in that instance."

"And provide indisputable testimony to the court. Such evidence was used recently in a murder trial up in Scotland."

Lestrade nodded to himself, obviously pleased with the case I recounted. "And I would think that a missing hand or leg would be the most convincing evidence."

"Quite so, for one cannot grow another limb, and if a prosthesis has been substituted, it is easily discerned," said I.

"Let us hope the burned corpse's skeleton reveals such a marking, although my natural pessimism tells me that we shall not be so fortunate."

"To the contrary, Inspector, for in the majority of similar cases I have been involved with, the individual's bones have left behind a personal signature."

"Then we should proceed with that assumption in mind," Joanna interjected. "Our next steps are for Lestrade to obtain the court order required for exhumation, and for John and I to travel to Wormwood Scrubs to interview the governor and review the prison's records of Harry Edmunds. Please be good enough, Inspector, to call the governor and inform him of our imminent arrival."

Reaching for the phone, Lestrade said, "He may well inquire as to the purpose of your visit."

"Tell him it is because I believe he has buried the wrong man."

14

Wormwood Scrubs

Mr. George Bradshaw, the governor at Wormwood Scrubs, met us with a cold greeting and a limp handshake, obviously none too pleased with our visit. In his sparse office, he sat behind a neat, wooden desk and gave the appearance one might expect to see in a funeral director. He was tall and thin, nearly to the point of being gaunt, with a somber expression that had not even a hint of warmth.

"This is most unusual," said he.

"So is burying the wrong body in a potter's field," Joanna countered.

"Do you have proof of this?"

"Enough to request an exhumation which will shortly be granted."

"Do you care to share this evidence with me?"

"I am afraid I cannot, for such evidence must remain confidential until it has been submitted before a court," Joanna replied easily. "Furthermore, there may well be other related clues we uncover in your prison that must be added to the legal brief, which explains our presence here today."

"May I ask where you anticipate finding these clues?"

"In your prison records, as they pertain to one Harry Edmunds and the explosion that supposedly took his life."

"A most unfortunate accident," Bradshaw noted indifferently.

"And a most convenient one," said Joanna. "May we see his prison file?"

Bradshaw handed across a thin folder which when opened revealed only a few loose sheets. "As you can see, his reports are quite meager, for he was only with us several months before his untimely death."

Joanna quickly scanned the file that contained Edmunds's medical record, death certificate, and accounts of his behavior while incarcerated. "It appears he was a model prisoner."

"He was indeed," Bradshaw confirmed. "He never caused a spot of trouble and worked diligently in the furniture restoration shop where he seemed to enjoy his time."

"What becomes of the furniture once it is restored?" Joanna asked.

"It is sold, with the proceeds used to buy the tools and equipment required for the restorations. Each prisoner receives a shilling for his work once the sale is done, which gives them added incentive. They spend the money quickly for tobacco and such, and of course for gambling that we do our best to discourage."

"Was Edmunds involved in any fights or brawls?"

"None whatsoever."

"Any attempts to escape?"

"There is no escape from here, for it is the most secure prison in all London," Bradshaw answered. "Moreover, most of our prisoners are nonviolent offenders with relatively short sentences, and any attempt to escape would add significantly to the time they needed to serve. This of course dissuades them from any such activities."

Joanna glanced at the inmate's medical record briefly before handing it to me. "John, here is the physical examination done by the prison doctor on Harry Edmunds when he first arrived. Read it aloud while you search for a signature marking."

"What is a signature marking?" asked Bradshaw, showing sudden interest.

"It is a finding which belongs to Harry Edmunds and no one else."

I read through the entire document before speaking, for I wished to make certain it was authentic and done by a physician who was competent to perform such an examination. The terms he used indicated he was an experienced doctor who did not mince his words.

"Well?"

"The examining physician knows his anatomy."

"Excellent. Please proceed."

"The report begins as follows: the patient is a forty-five-year-old male who appears to be his stated age. His blood pressure is one hundred twenty-five over eighty-five, and he has an even pulse of seventy per minute. Examination of the head, eyes, nose, and throat reveals severe psoriasis involving the entire scalp, with lesions extending down well into the posterior neck. Only a few psoriatic plaques are present on the torso. The intense smell of coal tar permeates the entire area. His dental hygiene is good, but several bottom teeth are missing. The heart and lungs are clear, with no abnormal sounds or murmurs. However, on the left lateral chest wall there is a five-by-five-inch black-and-blue area most likely caused by trauma." I glanced over to Joanna and remarked,

"We should determine if the burned corpse has fractured ribs in that location."

"Does the examining physician believe they are broken?" Joanna asked quickly.

"He only states that the area was tender and that could indicate the ribs were only bruised," I opined, before continuing on. "The liver and spleen cannot be felt, nor are there palpable lymph nodes in the inguinal region. His extremities are unremarkable, other than he has an amputated small toe on the left." I could not help but smile at the seemingly insignificant finding. "A missing toe!"

"The signature," Joanna noted, nodding in satisfaction.

"Indeed."

Bradshaw was not impressed, saying, "A missing toe is hardly conclusive evidence."

"It is if the prisoner you buried has all ten of his," Joanna informed.

Bradshaw appeared to sink into his chair. "Your point is well taken."

"And this finding may yet beg another question for you to answer," said Joanna.

"Which is?"

"Who is the man you buried?"

"And how does he fit into this scheme," I added.

"That, too," Joanna concurred and arose from her chair. "Now I would like to examine the restoration workshop where the explosion took place."

"I am afraid it remains in a bit of a mess," Bradshaw said.

"So there has been no cleanup?"

"Not as yet."

"Excellent, for an untouched crime scene serves our purposes best."

"Why are you so convinced that a crime has occurred?"

"Because I have a nose for it."

We strode down a very long corridor, passing through a series of locked doors, then took two flights of stairs down before reaching the furniture restoration workshop. It was a large room that held shelves filled with numerous unopened jars and cans, all neatly stacked together. A rack on the wall had protruding pegs upon which various tools could be placed and secured. The air still smelled of burnt wood and yet another pungent odor that I surmised was emitted by the flammable solvent which has taken someone's life.

"This is the area where the explosion occurred," Bradshaw said, gesturing to a badly burned table and then to a scorched, blackened cabinet that rested upon it. "Edmunds was mixing up his specially prepared solvent when someone came too near with a lighted cigarette."

"Specially prepared?" Joanna inquired. "Did he make his own solvent?"

"He insisted on it, for it was in his opinion far superior to those that are commercially available," replied Bradshaw.

Joanna moved closer to the badly charred cabinet and seemed to be most interested in its position on the workbench. It appeared to be at an angle so that it faced another similar workbench upon which stood a chair that had also been scorched by the flames. "Where were the witnesses located at the moment of the explosion?"

"There was only one witness, Robbie Gates, who was sanding a chair on the adjacent table," Bradshaw answered.

Joanna paced off the distance between the charred cabinet and the scorched chair. "Fifteen feet apart," she announced.

"Which is surely close enough for a clear recognition," said Bradshaw. "In addition, Gates has quite good vision and does not wear glasses, which I suspect was to be the answer to your next question."

"It was," Joanna responded. "Nevertheless, I wonder if it would be possible for me to speak to Mr. Gates."

Bradshaw signaled to a nearby prison officer. "Please bring Robbie Gates down to the restoration area."

I could see that Governor Bradshaw was somewhat annoyed by Joanna's request, for it would appear she did not trust his word. Which of course was the case, for one of her cardinal rules was to never accept the assessment of another until she herself had confirmed it.

Joanna strolled over to a shelf that held the various ingredients necessary for furniture restoration. She briefly studied the labels on large bottles of acetone and hydrogen peroxide and checked to make certain their tops were secure. "Ah, the individual components required to make the solvents. It is wise to keep them well apart, is it not?"

"Quite so, madam, for the restoration supervisor is aware that when the two are combined together they form an unstable, most dangerous mixture."

"The mixing produces acetone peroxide which is highly explosive," Joanna noted.

"You are informed on chemistry?" Bradshaw asked, taken aback by Joanna's knowledge of science.

"Only as it applies to crime." Joanna moved farther down the shelf and came to large glass containers of flour and salt. She pried off their tops and sniffed at the contents before dipping her finger in to take a taste. "Flour and salt," she confirmed.

"I have no idea what purpose they serve in restoration."

"They are the major components of glue."

"Is that all that is required?"

"You can add a bit of vinegar to make for a firmer adhesive," Joanna said and pointed to a nearly empty bottle of white vinegar.

At that moment, a grizzled prisoner in his late middle years entered the restoration area and made his way over to us. He kept his eyes averted as is commonly done by individuals about to face someone in a position of power. His posture was decidedly stooped, but he had no other distinguishing features.

"This is Robbie Gates," Bradshaw introduced. "It was he who witnessed the explosion that took Harry Edmunds's life."

"I did indeed, guv'nor, for it happened right before my very eyes," Gates said in a cigarette-induced hoarse voice. His clothes carried an overwhelming odor of stale tobacco smoke. "Went up in a ball of flames, he did."

"How close were you to him?" Joanna asked.

Gates hesitated and only answered when Bradshaw gave him an approving nod. "Ten, twelve feet or so. Maybe a little more."

"Please take the position you had at the moment of the explosion," Joanna requested.

Gates again waited for Bradshaw's permission before walking over to the workbench that held the scorched chair. "Here I was, madam, when Harry and his cellmate were mixing up their brew."

"Then you must have seen them quite clearly," said Joanna, picking up a blackened chisel to examine, but as she did so it seemed to slip from her grasp and land on the floor. Gates hurried over and retrieved the tool, then handed it back to Joanna.

"Oh, thank you, Gates," she said, placing the chisel down.

"You are welcome, ma'am."

So Gates had passed the vision test, I thought at once. A man who could see a falling chisel at fifteen feet could surely recognize a face at that distance.

"Side by side, they were," Gates replied.

"I take it you knew Edmunds's cellmate."

"Everyone knew old Derrick Wilson who is now breathing the fresh air of London, having served his sentence."

"Are you certain that Derrick Wilson was standing next to Edmunds at the moment of explosion?"

"Oh yes, ma'am. I saw the two chatting and what have you, then went back to sanding the varnish off my chair. A moment later I heard a terrible bang and saw the flames engulfing the workbench."

"Did you actually see Harry Edmunds on fire?"

"I saw a man with his clothes aflame and waving his arms furiously to put out the fire," Gates recalled. "It was a horrible sight to see, it was. But I saw no more as I ran for the door, like all the others did."

"But did you clearly see Harry Edmunds's face?" Joanna pressed.

"I do believe it was him," Gates insisted. "And when I saw his cellmate later on that day, I knew it was poor Harry who had perished in those bloody flames."

"Was Derrick Wilson not burned by the flames?" Joanna asked. "After all, he was quite close to Edmunds at the time of the explosion."

Gates considered the matter before answering. "His thick beard and moustache were badly singed and his nose was red from the flames licking at it. Also, his hands had some blisters."

"Did you know Wilson well?"

"I do not think anyone knew that bloody Scotsman well, for he was a rather rough character who spent most of his time alone."

"Did he and Harry Edmunds, being cellmates, get along?"

"So-so," Gates said with a shrug. "Like most cellmates,

they could be friends one day and at each other's throats the next. They did seem to argue a lot about cheating when they gambled at cards, with Wilson dominating and often threatening Harry."

"Which is forbidden," Bradshaw interjected.

"Right you are, guv'nor," Gates said in a neutral voice.

"I have one final question," Joanna continued on. "Was Derrick Wilson, being such a rough and domineering character, much larger than Harry Edmunds?"

"Both were about the same size, but easily told apart, for Wilson had a thick beard and moustache that gave him a mean look," Gates recounted. "The beard covered most of Wilson's face and in particular covered up his busted cheek."

"Busted cheek, you say?" Joanna asked immediately.

"That would be a polite term for it," Gates described. "Apparently some years back, Wilson was involved in a terrible fight and caught a vicious punch that crushed his upper cheek bone. It left a dent and scar that Wilson tried to hide behind his thick beard. You didn't notice it that much unless you were up close, and most people tended to keep their distance."

"Thank you for your helpful information," said Joanna.

Gates bowed awkwardly, obviously unaccustomed to being appreciated.

We departed the restoration area and were accompanied to the imposing gates of Wormwood Scrubs prison by its governor, who was most inquisitive about the success or failure of our visit. Unlike my first impression of the man, he now appeared overly concerned that a bad mark would suddenly appear on his record.

"Were you able to uncover any clues that might prove important?" Bradshaw asked anxiously.

"None that would sway an official inquiry, if that is your question," Joanna replied.

Bradshaw breathed a sigh of relief as the worry left his face. "Good, then. But if I can be of further assistance, you must let me know."

"We shall."

We bade farewell to Bradshaw and proceeded through the gates of Wormwood Scrubs, and onto Du Can Road where the car and driver that Lestrade had provided awaited us.

"Our vandal is very, very clever," Joanna remarked.

"Even more than we originally thought?" I queried.

"Much more."

"What led to this conclusion, might I ask?"

"The ingredients for glue in the workshop," Joanna said and hurried for the car as a light rain began to fall.

15

Two Vandals

On our return to 221b Baker Street we learned that the specimen sent to St. Bartholomew's had tested positive for cholera and that Johnny had surely been afflicted with this dreadful disease, but he was now totally well and asymptomatic, which gave us great joy. With the full recovery of his body came the resurgence of his most inquisitive mind, causing him to ask one question after another in our absence regarding the case of the art vandal. Like his mother and grandfather before him, he was fascinated by crimes and those who committed them.

Yet, as he listened to Joanna expound upon our new discoveries, he made no comment nor raised any inquiries, only nodding at one clue and squinting his eyes at another.

"Now to the most striking finding," she recounted, looking directly at my father and awaiting his reaction. "There was in fact an individual with severe dermatitis of the scalp and neck who was previously employed at Hawke and Evans, according to Simon Hawke."

"How could this be?" my father asked, his eyebrows lifting

in surprise. "Hawke was questioned about such a person and gave a negative response."

"Then Lestrade either phrased the question incorrectly or Hawke misunderstood it," Joanna said. "For the man with the skin condition is Harry Edmunds, who once worked at the gallery as a restorer."

"Then we have our vandal," declared my father.

"But here arises a problem, for we were earlier told that Edmunds was currently imprisoned at Wormwood Scrubs, having been convicted of art forgery."

"Has he somehow managed to escape?"

"In a manner of speaking he did, for Harry Edmunds died in prison three weeks ago and is now reportedly buried in a potter's field."

"Then we have selected the wrong man to be our vandal."

"I think not." Joanna described in detail the explosion in the workshop that supposedly took the life of Harry Edmunds. She gave particular attention to the highly volatile solvent, the ingredients of which were being mixed at the moment the fire broke out. "It was said to be caused by someone nearby holding a lighted cigarette," she concluded.

"But Edmunds was an experienced restorer who would be familiar with the dangers of mixing a solvent, would he not?" my father asked.

"Quite familiar," Joanna replied.

"He would have never prepared his solvent in an area where people were smoking," my father said with certainty.

"Excellent, Watson!" Joanna lauded. "For you have named the first clue that is telling us all is not what it appears to be. Edmunds would have demanded the preparation of the solvent be carried out in a safe area, but he did not and for good reason."

"He intended the explosion to occur," I deduced.

"He did indeed." Joanna went on, "It would not surprise

me if he had convinced his cellmate, Derrick Wilson, to perform the actual mixing while the idiot was smoking. With this
scenario in mind, Edmunds would stand behind Wilson, so that
the cellmate would absorb the flames and blast of the explosion.
Allow me to draw your attention to the fact that the eyewitness
did not see Edmunds on fire, but only an individual engulfed in
flames, with that individual no doubt being Derrick Wilson."

"But the eyewitness clearly stated that he saw Derrick
Wilson later that day," my father argued.

"Another contradiction which must be overcome," I
agreed.

"Which brings us to the ingredients for glue that I noted
on a shelf in the workshop," said Joanna. "Flour and salt, with
a touch of vinegar, produces a sticky paste that can serve as
glue, but it will not be a very strong adhesive and one that
would never be used on furniture. So then, what purpose
could it possibly have?"

Joanna waited for a response and when one was not forth-
coming, she gave us another clue. "Please recall that Edmunds
and Wilson were quite similar in size and frame. Also keep in
mind that Wilson was a rough character from Scotland, who
was a loner and spent most of his time away from others."

Neither my father nor I could grasp the direction she was
leading us in.

"What was the single, most distinguishing feature that
Derrick Wilson possessed?" Joanna prompted.

"His thick beard and moustache," I answered without
thought, but then all the pieces of the puzzle came to me in
a rush. "Harry Edmunds pasted on a beard and moustache,
using the glue he made in the workshop!"

"Bravo, John," Joanna praised, then continued on. "Wilson
no doubt trimmed his beard in his cell, where Edmunds could
have easily and slyly gathered and hid the clippings."

"And in the disruption caused by the explosion, he could have hurried back to his cell and applied the clippings to his face unnoticed by anyone," I added.

"The pasty glue made in the workshop would have been well suited for that purpose, and thus Edmunds could have taken on the appearance of Derrick Wilson who was soon to be discharged," Joanna continued on. "You should also recall they were cellmates, so Edmunds knew all of Wilson's mannerisms and ways, including his Scottish accent which could be copied with practice."

"Thus, Harry Edmunds was able to take the place of Derrick Wilson and walk out of Wormwood Scrubs a free man," my father concluded. "And conveniently left behind an unrecognizable charred body to be buried in a potter's field. Of course all this needs to be proven beyond a doubt."

"And so it will, Watson, for at this very moment Lestrade is soliciting the court for permission to exhume the body," said Joanna. "I am confident examination of the corpse will back up the evidence we now have and will put a face on our vandal."

"But will this new information lead to his apprehension?" asked my father.

"Let us hope so, for time is now very much against us," Joanna replied. "You see, the vandal has narrowed down the list of paintings that could be hiding the masterpiece."

"How did he manage that?"

"By examining the file that Simon Hawke keeps in his office." Joanna described the folder containing the names of all the paintings restored over the past few years. On separate pages, the defects in each work of art was detailed and signed by the owner as well as the restorer. "The restoration performed during a given time period will hold the treasured masterpiece."

"How did Edmunds gain access to the file?" my father asked.

"By entering Simon Hawke's office during one of the break-ins," Joanna replied. "I questioned the lockpick involved and he distinctly remembered the sound of pages being flipped while Edmunds was in the office."

"The sound, you say?"

"The sound," Joanna repeated. "I should mention that the lockpick is virtually blind and depends on his sharpened hearing and other senses to get around in his sightless world. He clearly recognized the noise made by flipping pages."

"Were you able to obtain the titles of the listed restorations?" my father inquired.

"I thought it best not to do so in the presence of Simon Hawke."

"Why so?"

"Because I am not convinced of his innocence."

My father nodded, with a thin smile. "Like your father who believed that innocence must be proven before a suspect can be excluded."

"Precisely," Joanna concurred. "In addition, I have now concluded that it was the other restorer, and not Harry Edmunds, who discovered the hidden masterpiece and knows the painting which hides it."

"Based on what?" asked I.

"A deduction I should have made earlier," Joanna responded. "It is the simplest of deductions, based on the simplest of observations. You must remember that it is Harry Edmunds who travels from place to place, slashing up portraits of women, which informs us that he doesn't know which painting conceals the masterpiece. Thus, he could not be the one who found the hidden masterpiece during a restoration, yet he knew of it. How could this be so? Obviously the other restorer told him of the fantastic find, and the other restorer had to be James Blackstone, with whom he worked and was no doubt close to. I suspect they were partners and planning to sell their ill-gotten gain on the black market, which they no doubt were familiar with. You will recall both were arrested and convicted of selling their forgeries in such a marketplace."

"But why leave the masterpiece in its concealed location?" my father inquired. "Why not remove it and secure it somewhere away from the art gallery?"

"An excellent question, Watson, and one that I, too, pondered over," said Joanna. "There are several possible explanations. First, the masterpiece may be too fragile to move and carry about. Remember, in its current location, the atmosphere is dry and away from light, which protects it from degrading. Exposing it to humid air and ultraviolet rays could damage it further and reduce its value substantially. Thus, finding another suitable place to conceal it is no easy task and carries risks. But it is the second reason for not moving the masterpiece that I favor. They were thieves and simply did not trust one another. In the art gallery, where it was hidden behind a restoration that could take months, both knew where their share of the projected fortune was located. Here, they could keep an eye on each other. But their plans fell apart when the two were arrested for forgery, with Edmunds going to prison and Blackstone reportedly fleeing to Australia."

"Mother, he has not fled," Johnny interrupted. "In all likelihood James Blackstone remains in London."

"How did you reach that conclusion?" Joanna asked, but the pleased look on her face told me she had the very same thought.

"Why flee to Australia while on the run, when a once-in-a-lifetime fortune awaits you here in London?" Johnny explained. "Your partner is in prison and you are free, thus giving you the opportunity for sole ownership of a true masterpiece. So you see, Mother, he is still in London searching for the treasure, as any thief worth his salt would."

"Are you suggesting we are dealing with two vandals rather than one?" I proposed.

"It is a distinct possibility," Johnny answered.

"But James Blackstone would have no need to resort to vandalism, for he *knows* where the masterpiece is hidden, does he not?" my father countered.

"Perhaps it was subsequently moved," Johnny suggested.

"By whom?" my father inquired. "Only the two restorers, Harry Edmunds and James Blackstone, know of the hidden treasure. If Edmunds had moved it, he would be aware of its location and would not be frantically slashing the other paintings. And if the transfer was done by Blackstone, he would know precisely where it was concealed and would have fetched it by now."

We considered the matter further in silence, but could not explain why James Blackstone had not gone directly to the source and made off with the masterpiece. He could have done so easily, with his partner out of the picture and securely locked up in Wormwood Scrubs. "Of course all this conjecture is dependent on Johnny's assumption that Blackstone remains in London and did not flee to Australia," I said finally.

"An assumption I believe to be correct," Joanna asserted. "The temptation of such a great fortune would be far too great to leave behind."

"Then why does Blackstone not have the masterpiece in hand?" I challenged.

"I can think of a number of reasons," said Joanna. "But the most likely one is that Blackstone does not know where the treasure is at this moment. Keep in mind that he discovered the masterpiece behind a painting of a woman which required restoration. Now suppose, just suppose, the restoration was completed and returned to its owner who sold it to another gallery or perhaps to another individual. Blackstone, fleeing for his freedom, would have no way of following the trail of the painting to its current location."

"He could have broken into Hawke and Evans and searched through the restoration and receipts folders," I submitted.

Joanna shook her head at the suggestion. "It is Edmunds, not Blackstone, who is the master criminal. It was he who arranged for the forced entry into Hawke and Evans and into the Dubose home. And it was he who cleverly arranged for the death of a cellmate so he could gain his freedom. It was because Blackstone was such a novice at crime that he brought Edmunds in on the theft."

"So the masterpiece is still out there," I concluded.

"And so is James Blackstone," Joanna noted, then abruptly waved away the ideas under discussion. She reached for a Turkish cigarette and, after lighting it, began pacing back and forth in front of us. "We are on the wrong track here. Of course James Blackstone would know which painting hid the masterpiece, but he was far too clever to conceal it behind a portrait belonging to a gallery, from where it could be sold and sold yet again, making it very difficult if not impossible to trace. Being the clever fellow he is, he would hide the masterpiece beneath a painting that belonged to a person of wealth and status, who would never dream of parting with it."

"Like the countess," I surmised.

"Precisely," Joanna agreed. "But all the evidence tells us it was Harry Edmunds, not Blackstone, who entered the Granville residence. So here we have Edmunds desperately slashing portraits while Blackstone bides his time. All of which informs us that Blackstone knows where the masterpiece is located, but Edmunds does not."

"But how did Blackstone keep the new location a secret?" asked I.

"It could have easily been done while Harry Edmunds

was not present in the restoration area of the gallery," Joanna answered. "Blackstone would never disclose the move had been made, for he apparently distrusted Edmunds."

"A fallout among thieves," I opined. "But why hasn't Blackstone retrieved the masterpiece?"

"Most likely it is in a quite secure place which compounds the difficulty," Joanna replied. "Besides, he was in no rush, with Harry Edmunds locked away in Wormwood Scrubs."

"But with all the recent portrait slashings, Blackstone must be aware that Edmunds is now a free man."

Joanna nodded at my conclusion, saying, "And thus the race is on to see who reaches the masterpiece first."

"All this hypothesizing is well and good," my father interjected. "But you are neglecting the evidence Lestrade has which indicates Blackstone has in fact set sail for Australia."

"Pshaw!" Joanna waved away the voyage. "This so-called evidence consists of a receipt for a ticket found in Blackstone's lodging which indicated he had booked passage to Australia on the *Queen Victoria*. Let us see if his name appears on the manifest of that ocean liner when it left port."

"So it appears you firmly believe James Blackstone is still here in London," I said.

"I do, and for all the good reasons Johnny has laid out for us," Joanna affirmed.

"Might the two actually be competing with one another, Mother?" asked Johnny.

"If so, I would lay my wager on Harry Edmunds, for he is by far the more clever of the two," Joanna responded, then leaned back and tapped a finger against her closed lips, obviously in deep thought. This motion went on for a half minute or so, before she added, "We must place ourselves in the position of our two thieves. Both need more information on the possible whereabouts of the portrait of a woman which hides the masterpiece. How could they go about this?"

"They would search the folder containing the list of restorations!" I replied at once.

"That is the key," Joanna agreed. "For it not only lists the restorations done by Hawke and Evans, but who performed the work and when. With this in mind, we should search the folder for a female portrait that was restored by James Blackstone."

"But how do we accomplish this feat without Simon Hawke being aware?" my father asked.

"With guile, Watson," Joanna replied.

Before she could expound, there was a gentle rap on the door and Miss Hudson entered with a large platter that held a roasted goose which was accompanied by side dishes of baked potatoes and sprouts wrapped in crispy bacon.

Johnny rose quickly to his feet and exclaimed, "Ah, it is Miss Hudson with her fine goose dinner, the makings of which cannot be surpassed in all England."

He gave our landlady a most courteous bow that caused Miss Hudson to blush.

Joanna hurried over to her son and gave the lad a tender kiss on his forehead.

"What was the reason for that, Mother?" Johnny asked.

"For being so brave during a most trying time."

"That is because I am a Blalock," he said simply.

"And a Holmes," Joanna added.

"A most formidable combination," Johnny stated, with a hint of pride.

Joanna smiled broadly at the return of her son's health and good spirits, and for that brief moment all was right in the world.

16

The Exhumation

The grave to be exhumed was stark and unadorned, with only freshly turned earth and a numbered wooden stake to note its occupant. Surrounding the site on that cold, dreary morning were two diggers, a health official, Lestrade, Joanna, my father, and me. Both grim-faced diggers were wearing bright red, hooded caps, with white fur trimming, to honor Christmas which was rapidly approaching. However, no religious presence was required because the ground was not consecrated. With each shovelful being removed, I could not help but wonder what the condition of the corpse might be. A body dead for three weeks should demonstrate black putrefaction, in which the skin undergoes a blackish-green discoloration and the internal organs degenerate into a soapy pulp that emits a most foul odor.

As the digger's shovel scraped against the wooden casket, my presumption proved to be correct. A terrible smell arose from the grave and reached our nostrils. Everyone quickly stepped back and placed on masks to dampen the awful stench. With care, the casket was lifted out by the diggers and opened to reveal a blackened corpse, the ink-like color due in large measure to its charred cutaneous tissue. The lid was tightly replaced and the body and its casket lowered into a large, separate container called a shell and prepared for transport.

Suddenly a flock of ravens descended onto the grave site. Large and black as the darkest night, the birds landed and made hoarse, raucous squawks through their pointed beaks. The diggers swung their shovels at the aggressive ravens which backed off, but refused to fly away. Even more birds appeared overhead. Lestrade hurriedly took out his revolver and fired several shots into the air, missing the ravens but finally frightening them into full retreat.

"The smell of the dead does it," one of the diggers said. "They seem to be capable of picking up the scent a mile away."

"It is the carrion," Lestrade noted, securing his revolver. "Crows and ravens alike are attracted to it, but the flesh has to be rotten for them to be interested."

"Aye, guv'nor," the digger agreed, then turned his attention to the grave. "Shall we leave it open for the corpse's return once your studies are completed?"

"Yes, but you may wish to add a layer of soil to the bottom and so cover up the odor which attracted the ravens."

"We will do that, guv'nor."

Joanna watched with interest as the ravens flew high above and waited patiently for us to leave so they could return to the grave site. "I take it you have seen this kind of behavior on a number of occasions," she inquired of the digger.

"Oh, yes, madam," the digger replied, and pointed to a stand of trees in the far distance. "They house themselves over there until the scent of rotting flesh comes their way. I have heard they consider it a food of choice."

"That is not uncommon among animals, even those who are domesticated," Joanna said, smiling thinly to herself. "It represents a guaranteed meal, you see."

"And maybe they like it because the rotten meat is more tender," the digger surmised.

"That, too," Joanna said, as she continued to gaze at the noisy ravens flying above. "For them it might well be an irresistible delicacy."

"Quite right, madam," the digger concurred and then, with the help of his coworker, lifted the heavy shell and carried it to a waiting transport.

We rode to St. Bartholomew's in a Scotland Yard car, with Lestrade in the front seat next to the driver. He turned to face us as he told of the latest findings regarding the art vandal. New information had been gathered on the journey of James Blackstone to the land down under.

"There were two ocean liners that departed Southampton for Australia during that time period," Lestrade began. "There was HMS *Olympic* and HMS *Queen Victoria,* each carrying seven hundred and ten passengers in first class and four hundred in the second tier. We checked the manifest of both and found a James Blackstone listed on the *Queen Victoria*—first class, mind you—with a cabin reserved on the portside. Rather pricey by any standard, wouldn't you say?"

"Paid for by his forgeries, I would think," said my father.

"And planned well in advance," Joanna reasoned. "You will note he booked under his true name, which indicates he was not yet on the run and wanted by Scotland Yard. Thus, the passage must have been purchased before Edmunds's arrest, and that tells us Blackstone was already counting the fortune he and his partner would reap from the sale of the masterpiece."

"I thought along those same lines," Lestrade continued

on. "The cabin reserved by Blackstone was used during the voyage, as attested to by the serving members of the crew. None unfortunately could give us a clear description of the individual who occupied that cabin."

"What of the passengers who were listed in the nearby first-class cabins?" asked my father. "Perhaps they may have seen Blackstone."

"We are attempting to track down those individuals, but without success thus far," Lestrade replied. "In any event, after a long journey, the *Queen Victoria* docked in Sydney and seven hundred and ten passengers disembarked, none of whom were named James Blackstone."

"He must have used an alias," my father said at once.

"Spot-on, Dr. Watson," Lestrade agreed. "So we requested the Australian authorities to check the manifest from the *Queen Victoria* against the list of those who disembarked and registered in Sydney. All of the names matched except for a gentleman named David Hughes who no one seems to remember. He gave a local hotel as his address while in Australia, but no such guest ever showed at that hotel. The authorities there are of course searching for the whereabouts of one David Hughes, but have no identifying features to go on. They have asked us for a recent photograph of Blackstone and we are currently searching for one."

"They will never find him," my father said. "Australia is such a vast country, with an outback of uncountable miles and tiny towns so remote they are rarely visited even by the natives."

"The Australians did not sound very optimistic as well," Lestrade remarked.

"Is it possible that David Hughes is a real person who purchased the passage from Blackstone at a reduced price and used the forger's name to disguise his true identity at the time of boarding?" I conjectured.

"Why would he do such an act?" Lestrade questioned.

"To escape to Australia unnoticed where he could hide and begin a new life," I responded.

"To escape from what, may I ask?"

"That is a query that Mr. David Hughes alone can answer. But I think it worthwhile for you to run that name through your criminal files and missing persons section to see if there is a match."

"We shall indeed, but you must admit that is a rather long shot," said Lestrade, then looked over to Joanna who was gazing out a side window. "You have been very quiet on this matter, madam. What say you as to the whereabouts of James Blackstone?"

"He remains in London," Joanna replied.

"Even though our strongest evidence indicates he is in Australia?"

"Even though," said Joanna as our car pulled up to the curb outside St. Bartholomew's Hospital.

We gowned and masked ourselves before entering the autopsy room where the charred corpse awaited us. It lay on the dissection table and, under the bright light, had an even more disgusting appearance than before. The blackish-green body was now severely bloated as a result of enzymes and bacteria digesting the dead tissue and releasing noxious gases into all tissues. We quickly placed small dabs of menthol cream under our masks in an attempt to dampen the awful stench arising from the corpse. I decided against opening the abdomen or thorax, for at this stage of putrefaction their organs would be unrecognizable and little more than liquefied tissue.

"John, please describe the remarkable findings as you come across them," Joanna requested.

"Let us begin with the body in general," said I, snapping on rubber gloves. "The corpse is that of a male, as evidenced by the external genitalia, but none of his other features are recognizable because of the severe burns which have charred every inch of his skin. Putrefaction has bloated the body, most notably the abdomen, and added a greenish tint to its surface."

"I take it these findings are consistent with a body that has been dead for three weeks," Joanna inquired.

"Quite so," I replied and moved to the corpse's head. "The face is deeply burned, with charred tissue resting upon scorched bone. Most of the hair is gone, but I can still see stubbles beneath the nose and on the chin, indicating that a beard and moustache of some thickness were once present. The skull appears to be intact, but there is definite evidence of a healed fracture of the zygomatic arch on the left." I clarified this finding for Lestrade. "Inspector, the zygomatic arch comprises most of the cheekbone, and here it is distorted, with irregular healing and dense deposits of calcium. So we can conclude it is from a long time ago and was quite disfiguring."

"Easily noticeable, then," Lestrade noted.

"And difficult to hide, even with a most thick beard," I added. "It would have shown itself as an obvious indentation, with a covering scar."

"Can you determine its origin?"

"Not with any degree of certainty, for no foreign bodies were present, but a fall or fight would be the most likely cause."

Joanna interjected, "Inspector, you should be aware that

Harry Edmunds had no such disfigurement, whilst his cell-mate Derrick Wilson was so damaged."

"Are you certain of this?" Lestrade asked.

"Beyond any doubt," Joanna assured. "Derrick Wilson's disfigured cheek was described to us by another inmate we interrogated during our visit to Wormwood Scrubs."

"And Harry Edmunds had no similar facial damage?"

"Not according to the physician who performed a thorough physical examination on Edmunds upon his arrival at the prison."

I next went to the neck where the cutaneous tissue had been completely burned away, exposing a melted and collapsed trachea. "His airway was completely blocked off by the intense flames, and he most likely died immediately of suffocation which is not unusual in severe burn cases. So, in addition to the agony of the burns, such patients literally choke to death."

I moved past the bloated abdomen and charred genitalia to the lower extremities that showed more evidence of significant trauma. One of the kneecaps had been fractured, but had healed well and would cause no disfiguration. Then I arrived at the feet and saw the signature marking we expected to find. "All ten toes are present!" I announced. "This finding is of critical importance, Inspector, for Harry Edmunds had a missing small toe, whilst our charred corpse has no such defect."

Joanna stepped in for a closer look and recounted the phalanges. "I must admit that I was concerned the intense fire together with the putrefaction process might have caused the digits to drop off, which would have presented quite a problem."

"You raise a good point," I stated. "But fortunately the

fire did not burn through the ligaments that keep the toes attached to the foot, and in fact rarely does. The putrefaction process itself will not be a cause for worry, for the ligaments do not disappear until many months have passed. Had that occurred, we would be looking at a jumble of small, disjointed bones. So, when all is said and done, we have a charred corpse with a facial disfigurement and all ten toes, and thus can say good-bye to the plausibility that these remains belong to Harry Edmunds."

"And we can say hello to Mr. Derrick Wilson."

We quickly disrobed and walked out into the corridor to further discuss our findings, but were interrupted by a sergeant from Scotland Yard who urgently signaled Lestrade aside.

"Harry Edmunds is a most clever devil," Joanna remarked whilst we waited for Lestrade. "It was an ingenious plan and he nearly got away with it."

"Yet from the start, I had the feeling you never truly believed Edmunds died in that fire," said my father. "Were there clues we overlooked?"

Joanna shook her head at the question. "You observed the same clues as I did. First, as you noted earlier, Edmunds was an experienced restorer who was very familiar with solvents and their flammability. He was far too smart to allow a lighted cigarette to be in the vicinity where a solvent was being prepared. And secondly, there was the incontrovertible evidence that Harry Edmunds, with his severe psoriasis and coal tar lotion, was the vandal who was committing crimes weeks after his reported death. Putting these two observations together, one can only conclude that Edmunds did not die in that fire, and thus someone else must have. And that someone else was his cellmate Derrick Wilson, with whom he shared a number of physical characteristics."

"Edmunds picked the ideal subject to die for him," my father noted.

"Except for the fact his ideal subject has ten toes," said Joanna.

Lestrade hurried back to me with the newest developments. "The art vandal has struck again. This time at the Stewart and Son gallery in Kensington. But on this occasion he turned violent."

"How so?" Joanna asked.

"He stabbed a security guard who attempted to intervene."

"On the vandal's way in or out?"

"Out, for he escaped with a framed painting securely tucked under his arm."

"The masterpiece," my father muttered in a whisper, as the very same thought echoed in all our minds.

17

The Stewart Gallery

On our ride to the Stewart and Son gallery, we had to face the disheartening fact that Harry Edmunds had won the battle. He now had the masterpiece in his grasp and would soon disappear once it was sold on the black market.

"He must have discovered which painting held the masterpiece," Joanna surmised, raising her voice above the noise of the four-wheeler we had hired. "There was a marking of some sort that served as a clue."

"Do you have any idea what this marking might be?" I inquired.

Joanna shrugged. "It could have been made in a dozen different ways. Perhaps there was a scratch on the corner of the frame that James Blackstone had mentioned. Or perhaps there was some irregularity in the varnish which was difficult to detect. But then again, it may not have been a marking that led to the masterpiece, but rather that Edmunds recalled the painting which was being restored when the treasured canvas came to light. Or even more likely, he narrowed down the possibilities by reviewing the list of restorations in the folder on Simon Hawke's desk."

"Whatever the clue, he knew it well beforehand," my father said. "That is why he advertised on the black market that the masterpiece would soon be available."

"Yet all may not be lost," I thought aloud. "Could we not set a trap for him on the underground market?"

Joanna shook her head quickly. "To set a clever trap requires an irresistible bait, which we lack. And even if such bait was available, it might well prove useless since the auction we presume is taking place may be over and a deal struck. That being the case, any clever trap would be totally ignored."

"The tide is now running entirely against us," my father said unhappily. "And it appears to be reaching the stage where it cannot be reversed."

"We have lost a battle, Watson, not the war," said Joanna.

We arrived at the Stewart and Son gallery and hurried into a large, well-appointed display room that had every wall covered with eye-catching paintings, all of which seemed to come from a long gone past. The owner, Mr. Miles Stewart, was not available, for he was bedridden with severe bronchitis. However, his son Samuel was minding the gallery and greeted us with suspicion until we were formally introduced. He seemed most pleased to meet Joanna.

"Ah, the daughter of Sherlock Holmes whose exploits I have read about," said he. "I would be forever grateful if you could somehow arrange for my painting to be returned, for it will be dearly missed."

"Am I correct in assuming the painting is quite valuable?" Joanna asked.

"That is the strange part, madam," Stewart replied. "It was surrounded by works far more precious, yet he chose the one of considerable less value. It is beyond me why he would do such a thing."

"Was there anything unusual about the painting?"

"It is the artist who was unusual."

"How so?"

"It was painted during the Italian Renaissance by a woman named Saint Catherine of Bologna, and depicts a nun at prayer in full habit," Stewart described. "Saint Catherine was so revered as a religious personage that her body was exhumed shortly after death and preserved, and it remains on display to this very day. But I can assure you that feature does not add to its value. From an artistic standpoint, the work is not very impressive."

"Yet you hang it in your very fine gallery," Joanna noted.

"Only briefly, for the owners who requested the restoration will return from America tomorrow, and sadly find their treasured painting missing."

Joanna's brow went up. "Restoration, you say?"

"Limited, but nonetheless expensive," Stewart replied. "The owners thought the faded, multicolored flowers in the background detracted from the portrait and were willing to pay a rather handsome fee to have it restored."

"At Stewart's?"

"Oh no, madam. The work was done at Hawke and Evans who have the finest restorers in all London."

I nodded to myself, for here was yet another connection of the vandal to Hawke and Evans. I wondered which of the restorers performed the recoloring and asked, "Were you given the name of the restorer?"

"I was not," Stewart answered. "The decision was left up to Simon Hawke whose judgment we trusted implicitly. The work was quite well done, but at a cost that nearly exceeded the value of the painting."

"Do you have any idea why the owners were so attracted to an unimpressive portrait of a nun?" I asked.

"I did not ask, but perhaps they are of the Catholic persuasion," Stewart replied. "Those are the ones who would show the most interest."

We turned as the security guard, with his bandaged arm in a sling, came back into the gallery. A thin man, in his middle years, he appeared to be quite shaken by his ordeal. Taking slow steps, he walked over to a chair beneath a painting of St. Peter's Square and sat down heavily.

"That is Armstrong, our security guard, who was injured in a scuffle with the thief," Stewart told us. "We of course immediately sent him to a nearby surgery for medical attention, but asked that he return in the event Scotland Yard had further questions."

"Most wise," Joanna said and led the way over to the injured security guard who was gently rubbing at his bandaged arm. "I realize you have had a rough time of it, but we require more information and wonder if you could help us with that."

"I shall try, madam," the guard said.

"Very good," Joanna went on. "Please describe every detail from the moment you became aware of the intruder until he fled carrying the portrait with him."

"Well, madam, it was a calm and peaceful night as I made my rounds on each of the two floors and the loft," the guard began. "I was in the loft when I heard a sound below that resembled a piece of furniture being moved. It did not recur, but I thought it best to have a look-see. I went down and shined my torch around the gallery and saw nothing amiss. Next I took the stairs to the bottom level that is used for storage and again saw nothing out of place. I then returned to the main floor, and that is when I noticed a moving shadow and called out a warning."

"Were you armed?" Joanna asked.

"No, madam, I was not, but I do carry a whistle that can alert patrolling constables," the guard continued. "I was reaching for my whistle when the bloody thief attacked me. In the struggle he stabbed me with a knife I did not see, and next came at me with a framed painting. He proceeded to crack me on the head and, as I went down, he bolted for the side door with the painting tucked under his arm. It required some time for me to regain my senses and rise up, but by then he was long gone. It was at that moment I became aware of my wound and the blood coming from it."

"How much time went by before you whistled for the constable?" Joanna inquired.

"I cannot be certain, for I was dazed by the blow to my head," the guard replied and gently massaged the crown of his skull. "He must have given me quite a knock, for it continues to throb."

"I take it you did not have a good look at him."

"In the darkness, I saw only shadows."

"During the scuffle, did you notice any peculiar odor about the thief?"

"No, madam, but then I was fighting for my life and just trying to survive."

"As would anyone in that situation," said Joanna, as the guard went back to rubbing his bandaged arm. "Is the wound painful?"

"A bit, madam."

"Then perhaps you should retire to your home and rest," Joanna suggested.

The guard glanced at Stewart for consent and, once given an approving nod, walked slowly to the front entrance, still unsteady on his feet.

Joanna said quietly to Stewart, "You may wish to hire a hansom to make certain your guard reaches home safely."

"Of course," Stewart agreed and hurried over to assist the security guard.

With the pair not yet out of hearing distance, I guided Joanna and my father to a nearby staircase and said, "I find it odd the vandal thought it necessary to carry out the entire painting. Why not just slash it open and grab the masterpiece?"

"I can think of several good reasons," Joanna replied.

"Yet the vandal must have an irresistible impulse to snatch the masterpiece and be gone once and for all," said my father.

Our voices must have carried, for Lestrade heard the end of our conversation as he ascended to the top of the staircase. "Masterpiece? What masterpiece?" asked he.

"We believe there is a masterpiece, a painting of immense value, hidden behind one of the restored canvases, and it is for this reason the vandal has slashed them open," Joanna explained. "We further believe that two restorers at Hawke and Evans discovered the hidden masterpiece and were planning to sell it on the black market, then flee with their newly acquired fortune."

Lestrade started at Joanna in astonishment. "Do you know this for a fact?"

"All evidence points to that conclusion," Joanna asserted. "There is no other explanation."

"So we are not dealing with simple vandalism, but with two thieves desperately searching for a concealed masterpiece," Lestrade said, while he quickly assimilated the information. "This would explain why Harry Edmunds was so eager to escape from Wormwood Scrubs and why James Blackstone is in all likelihood still in London. They were racing against one another in an effort to reach the valuable prize first."

"Spot-on, Inspector," Joanna concurred.

Lestrade rubbed at his chin, thinking the problem through. "But why are they slashing only portraits of women?"

"Because that must be the clue to which painting hides the masterpiece," Joanna replied, keeping an eye on Samuel Stewart who remained near the front entrance. "That is the only plausible—"

"Hold on," Lestrade interrupted. "If they knew where the masterpiece was hidden, why all the slashing?"

"Because we believe it was James Blackstone who discovered the hidden painting, and he partnered with Harry Edmunds but never told him of its exact location," said Joanna.

"Only that it was behind a restoration showing the portrait of a woman," Lestrade concluded, as the complete picture came to him. "So Harry Edmunds was running around slashing portraits, whilst James Blackstone was biding his time and waiting for a good opportunity. And now it would seem that Edmunds has won the contest and has the masterpiece in hand."

"So it would appear, Inspector."

There was a sudden commotion at the side entrance of the gallery. We turned to see a constable rushing in and holding up a badly damaged painting that had a broken frame and a deep slash across its colorful canvas.

The constable hurried over to Lestrade and held the painting up for all to see. A vertical cut bisected the praying nun in two equal parts.

"The missing painting!" I proclaimed.

"I found it in a rubbish bin a block over," the constable reported.

"In the open?" Joanna asked at once.

"No, madam. It was beneath a tin overhang that must

have protected it from the early morning rain. As you can see, it is not wet."

Joanna reached for her magnifying glass and, after peeling back a thick edge, examined the undersurface of the tear, then the area behind the damaged canvas. "The backing has been damaged, with a deep cut that has a streak of blood upon it."

"What does that tell us?" Lestrade asked.

"Everything," Joanna answered.

Samuel Stewart dashed in from the outside and, upon seeing the condition of the painting, gasped in horror. "Ruined! It is ruined!"

"Is there any hope of restoration?" asked Joanna.

"Perhaps, but at a cost far, far beyond the value of the painting," Stewart replied and, moving in closer, gently touched the distorted face of the nun. "Who would commit such a senseless, cruel act?"

A vicious killer who now has a fortune in hand, I thought, but held my tongue.

"The crazed vandal who is plaguing the west side of London," Lestrade replied, and was wise enough not to give any particulars. "It is clear he has struck out again."

"You must put a stop to this, Inspector," Stewart demanded and, with the broken portrait in hand, retreated to his office.

Lestrade sighed resignedly and waited for the constable and Stewart to be well out of earshot before saying, "I am afraid the sliced and discarded painting tells us that Mr. Harry Edmunds is now in sole possession of the priceless masterpiece."

"I think not," Joanna said. "All of the evidence points to the contrary."

"Pray tell how did you reach this conclusion?" Lestrade asked.

"Allow me to draw your attention to the backing of the nun's portrait," replied Joanna. "It reveals a deep cut with bloodstains on its edges. Recall that all of the other vandalized paintings had pristine backings, so that the slashing would not damage the concealed artwork. But on this occasion it appears he cut through the canvas all the way to the backing, which would have surely sliced into the hidden masterpiece."

"Why would he do such a foolish act?" I asked quickly.

"That is the point, John," Joanna replied. "Harry Edmunds is no fool and did not commit the deed as you and the inspector described."

"I am confused," I confessed.

"As am I," said Lestrade.

"You must concentrate on the bloody knife, for it tells us the all-important sequence of events," Joanna elucidated. "Harry Edmunds had the portrait in hand when he encountered the security guard and stabbed him. There was no blood on his knife until that moment, yet the blade left its bloody mark on the backing of the portrait, which indicates he slashed the canvas open outside the gallery."

"Why would he do that?" my father asked.

"Because he was surprised by the guard in the gallery and had no chance to cut open the canvas," Joanna went on. "So he ran, with the painting in hand, but the guard blocked his exit and a struggle ensued. Harry Edmunds then stabbed the guard, thus bloodying his knife. For good measure Edmunds brought the painting down on the guard's head, the force of which dazed the guard and damaged the frame of the canvas."

"And Edmunds used only a sharp corner of the frame so as not to cause harm to the concealed masterpiece," I noted.

"Precisely, John," said Joanna. "For only a corner was

badly cracked and not shattered, and thus what lay beneath it remained safe. So now we have Harry Edmunds running for his life, the nun's portrait in one hand, the bloodied knife in the other. He would be an obvious figure, a man dashing about in the early morning hours carrying a large, framed painting. People would be beginning to stir, some up and around, and would take notice, so Harry Edmunds has to determine if the portrait holds the masterpiece. He arrives at the tin overhang the constable described and slashes the painting open, and finding no hidden treasure, lashes out and stabs the painting itself and inflicts a bloody gash on its backing. I also observed a bit of blood on the edges of the torn canvas and that tells us the slash was made with a bloodied knife."

"Let us say the sequence of events you described is correct—is it not possible that Edmunds did in fact find the masterpiece and stabbed the backing out of joy rather than rage?" Lestrade challenged.

"Most unlikely when you consider the rain," Joanna responded. "Keep in mind that Edmunds sought the shelter of a tin overhang before slashing the canvas. He did this with the singular purpose of protecting the masterpiece, for it is undoubtedly old and fragile and exposure to rain would result in irreparable damage. Harry Edmunds, being an experienced restorer, would have never taken such a chance. Even if the masterpiece was found, he would not have removed it in this weather, nor would he have folded or rolled it up, for that could cause significant damage to an ancient work of art. Being such a clever fellow, he would have wrapped the painting under his scarf and hurried along his way."

"I still see an obstacle in pinning this entire adventure on Harry Edmunds," said my father.

"Which is?" asked Joanna.

"The odor of coal tar which the guard did not detect," my father replied. "It is impossible to miss that pungent aroma close up."

"But not when one is fighting for one's life," Joanna rebutted.

"Yet the smell is so overpowering," my father emphasized. "With this in mind, could the villain here be James Blackstone who came out of the shadows to reclaim his treasure? In the darkness, it would be the odor which distinguishes Edmunds from Blackstone."

"A very good point, Dr. Watson," Lestrade concurred, nodding at my father's assessment.

"It is except for the fact that James Blackstone is dead," said Joanna.

Lestrade's eyes suddenly widened. "Have you seen the body?"

"Not as yet," Joanna replied. "But I know its location."

"Would you care to share that secret with us?"

"Only after you have obtained a special search warrant."

"Special in what regard?"

"One that allows for demolition at a crime scene."

18

The Hiding Place

Business at Hawke and Evans was by all signs improving, with a half dozen or so people milling about and inspecting the works of art on the first floor of the gallery. I attributed this increase to the fact that stories of the art vandal were no longer on the front page of London's newspapers, having been replaced by sad news from the Great War on the continent. Simon Hawke seemed pleased with the turnout of potential customers and readily consented to Joanna's request that we be allowed to review the folder containing all the artwork restored by the gallery over the past year. However, he was none too happy when Joanna insisted that Giuseppe Delvecchio be permitted to assist her in a search for other clues or markings that might indicate where the vandal would strike next. At the moment Delvecchio was restoring a fine painting by Monet that would bring in an extraordinary fee, and Hawke was reluctant to waste hours of the restorer's time on a nonprofitable review. But Joanna persisted and Delvecchio was eager to join in, so Hawke finally gave his permission, with the proviso that the restorer spend no more than one hour at the task.

It soon became clear that Delvecchio's presence was not only necessary but invaluable, for most of the restoration projects listed in the folder were done on paintings from the Italian Renaissance period. Delvecchio had a remarkable familiarity with those works of art, as well as with their artists whose names rolled off his lips like they were members of his family.

"Ah, Fabriano," he was saying with affection. "Gentile da Fabriano was from the Early Renaissance and unfortunately most of his works did not last through the ages. But this one, *Madonna dell'Umiltà* survived and represents one of his very best works. Note the description of the Madonna's lovely brown eyes and her perfect lips with her enigmatic smile, all of which required restoration."

"It bears some resemblance to the *Mona Lisa*," Joanna remarked.

"Others have made a similar comment," Delvecchio said. "But da Vinci's portrait was a gift from the gods and this is not. It is possible of course that da Vinci saw Fabriano's earlier work and used it as a model. But only the smile of course."

"Of course," Joanna agreed and studied the restoration note at length.

It was not so much the colorful description of the painting that drew her interest, but the fact it was restored by James Blackstone. She was searching for some detail written down by the restorer that might indicate a marking he could use in the future.

"John," she said, looking up, "please see if you can find a picture of the portrait by Fabriano."

I opened the quite large reference book we had purchased at the suggestion of Edwin Alan Rowe, and began turning pages. The volume contained pictures of the more important works done by artists during the Italian Renaissance period, including extensive biographies on each of the painters. We had carefully studied the photographs of the vandalized portraits the night before, searching for similarities other than female depictions, but found none.

"Here it is," I said and passed the reference book over to Joanna and Delvecchio.

"It is quite beautiful," Joanna admired, as her gaze swept over the portrait. "I can see why its owners wished to have it restored."

"But only by the best of restorers which Blackstone was, and Edmunds was not," Delvecchio stated without malice.

"Did you determine that by simply reading the descriptions they signed?" asked Joanna.

"No, madam," Delvecchio replied. "I have had the privilege of examining some of their unfinished restorations, which I will eventually complete. It is clear that it is Blackstone who is the master."

Joanna's eyes widened, as did mine, at the casual mention of unfinished restorations by both men. But it was James Blackstone's name that drew our immediate attention, for what better place to hide a masterpiece than in a work in progress that had been put aside and perhaps intermingled with others?

"Is it common for restorers to work on more than one painting during the same time period?" I inquired.

Joanna smiled briefly at my question, for I believe it was one she was about to ask.

"That depends on the restorer and the painting itself," Delvecchio answered carefully. "Many restorers, for example, prefer to let their work stand for a while and allow the oil paints to set, for then it may take on a different quality. During this time, they may go to another work."

"Does *set* have the same meaning as *dried*?" asked Joanna.

"To a large extent," Delvecchio replied. "A wet red will reflect the light differently than a red that is settled and completely dried."

"Most interesting," Joanna said. "I would very much like to see Blackstone's unfinished restorations, if it presents no bother."

"No problem at all," Delvecchio told her. "There are only two partial restorations and they are safely tucked away in a far corner."

"They have been there for a while, then?"

"From the dust beginning to collect on their surfaces, I would say the answer is yes."

"Let us move on to the next restoration, for Simon Hawke has limited the time you can spend with us," Joanna urged.

"He is always in a hurry," Delvecchio said, unconcerned, and reached for the next item in the folder. "Ah, this is a very special work by Guido Reni from the late Italian Renaissance period. Of all his paintings, this, the portrayal of *The Archangel Michael Defeating Satan,* is his very best."

I quickly turned to the section on Guido Reni in the reference book and found myself struck by the beauty of the painting Delvecchio had just mentioned. It showed a fierce, but majestic warrior about to slay a vanquished, humanized Satan. Yet the most stunning feature was the brilliant blues and reds of the Archangel's robe, which glowed in different shades. It was beyond me how an artist could paint such dazzling colors, but then I remembered this work came from the age that produced Michelangelo and Leonardo da Vinci.

"I myself would have loved to work on this restoration," Delvecchio mused.

"Is this painting among Blackstone's unfinished works?" I asked.

"Unfortunately not."

We quickly went through the majority of the restoration documents without detecting a clue or marking that might indicate which painting was used to conceal the masterpiece. But the last three in the folder caught our interest because they were unusually thick as compared to the others.

"Why so voluminous?" asked Joanna, scanning the notes that had been written down by the restorer.

"Because of the stature of the artist and the greatness of their work," Delvecchio replied, turning back to the first of the three. "Here is the magnificent painting entitled *The Calling of Saints Peter and Andrew* by Caravaggio in which the beardless Christ needed to be restored. Note his expression of sadness and acceptance. It is beyond beautiful, and one Blackstone must have adored while he restored it."

"Lovely," Joanna agreed, glancing at the photograph of the painting before coming back to the document. "I see where the restoration took place a year ago."

"And no doubt took a month or more to complete," Delvecchio added.

With such a timetable, there was no way the painting could have been used to hide the masterpiece, I thought.

Joanna had reached the same conclusion, for she requested, "Let us move on to the next restoration."

The following artist was named Canaletto, a Venetian whose paintings centered on Venice and the Grand Canal that flowed through it. The work that had been restored showed an expansive view of the Piazza San Marco. "He is quite good, but not near the level of Caravaggio," Delvecchio commented.

Joanna studied the signature page of the document before asking, "I see where Simon Hawke is listed as a co-owner. Isn't that a bit unusual?"

"On occasion, an owner brings in a painting he wishes to sell, but the condition is such that it requires restoration," Delvecchio replied. "The individual may lack the funds necessary to have it restored, and Mr. Hawke agrees to do so for a percentage of the ownership."

"Is that commonly done?" Joanna inquired.

"It is a matter of need, madam," Delvecchio answered in a neutral voice. "For both of the concerned parties."

Joanna searched for the final document which was the thickest of all and remarked, "Ah, a Titian!"

"A true master." Delvecchio smiled broadly at the mere mention of the famous artist. "His true name was Tiziano Vecelli, and he was the most important member of the sixteenth-century Venetian school of art. None surpassed him, or even came close for that matter. The painting we restored was *Diana and Actaeon,* in which the hunter Actaeon bursts in while the goddess Diana and her nymphs are bathing. She of course is furious and Titian paints her fury in such detail that you can sense every ounce of her emotion."

"*We* restored?" Joanna asked at once.

"I was referring to the gallery, madam, for I had not arrived when the restoration was done," Delvecchio clarified, and pointed to the date on the last page of the document. "It was completed several months before I stepped foot into Hawke and Evans. And next to the date, you will note the name of the most fortunate restorer, James Blackstone."

"From the sound of your voice, I take it you would have dearly loved to work on the Titian," Joanna surmised.

"It would have been an opportunity that comes along once in a lifetime, madam," Delvecchio said quietly, then added an optimistic note. "But, with the gallery's connection to the Royal Art Collection, from which the Titian came, one never knows what the future may hold."

"Indeed, the Royal Collection," Joanna repeated to herself, as her mind seemed to shift into another gear. She glanced at the restoration folder a final time before saying, "I think we are done here. Now, if it is convenient, I would like to see the partially restored paintings you mentioned earlier."

"Of course, madam, but first I should ask for Mr. Hawke's permission."

"Please do so."

Joanna waited for Delvecchio to leave the office, then quickly turned to me. "Be so good as to stay behind once the restorer and I depart. While Simon Hawke is otherwise occupied, I would like you to write down the name, date, and restorer of every item in the folder. Make no exceptions."

"What if Hawke attempts to interrupt?"

"Tell him we have Lestrade's permission."

"But we don't."

"We will shortly."

I busied myself with the task, all the while keeping my back to the outer gallery so as to hide my activity. Writing down the requested pieces of information, I could not help but wonder if Joanna had detected a clue to the possible whereabouts of the masterpiece. But why copy down a list we had just studied in detail? Title. Date. Restorer. Where could the hidden clue lie in those bare facts?

I glanced over my shoulder and saw Joanna and Delvecchio in conversation with Simon Hawke. I could not hear their voices, but the stern expression on Hawke's face, together with his other body language, indicated he was displeased with Joanna's further requests. With some urgency, I hurried with the compilation, always double-checking the data from each restoration before I went to the next.

Now Simon Hawke was raising his voice and I could feel his eyes on my back. I straightened up briefly and appeared to be stretching my spine, all the while glancing out at the gallery in my peripheral vision. Joanna had positioned herself in front of Hawke, and was partially blocking his view of the office as she spoke to him in a commanding tone. "I need fifteen more minutes of Delvecchio's time. You can allow it now or later when the police arrive. Either way, I can assure you I will have those fifteen minutes."

I returned to the restoration list and scribbled down the information as rapidly as possible, suddenly wondering if Delvecchio's time was the excuse rather than the reason for Hawke's obstinacy.

A loud voice abruptly came from behind me, but it did not belong to Hawke or Joanna. It carried the distinct bark of a no-nonsense Inspector Lestrade.

"This is an official search warrant for the premises and all structures within," Lestrade announced. "You will be reimbursed for all damages should no criminal activity be discovered."

I turned to see Lestrade at the front of the gallery, with two constables at his side, each armed with a pickax. The few customers in the art gallery hurried out past a third constable who stood guard at the entrance.

"What kind of nonsense is this?" Hawke demanded.

"It would be in your best interest to cooperate," Lestrade said and, without waiting for a response, added, "Be good enough, Mr. Hawke, to lead the way down to your restoration area."

"You shall hear from my solicitor!" Hawke threatened.

Lestrade was unmoved. "You may wish to protect those works of art that are in the process of being restored," he cautioned.

With that warning, Hawke hurried to the staircase, with Lestrade, two constables, Joanna, and Delvecchio only steps behind. Not wishing to miss even a minute of the action, I rapidly copied down the data on the final documents describing the works of Caravaggio, Canaletto, and Titian. After a quick double-check, I found I had written down an erroneous date on the Titian and corrected it. Then, gathering up all the information, I dashed for the stairs.

In the restoration area, the two constables had removed their coats and were carefully rolling up their shirtsleeves. I could not help but notice their pickaxes which were leaning upright against the brick wall that enclosed the central heating furnace. All was eerily silent as Hawke and Delvecchio busily placed shrouds over paintings that had been or were in the process of being restored. My father stood off to the side of the brick enclosure where he had been stationed earlier to make certain it remained secure.

"I trust you are not planning to destroy the protective brick enclosure," Hawke called to Lestrade.

"Only its door, if you refuse to open it," Lestrade said.

"It is tightly bolted and closed off, so no soiled air can seep through," Hawke informed. "But it can be unlocked."

"Then please do so."

Using two keys, Hawke opened the steel door and stepped back as clear but fuel-laden air escaped into the restoration area. Once the odor had dissipated, Lestrade led the way into a spacious room that was enclosed by brick walls on all sides. In its center was a large furnace with an ample, open area around it, which would allow workmen to perform maintenance and needed repairs. The bare floor of the space was made of solid cement, and its walls were uninterrupted except for a wide, bricked-in fireplace.

"Surely you do not plan to break through the sturdy floor and walls, which would wreak havoc on our climate control," Hawke said in a pleading voice.

"The walls and floor do not interest us, but your bricked-in fireplace does," Lestrade informed and signaled to the constables to begin their work.

"If you turn up nothing, your expense will be considerable," Hawke warned.

"I suspect your expense will be far greater," said Lestrade.

The constables drove their pickaxes over and over through the thick, red bricks that covered the fireplace. In the process, they displaced large pieces of the stonework and pushed them aside until they reached the darkened space that lay behind. Lestrade stepped in and illuminated the fireplace with a bright torch. Everyone leaned down to peek in and all saw the same horrific sight. A mummified human figure was curled up within, with its knees flexed and tightly pressed against its chest. The body was completely covered in brown, leatherlike skin, but its skeletal head had no recognizable features.

"Oh, my god!" Hawke gasped, his face losing color.

Delvecchio quickly brought a hand up to his lips to suppress a wave of nausea.

The rest of us had seen our fair share of dead bodies in various conditions and stages of decomposition, and were more interested than moved by the gruesome sight. In particular, the mummified remains were still wearing his clothes and shoes which might allow us to positively identify the corpse. Such items as a wallet would be of great importance. Of additional significance was the absence of a foul odor which indicated the body had passed through the final stages of the putrefaction process and was now skeletonized. From a forensic standpoint, this meant the corpse had to be at least two months old. But a proper, thorough examination required that the corpse be removed from its cramped hiding place.

"The body has to be taken out with great care," I instructed Lestrade and the constables. "We are in fact dealing with little more than skin and bones."

"How should we then proceed?" asked Lestrade.

"The corpse must be handled with kid gloves, otherwise all could fall apart," I cautioned. "Please have the constables place their hands under the head and neck at one end and under the pelvis and knees at the other, then gently lift and place the remains on a shroud that Mr. Delvecchio will provide."

Delvecchio rushed out and came back with a thick shroud which he spread out on the cement floor. Then he stepped back as did the rest of us, except the two constables who reached into the fireplace, but quickly withdrew their hands.

"Sir," the taller of the two constables addressed Lestrade. "What should we do with the bricks atop the corpse's lap?"

Lestrade turned to me. "What say you, Dr. Watson?"

I gazed into the fireplace and saw a short stack of dust-covered bricks that rested upon the corpse's lap and pressed its arms against its torso. It required a moment for me to realize the purpose of the bricks. "I believe the bricks were so placed to prevent the dead man's arms from dangling out of the fireplace. He was literally stuffed in."

"How should the bricks be removed?" Lestrade asked.

Joanna quickly interjected, "With care, for they no doubt were handled by the killer who may have left his fingerprints on them."

The constables covered the dusty bricks with their handkerchiefs and carefully removed them from the corpse's lap and placed them on the cement floor.

Joanna moved in and examined the tops of the extracted bricks with her magnifying glass. "There are fingerprints on several of the bricks," she announced.

"I'll wager those prints belong to Harry Edmunds," said Lestrade.

"Which is a wager you would no doubt win," Joanna agreed, and looked to me with a request. "John, please measure the body's exact height at autopsy."

"Of course," I said, but had no idea why such a measurement would be important.

"Well then, let us proceed," Lestrade ordered somewhat impatiently, and gestured to the constables.

Once the corpse was extracted, I performed a more detailed examination, but could not discover any feature that might lead to its identification, other than it was a male as established by its clothing. The mummified skin showed no large scars or tattoos, nor were there any fractures of large bones. The pockets in his well-worn clothes were empty.

"It is most likely James Blackstone, but the proof is lacking," I opined.

"What causes the peculiar condition of the skin?" Lestrade inquired.

"He became mummified because he was exposed to a constant dry heat that desiccated the body's tissues and turned his skin into a dark brown leather," I explained. "In some ways it resembles the process used in Egyptian mummies, except our corpse's internal organs were not initially removed."

"Can you give us the length of time the body was in the fireplace?"

"Not with any degree of accuracy, for the dry heat inhibits the putrefaction process to a large extent which accounts for the body's appearance and lack of odor. But for certain he has been dead for some months." I carefully removed the corpse's shoes to further my inspection for identifying features, such as old fractures, deformities, and missing toes, but none were seen. I glanced over to Simon Hawke and asked, "Did James Blackstone have any physical ailments?"

Hawke pondered the question briefly. "None that I was aware of."

"Any tattoos?"

"Not to my knowledge."

"Any deformities?"

"None, although he did have a noticeable limp, particularly when standing on his feet all day."

"Describe the limp," my father requested at once.

"He simply favored one leg a bit," Hawke said and, after a moment's thought, added, "I believe it was the left one, for that was the one he tended to rub."

"Did he say he had arthritis?" my father probed.

"That was not the case," Hawke responded. "He once stated that he had been wounded in the Second Boer War which left him with a permanent weakness."

My father and I exchanged knowing glances, for that war wound could play an important role in identifying James Blackstone.

Hawke stared down at the corpse and shuddered, then peered into the depth of the fireplace before turning to Lestrade. "How could you possibly know the body was hidden in there?"

"I did not, but the daughter of Sherlock Holmes did," the inspector replied. "I believe Edgar Allan Poe would have been delighted with her conclusion which was based on a flock of ravens."

"Ravens, you say?" Hawke asked quizzically.

"It was the manner in which they behaved at a recently exhumed grave site," Joanna elucidated. "The birds were greatly attracted by the stench of the rotting flesh that arose from the casket. To them, it represented a kill and an easy meal. Their attraction was so great it required several shots from Lestrade's revolver to frighten them away. This type of behavior is commonplace, even among dogs that have been domesticated."

"My Mimi!" Delvecchio cried out.

"Indeed, it was your dog that detected the scent of dead tissue behind the brick wall and desperately tried to reach it. That was the reason she barked at the wall and attempted to paw her way through. It all became clear when I saw the ravens at the grave site, screeching with their raucous caws."

"It was like Mimi's bark," Delvecchio recalled.

"She was trying to tell us something, as were the ravens at the exhumation," Joanna said. "And so were the ravens in Edgar Allan Poe's poem, *The Raven*. They kept saying, 'Nevermore,' to a distraught lover on the loss of his love. The ravens at the grave site, on the other hand, were screaming, 'The dog! The dog!' Which brings me to the next important question—namely, who bricked in the fireplace?"

"It was Harry Edmunds," Hawke replied, without hesitation. "The company that placed the central heating furnace strongly advised we brick off the fireplace to stop the loss of heat which was considerable. I was not prepared to spend yet more money on the masonry, and put it off for a future date. That is when Edmunds, who had worked as a bricklayer in his younger days, offered to perform the task at a minimum labor cost."

"Again, planning ahead," Joanna muttered under her breath.

"What was that?" Hawke asked, not hearing the utterance.

"It was of no matter." Joanna waved away the comment and gazed down at the leathered corpse. "Now, how did James Blackstone's life come to an end?"

"A postmortem examination will hopefully reveal the

cause," my father said. "There are only a limited number of ways to kill in any art gallery without others being aware."

"A gunshot would be far too noisy," Lestrade stated the obvious.

"Poison too unpredictable," said I.

"A knife wound too uncertain unless wielded by an expert," my father surmised.

"Blunt force to the head would be a more likely possibility," Joanna asserted. "But what was the weapon and where would he hide it?"

She peered into the restoration area and searched for the instrument or tool that could be used as a lethal weapon, but found none. Next, her gaze went to the fireplace. Something caught her attention and she moved in closer to it. "A brick," Joanna noted, pointing at the masonry. "He could have done the deed with a solid brick."

"And used it in blocking off the fireplace," Lestrade added.

Joanna shook her head immediately. "That would be too risky, for the brick might have the victim's blood spattered upon it. Moreover, the smart move would be to bury the weapon along with the corpse." She reached for a pickax and said, "Let us see if Harry Edmunds is as clever as we believe him to be."

"You seem to be convinced that Harry Edmunds is the killer," Lestrade stated.

"That is because he had the most to gain," Joanna responded and used the pickax to stir the ashes heaped up in the fireplace. Upon hearing the sound of metal scraping against metal, she dug deeper and exposed a sturdy, dust-covered knife. "Hello there!"

Lestrade shined his torch in for added illumination which

allowed Joanna to extract the blade using the end of the pickax. With care she blew away the thick, covering ash, and this revealed a handle which had a dark brown stain that was most likely old blood.

"It looks as if Edmunds left behind a little memento for us," Lestrade noted.

"He left behind more than that," Joanna said and pointed to a fingerprint embedded in the dust on the knife's handle. "Chances are it will match the prints on the brick."

"Are you not surprised Edmunds used a knife to kill?" my father asked. "After all, a misplaced stab and all would be lost."

"He would not misplace," Delvecchio interjected. "For like many restorers of Italian Renaissance art, Mr. Edmunds no doubt studied anatomy so he could work with confidence on the human figures that were painted by the magnificent artists of that period."

"Did you yourself study anatomy?" Joanna inquired.

"I took classes at the University of Bologna for that very purpose," Delvecchio answered. "I would have no problem finding a vital spot."

"This Edmunds fellow is more than clever," Lestrade pronounced.

"And more than dangerous," my father cautioned. "For now he has committed a hanging offense and will stop at nothing to escape the gallows."

"All well and good," said Joanna as she stared down at the mummified corpse of James Blackstone. "But there is one most important question that remains unanswered."

"Which is?"

"Why kill the only person who knows the precise location of the masterpiece?"

19

Dubious Identification

The autopsy at St. Bartholomew's was quiet and still until Professor Peter Willoughby, the director of pathology, barged in and glared at us with a look that told of his displeasure.

"Really, Watson," he said to me, "you are taking up entirely too much time with these nonacademic matters."

"But this case is a special request from Scotland Yard," I informed.

Willoughby came over to study the body, but not before giving Joanna and my father an unwelcome stare. As was his custom, he chose not to touch the corpse, but rather to view it at a distance. "Been in the ground for quite a while, I see."

"Actually it was discovered tucked away in a fireplace," said I.

"Hmph," Willoughby grumbled under his breath as he circled the corpse, stopping only briefly to study its skeletal face. He made a few guttural sounds while performing a superficial examination, but made no mention of any findings.

For some reason Joanna found Willoughby's presence of

interest, for she seemed to be watching every step he took. I saw nothing unusual about the man who treated his subordinates so harshly and went out of his way to harp incessantly on the smallest of their mistakes. It was said by all that his physical appearance matched his temperament. He was of short, wiry stature, with piercing dark eyes and unsmiling thin lips that seemed pasted together. The suit he wore fit poorly, and had sleeves so short they allowed most of his shirt cuffs to show. I had to admire his new shoes, but not the stained, red tie he favored so often.

"There is nothing here of note other than his leathered skin," Willoughby said brusquely. "With this in mind, I would expect the autopsy to be a brief one."

"It cannot be brief, for this is a case of murder," I objected mildly.

"Based on what?" Willoughby asked incredulously.

"On the location of the body," Joanna answered.

"May I remind you that a body found in a fireplace does not necessarily signify murder," Willoughby challenged.

"It does when the fireplace is bricked in," Joanna countered. "Unless, of course, you can describe a mechanism by which a person crawls into a fireplace, bricks it off from the inside out, then conveniently dies, but not before removing all forms of identification."

Willoughby's face hardened. "I should have been given this information earlier."

"You should have asked for it earlier," Joanna said easily. "But let us stop wasting time and allow the younger Dr. Watson to proceed with the autopsy. Before the final report is submitted, however, I believe it would be wise for you, as director of pathology, to carefully study it and make certain all is in order."

Willoughby was taken aback by Joanna's generous offer,

for there was a mutual dislike between the two that dated back to their initial encounter over a year ago. Moreover, the offer seemed to indicate that the mean, little man would have the final say in the autopsy report when in fact nothing could be further from the truth.

"Assuming you can spare the time from your most busy schedule," Joanna added.

"That will present no problem."

"And of course all matters regarding this matter must be kept entirely confidential from prying eyes, for the case may well end up in a court of law, where experts, such as yourself, should not have their testimony tarnished by unfounded rumors or unsupported hearsay." Joanna gave Willoughby a moment to nod, then nodded back. "Thus, it will be in your best interest and ours for not a word of this autopsy to go beyond the walls of this room."

"I will see to it," Willoughby affirmed.

"Excellent," Joanna said. "And, as you leave, please permit us to wish you a most happy birthday."

"It—it was last week," Willoughby stammered, caught off guard.

Joanna's face took on a pleased expression. "Better late than never."

"Indeed," Willoughby said, and hurried out before we could dwell on the hint of his smile which came and went.

I waited for the door to the autopsy room to close before turning to Joanna. "I think you managed to pacify that most unpleasant man."

"My intent was not to pacify him, but to keep his lips sealed," said Joanna. "He is the talkative type who needs to prove his importance to all who will listen. He no doubt would take great delight in spreading the word of the murdered man in the fireplace and the role he, as head of pathology, will play in the investigation. In that regard, he is much like Lestrade, both of whom yearn for the spotlight."

"They are cut from the same cloth," my father noted.

"And of course the newspapers would gladly print their stories," I predicted. "Which would no doubt reach our murderer's eyes and give him fair warning we are in pursuit and closing in."

"Which would surely work to our disadvantage," my father grumbled.

"I do not trust Willoughby to remain silent," said I.

"Nor do I," Joanna concurred. "But we may have further need of him as well, so it is best we have him on our side. For example, if there is any evidence to indicate the victim was poisoned, we would wish to identify the agent immediately. The chemists at St. Bartholomew's would give such studies their urgent and utmost attention if demanded by Willoughby, who wields considerable power despite his most disagreeable nature."

"Unfortunately true," said I, then smiled at my lovely wife and asked, "How in the world did you know it was his birthday?"

"His shoes."

"But new shoes on a middle-aged man does not necessarily signify a birthday."

"It does in this instance, for those shoes come from Northampton, the cobbler capital of all England," Joanna disclosed. "They are unique and easily recognized by their Goodyear Welt, which is a process of stretching thin strips of leather across the shoe in its middle area for added comfort and durability. They are considered to be high-end and very expensive indeed. Willoughby would never purchase these shoes on his own."

I nodded firmly at Joanna's conclusion. The man was a miser to the nth degree, who dressed accordingly in ill-fitting suits and threadbare shirts. "For a person who pinches every farthing, purchasing such costly shoes would be out of the question. Thus, they must have been a gift."

"But why a birthday gift?" asked my father.

"Because it is not yet Christmas, and the only other occasion that would merit gift-giving in a middle-aged man would be his birthday," Joanna replied. "However, you must remember that men in general place no value on their birthday, while women keep a close eye on such dates. For this reason, men neither expect nor receive gifts on their birthday except perhaps from someone dear to him."

"Then it was given by a loving wife," my father surmised.

"He does not have a *loving* wife," Joanna said. "A wife such as that would never allow her husband to appear in public so poorly dressed. His attire is so unseemly it caused me to wince. There is no love between the two."

"Are you implying a girlfriend was responsible for that gift?" I asked.

"Never," Joanna replied at once. "Most girlfriends or mistresses could not afford Northampton shoes and, even if they could, Willoughby could not wear them. His wife would surely notice and demand to know their origin."

"So, neither the wife nor a girlfriend could be the givers of such shoes," I concluded. "Where then did they come from?"

"The wife."

"But you just said—"

"I said they could not come from a *loving* wife," Joanna corrected. "In all likelihood, she gave him the shoes as a wonderful surprise, but not for love."

"For what then?"

"Here, I would be guessing," Joanna said, with a mischievous smile. "But an extraordinary gift is a clever way to atone for a guilty indiscretion."

"Oh, come now, Joanna," my father rebuked mildly. "Such a remark is surely beneath you."

I lowered my voice and said, "Father, there has been a rumor floating around St. Bart's suggesting a liaison of that sort does exist."

"Rumor, you say?" my father asked.

"Backed up by a sighting, I should add."

My father groaned at the unpleasant revelation.

"Which is a reminder, Watson, that all in this world is not what it appears to be," said Joanna, as the smile left her face. "Now let us return to our mummified corpse and determine what else is not what it appears to be."

The body of James Blackstone remained curled up on the autopsy table, so with force I straightened the extremities, although some degree of flexion persisted. I began my inspection at the head and planned to slowly work my way down. The skull itself was entirely skeletonized except for a few sparse areas still covered with leatherlike skin. The absence of skin was important here, in that it removed any cutaneous evidence of trauma. Without dermal tissue, important signs such as abrasions, lacerations, and ecchymotic bruises would have disappeared. I proceeded to the skull bones and found all intact, with no fractures or indentations. A full set of teeth was present, with none being cracked or out of place. As I moved to the neck, I tested the mobility of the cervical spine and found it surprisingly lax. After turning the body on its side, I began a careful countdown of the seven cervical vertebrae. But midway through, I encountered a strand of thin wire that encircled the entire neck. Bits of leatherlike skin were embedded into the delicate garotte.

"They strangled him," I pronounced and stepped back for others to see.

"The wire sliced through the skin," Joanna noted. "And probably through the trachea as well."

"But not through the cervical spine itself," said I. "There is a looseness of the spine, however, which I cannot explain."

"Perhaps a broken neck," Joanna suggested.

"A good thought, but there is no evidence for such," I informed. "As you can see, all the cervical vertebrae are intact and nicely aligned."

"Would the decomposition process allow for cervical laxity?" my father asked.

I shook my head. "The supporting ligaments are still very much intact."

"Could they have become stretched over time?" my father proposed.

"Not to this extent."

I returned my attention to the corpse's neck and once more began counting down the seven cervical vertebrae, starting with the first vertebra where it attached to the base of the skull and was referred to as C-1. Then came C-2, C-3, C-4, C-5, and C—! The explanation for the cervical laxity suddenly stared up at me. The cartilaginous interspace between C-5 and C-6 was gouged out and left a wide opening that partially disconnected the two.

"It was a double kill," I disclosed.

"How so?" Joanna asked at once.

"First, he was strangled and then, while bent over, a knife was plunged into the C-5, C-6 interspace," I replied and pointed to the gaping opening between the two vertebrae. "That thick blade was no doubt twisted in place, so it would inflict maximum damage and, when driven deep enough, would cause the spinal cord to be severed. It was a most brutal killing."

"Done by an expert who wanted to be certain no sign of life remained," Joanna envisioned.

"But after a thorough garroting, why bother with the knife?" my father asked. "Was it out of some perverse pleasure?"

"That is a possibility," Joanna answered. "But more likely the strangulation came first, and afterward Blackstone showed a flicker of life, like a choking sound or muscle twitch. That was when the killer ended it once and for all."

"Beyond gruesome," my father noted.

"And obviously necessary in the killer's mind," said Joanna. "But then again, why dispatch the one and only person who knew the precise location of the masterpiece?"

Like before, we had no answer to that most important question and, putting it aside for the moment, I continued with the postmortem examination on the mummified corpse. Its chest wall and abdomen were unremarkable, as was the normally structured pelvis. I was attempting to move an arm for a better view of the inguinal area when I noticed a disjointed thumb. On closer inspection, it was clear that multiple fingers had been broken or smashed into bony splinters. The other hand revealed similar findings. Taking in a deep breath, I announced, "They tortured him and were in no hurry to do so."

I pointed to the disjointed fingers, in particular to the thumbs which were badly fractured, with sharp ends of bone piercing through the leathery dermis. "The pain must have been unbearable."

"What sort of human being would commit such an evil act?" my father asked, grimacing briefly at the brutality.

"It was done by more than one, Watson," Joanna said and leaned in for a closer examination. She showed little emotion as she studied the wrists and ankles of the corpse. "I see no ropes or marks left by them, but surely he was securely tied down for this type of pain to be inflicted, and it required more than one man to do the holding and tying. Moreover, the size of the victim's body tells us this horrific deed was done by at least two and more likely three individuals."

My father looked at Joanna incredulously. "Three? Pray tell how did you reach that conclusion?"

"It is a straightforward deduction, Watson," she replied. "The skeletal remains indicate the victim was a relatively tall man, perhaps as much as six feet in height. John, if you would, please measure the mummified corpse and give us a more accurate reading."

Using a tape measure, I determined the victim's height to be just under six feet, although this may have been a slight underestimation because of the flexed lower extremities. "At least six feet in height," I calculated.

"So we have a six-foot-tall victim, whose clothing tells us he was well proportioned," Joanna continued on. "With this in mind, please tell me how many men would be required to stuff such a body into a normal-sized fireplace."

"Two strong men," my father answered. "One would be needed to hold the lower extremities up, while the other pushed the head and shoulders in and upward."

"Even then it would be difficult, for the weight of a heavy, sagging torso would work against such an action," Joanna proposed. "To cram such a large body into the fireplace, a total of three would be necessary. The two Watson mentioned and a third to support and push the torso forward."

"We know Harry Edmunds was one, but who were the other two?" I asked.

"That is to be determined," Joanna replied. "But what can be said with certainty is that Harry Edmunds did not work alone. He had at least one and perhaps two accomplices to help subdue and securely tie the victim."

"To a chair no doubt," my father surmised. "And one or more men had to hold the chair down, for the tortured James Blackstone would have surely rocked away from the torturer."

"He had to be gagged as well to prevent his screams from being heard," Joanna added. "And I suspect they turned up the furnace to full blast, so that its noise would drown out any muffled groans of agony."

"I cannot begin to imagine the pain he suffered," my father thought aloud.

"Yet he held up under it," said Joanna.

"How can you be so certain of that?" I asked.

"Because the torturers were required to break multiple fingers, one at a time, in an effort to break the poor man," Joanna reasoned.

"Are you saying he was able to withstand the pain and not give them the information they desired?" I asked.

Joanna considered the question before answering. "The autopsy tells us that the torturers smashed two thumbs and four other fingers, for a total of six. Blackstone did not surrender after the first fractured digit, which necessitated the torturers proceeding to the five others. Furthermore, had Blackstone given up the location, Edmunds would not have had to go about the business of slashing a bunch of paintings in his search for the hidden masterpiece. All of these findings indicate Blackstone held out until the very end."

"He was either very brave or very stupid, given his set of circumstances," I opined.

"Perhaps," said Joanna. "But he also realized they were going to kill him once they knew the location of the masterpiece. Thus, he may have thought it in his best interest to withhold the information and thereby stay alive."

"If I were in his place, I would have given false information to gain time and devise a possible plan of escape," I conjectured.

"What makes you so certain he did not?" Joanna asked. "After all, a false lead may have been the reason for his prolonged torture."

"All guesses," I said, with a shrug.

"I believe otherwise," Joanna countered. "For, although the puzzle is not yet complete, we have more of the pieces to work with."

"I take it these pieces are important," said I.

"Quite important if my assumptions are correct, and we shall determine that when more data is available," Joanna replied. "But for now, let us proceed with the autopsy and see what else Mr. James Blackstone has to offer."

My gaze went to the corpse's lower extremities that were flexed at the knee, yet appeared to be aligned and without deformity. Under the bright light, however, I saw a definite vertical scar on the left thigh that stood out from the shriveled leathery skin which surrounded it. Unlike normal skin, the scar would be composed of thick, fibrous tissue which would resist the mummification process far longer.

"The wound from the war," I noted and gestured to the midthigh area. "It is thin, straight, and even, all of which indicates it is surgical in nature, and not the result of bullets or shrapnel. Nonetheless, we should search for metal foreign bodies to make certain that is the case."

"From my experience in war, I might add other causes for such a straight scar," my father offered.

"Please do, Father."

"Although rifles were far and away the weapons of choice, the soldiers in the Second Boer War also employed swordlike bayonets, while the cavalry used lances. Either of these would result in a straight, even wound."

"Excellent," I lauded. "But would such a wound be responsible for the limp Mr. Blackstone apparently suffered with?"

"Unlikely," my father responded. "Unless the blade penetrated through the entire quadriceps muscle and shattered the femur."

"Let us see."

I incised through the length of the vertical scar and easily spread the leathery skin apart, for the quadriceps muscle had now disappeared. I could find no bullets or loose, foreign fragments in the scant soft tissue, but immediately encountered a metal plate that was screwed into the femur. These plates had been in use since the turn of the century and were used to fix the ends of the fractured bone together and allow for healing.

"There is an internal fixation plate in place," I announced.

"Is it corroded?" my father inquired.

"To a minimal degree," I observed after a closer inspection. "But for the most part it is clean metal."

"Then I am afraid the corpse we are viewing here does not belong to James Blackstone," my father said with conviction. "The time sequence is off by ten years or more."

"Please explain, Watson," Joanna requested at once.

"Last spring I attended a conference on internal fixation devices which was most informative," my father told us. "The initial plates were designed by a surgeon named Lane just after the turn of the century, but they fell out of favor because of corrosive problems that caused the plates to fail. Had James Blackstone's surgery been done during the Second Boer War, which ended in 1902, a Lane plate would have been inserted and by now be badly corroded. Our plate shows no such changes and thus was inserted much later on."

"When did the newer plates come into use?" Joanna asked.

"Ten years or so after the war ended," my father replied.

"And I can assure you, Mr. Blackstone did not walk about with an untreated badly fractured femur for all those years."

"Then we have a problem unless the plate we are viewing was in fact designed by Dr. Lane," Joanna said frankly.

I immediately reached for a screwdriver and went about the business of loosening the metal plate. It was a most difficult task, for the screws which held it in place were deeply embedded in the femoral bone. Slowly but surely it began to give.

"Can you determine the cause of the fracture?" asked Joanna.

"Not with any degree of certainty," I answered. "Nevertheless, the absence of metal fragments or excessive calcification suggest the injury was the result of a fall, perhaps from a horse."

"Or a kick from one," Joanna added.

As I tussled with the final screw, the metal plate cracked into two and exposed a fracture that had not completely healed and may well have accounted for a painful hip. I retrieved the broken pieces and retreated to a nearby basin where I scrubbed the grime and dried matter away. In the corner of the larger piece I saw a stamp mark, but could not make out the inscription even when held up to the light.

"I need a magnifying glass," I said to Joanna.

She hurried over and handed her large glass to me, then stepped back and waited.

I brushed away more grime and carefully studied the plate under the brightest light in the autopsy room. The name on the internal fixation plate read CARNEGIE 10. "Was there a surgeon named Carnegie who designed such plates?"

My father shook his head. "The surgeon who invented the plate was William Sherman, who was the chief orthopaedic surgeon for the Carnegie Steel Company in America. The reason I recall this information is that Dr. Sherman was the guest speaker at the medical conference I attended."

"And when did Dr. Sherman invent his plate?" Joanna asked.

"The same question was asked of Dr. Sherman and he replied that the first such plate was designed and used in 1912. This was a good ten years after the Second Boer War which ended in 1902. Thus it is safe to say the fracture and its plate cannot be from that war."

Joanna pondered the problem at length before asking, "What does the number ten on the plate signify?"

"I cannot be certain, but most likely it denotes the particular lot that was manufactured by the Carnegie Company at that time," my father replied. "I shall confirm that with an orthopaedic colleague."

"Please inquire if the stamp and number will allow us to track down the patient in whom it was inserted."

"I shall."

"But meanwhile we are faced with the very real possibility that the corpse in the fireplace is not James Blackstone," said Joanna. "And that, my dear Watsons, presents a most difficult conundrum."

"But who else could it be?" I asked.

"It has to be someone who was involved in the quest for the hidden masterpiece," Joanna replied. "There is no other explanation."

"Could it be the mysterious David Hughes who supposedly gained possession of Blackstone's ticket on the *Queen Victoria* and then disappeared into the wilds of Australia?" I queried. "After all, someone did occupy that cabin on the ocean liner, and it had to be either Blackstone or David Hughes. Perhaps it truly was James Blackstone who fled to Australia and we are at this moment staring down at David Hughes."

"But that does not fit," Joanna argued at once. "You are assuming that David Hughes knew of the hidden masterpiece, for there would be no other reason to torture him. Why would the two restorers bring in yet another to share in their fortune?"

"They would not, for there was no need to." My father spoke the obvious answer, then sighed deeply at our dilemma. "It appears we are facing a set of contradictory happenings. There is a corpse who should be James Blackstone and is not, and a mythical person named David Hughes who is believed to be hiding out in Australia, but may not even exist. It is a mystery upon a mystery."

"Which seems impossible to sort out," I thought aloud. "We have a corpse we cannot identify and a faceless man who may or may not be real."

"What do you make of it, Joanna?" my father asked.

"I do not propose to understand it yet," she said carefully. "But we have several different threads in our hands, and the odds are that one or the other will guide us to the truth."

"Which thread do you choose?"

"The corpse, for one way or another it holds the key to our mystery."

It was well past twilight when we departed from St. Bartholomew's and stepped out into a steady downpour which was beginning to flood the streets. Carriages were much in demand and we were fortunate to hail a taxi that was leaving a passenger off at the front entrance to the hospital. As we rode down Newgate Street, the rainfall intensified, forcing traffic to slow to a crawl. We remained silent, each of us grappling to answer the crucial question—who was the shriveled body in the chimney? All evidence pointed to James Blackstone, but the age of the metal plate inserted into the hip of the corpse said otherwise. And if it wasn't Blackstone, who could it possibly be and how did it relate to this most baffling case?

"Watson, are you quite certain about the age of the various

metal plates used to reunite hip fractures?" Joanna broke the silence.

"I am afraid so," my father replied. "The Carnegie plate was invented in 1912, long after Blackstone was wounded in the Second Boer War."

"It is a most important point," Joanna said, "Please consult with an orthopedic specialist and confirm the dates."

"I know several who could—"

My father's voice was drowned out by a large lorry that roared by us and abruptly swerved in front of our taxi. A moment later we heard an explosive noise that resembled an engine backfiring. Suddenly, the windshield of our taxi shattered, sending slivers of glass flying into the driver's face and causing him to shriek in agony. He tried desperately to control the vehicle, but it veered from side to side on the wet pavement despite the brakes being applied. We scraped against a parked motorcar, then another, before finally coming to a stop beneath a lighted lamppost. Ahead of us, the lorry sped down Newgate and disappeared into the heavy rain.

"I can't see!" the driver cried out.

My father quickly vacated the taxi, with Joanna and me a step behind, and all hurried over to attend the blinded driver. Using his hands to cup the falling rainwater, my father repeatedly washed the driver's eyes free of glass, and we all breathed a sigh of relief as his vision returned. Only then did the three of us begin to collect ourselves, now acutely aware of how close to death we had come.

"Someone obviously wanted us dead," Joanna said, with a quiver in her voice. "And he came frighteningly close to accomplishing his mission."

"Check yourselves for wounds," my father directed. "Sometimes in the heat of battle we do not sense pain until the aftermath."

I could not help but be impressed with my father's calm demeanor, but then I recalled his soldiering days in Afghanistan where he learned to control his nerves under the most trying of conditions.

"Are we all well?" my father inquired.

"I am fine except for a few cuts on my forehead from flying glass," I replied.

Joanna swiftly positioned me beneath the lighted lamppost for a more thorough examination. She ran a soothing finger over the area of the cuts, searching for glass slivers and finding a few. "Are you wounded elsewhere?"

"I am fine," I repeated.

"Do not minimize your injuries, John," Joanna said in a stern tone, but then her face softened and she embraced me tightly for a moment. "I have already lost one husband I loved dearly, and could not bear to lose yet another."

"I plan to be here for a while," I assured my wife and kissed her gentle hand.

"For a very long while," she insisted, with a sweet smile.

"What of you, Joanna?" my father asked. "Have you suffered any cuts or injuries?"

"None, and let us all thank the powers that be that the bullet did not find its intended mark."

"We were fortunate indeed, for the shooter was quite skilled," my father noted.

"Based on what evidence?" I asked.

"The fact that he was able to strike our windshield on the driver's side from the rear of a fast-moving lorry," my father answered. "I can assure you the shooter is a marksman."

"Who, under the circumstances, most likely employed a rifle," Joanna surmised.

My father nodded his agreement. "That he no doubt fired

from a prone position which allowed for steadiness in a moving lorry."

"Let us see if our assumptions are correct." Joanna hurried past our driver and opened the door of the taxi widely so that light from the lamppost shined into its front compartment. To the right of the driver's position was a small, round hole in the upper back of the leather-upholstered seat. Using a metal pen from her purse, Joanna carefully pried out a spent bullet and held it up for examination. "Note that it is relatively slender and long, which is characteristic of a bullet fired from a rifle as compared to one discharged from a pistol."

"I am surprised the bullet is not more distorted," said my father.

"That is because its route took it through the windshield whose glass offered minimal resistance," Joanna explained.

The taxi driver called out, "I feel yet more glass scratching my right eye, Doctor."

"Do not rub it, for that can cause more harm," my father cautioned and hurried over to the driver. Again and again he used handfuls of rainwater to cleanse the driver's affected eye.

All the while Joanna continued to study the bullet, now using her magnifying glass. It was the side of the bullet which seemed to draw her attention. "There are definite markings," she disclosed.

"Are they of importance?" I asked.

"Perhaps," Joanna replied, then told me of an unpublished monograph her father had written in which he predicted the day would come when markings on a spent bullet could prove or disprove whether it came from a specific weapon.

"How could that be done?"

"By comparing its markings to those on a bullet fired by that same weapon."

"Remarkable," said I, slowly shaking my head in admiration of not only the Great Detective, but at the daughter following in his footsteps. "I see the harrowing event we just experienced has not diminished your deductive reasoning. You seem steady as ever."

"Do not let my outer appearance deceive you," Joanna admitted in a quiet voice. "There was a long moment when I was consumed with the fear that I was about to die and leave my dear Johnny all alone. He has already lost a father, and I could not begin to fathom the depth of his sorrow were he to lose his mother as well."

"Nevertheless, you seem to be recovering nicely," I remarked.

"I am almost there," Joanna said, then her face hardened noticeably, as she stared back at the shattered windshield. "Let me assure you that whoever did this evil deed will soon pay dearly for it."

My father rejoined us and reported, "I believe all the glass particles have been washed out and the driver is now without symptoms."

"Well done, Watson," Joanna lauded, and again studied the bullet with her magnifying glass.

"Are there any significant findings?" my father asked.

"Only that we can say with certainty that the size and shape of the bullet indicate it was fired from a rifle."

"Which may have relevance in this particular case."

"How so?"

"Recall that James Blackstone fought in the Second Boer War and no doubt was experienced in the use of long rifles."

"Are you proposing that the shot was fired by Blackstone?"

"It would seem to fit."

"Except for the prospect that the corpse lying on the dissecting table may well belong to the very same James Blackstone."

20

An Unexpected Visitor

We had just finished a breakfast nicely prepared by Miss Hudson and were about to retire to our newspapers when she reappeared and hastily announced the arrival of a visitor.

"There is a Mr. Edwin Alan Rowe who wishes to see you on a most urgent matter," she said.

"Please show him in," my father requested.

Lifting a tray laden with dishes, she departed, after having been asked to start a new kettle for our guest.

"What in the world brings Rowe to our doorstep at such an early hour?" I inquired.

"It must be a happening of considerable importance," my father surmised.

"And one I can assure you brings the most unwelcome news," Joanna added.

"Who is Mr. Edwin Alan Rowe?" asked the ever-inquisitive Johnny.

"He is an art historian who is serving as a consultant for us," Joanna replied.

"In the case of the art vandal, then?"

"The very same."

"He would be quite the expert in the hidden masterpiece, I would gather," deduced Johnny who had been privy to our numerous conversations on the topic.

"Indeed, but you must not involve yourself in any way during his visit," Joanna demanded. "Not a word. Understood?"

"Even the most pressing of questions?" Johnny queried.

Joanna sighed resignedly as the door opened after a brief knock. In entered Rowe, bundled up against the cold, with some of the morning's snow showing on his hat and the shoulders of his topcoat.

"Here," my father offered, hurrying over. "Allow me to hang your outer garments."

"I trust I am not intruding despite the early hour," Rowe said.

"Not at all," my father assured.

"I fear that I am, but I thought it necessary once I saw the morning newspapers filled with your names and the story of the body in the fireplace."

"What!"

"And packed with details of the leather-bound corpse, curled up like an infant asleep."

My father rushed over to the table that held the morning newspapers and unfolded the *Daily Telegraph*. "The article is on the front page and is entitled THE CHIMNEY CORPSE."

He read aloud the gruesome details of the body that was hidden in the bricked-in chimney at the Hawke and Evans art gallery. The description was so accurate it had to come from someone who had actually viewed the corpse up close. My father groaned audibly when he came to the section dealing with the three of us. "And for good measure, the article states that now with Joanna Blalock-Watson and her colleagues involved, a quick resolution can be expected."

"It had to come from Willoughby," I said angrily.

"Or Scotland Yard," Joanna opined.

"Why Scotland Yard?" I asked.

"For two reasons," replied Joanna. "First, the macabre details assure front-page coverage and place Lestrade in the spotlight, a position he enjoys, particularly when a case is about to be solved."

"Which will allow him to soak up most of the credit," my father noted.

"Of course," Joanna agreed. "Why else would he do it?"

"And the second reason you mentioned?" I inquired.

"If the case is not brought to resolution, we shall have the discomfort of shouldering at least part of the blame, for our names are now attached to this rather nasty mystery."

"Lestrade," my father grumbled under his breath.

"Give him his due, Watson, for the good inspector knows how to manipulate the press to his advantage," Joanna said in a neutral tone. "But whatever the source, the information is now on public display, and has certainly reached the eye of the portrait vandal."

"And the eye of those of us in the art world, who are now aware the body must belong to James Blackstone, which is a great loss to us all," Rowe said sadly.

"But the man is—or rather was—a criminal," my father reminded.

"Do not judge him so harshly, Watson, until you have heard his entire story," Rowe said in a kind voice.

"Did you know him well?" Joanna asked.

"Quite well and for many years," Rowe replied. "I first met him in Paris after his return from the Second Boer War. He was an apprentice restorer studying at the Louvre under Auguste Curie, and even then he showed great promise. Some years later I learned he had taken a position with the Royal

Art Collection, and had the opportunity to interview him for a piece I was writing for *The Guardian*. He was remarkably informed on the artists from the Italian Renaissance and was most helpful in my future articles and research." A brief smile came to Rowe's face as he continued on. "His knowledge was so extensive that we would challenge one another with riddles on works of art from that period. For example, at our most recent meeting he gave me a brainteaser I have yet to unravel."

"When was the last meeting you had with James Blackstone?" Joanna interrupted abruptly.

"A few weeks before the warrant for his arrest was issued," Rowe answered.

"And the riddle?"

"It was Angels to a Perfect Angel," recited Rowe. "I could make little of it, for many of the paintings from the Italian Renaissance portrayed angels. But for some reason, James was quite curious to know if I had solved the riddle and asked me so on several occasions."

"Angels to a Perfect Angel," Joanna repeated, as if committing it to memory.

"Precisely," Rowe said, then waited to see if Joanna had further questions on the enigma, and when she did not he returned to James Blackstone's history as a noted restorer. "In any event, he was highly thought of at Windsor and continued on there until two years ago when to my surprise he was made redundant because of a supposed reduction in funding. He later confided to me that it was not a lack of funding which led to his departure, but rather the obvious fact that the head curator at the collection wanted the prized position to remain vacant until his younger brother could be prepared for that situation. The transition occurred within months of Blackstone's leaving."

"Was the younger brother as talented?" Joanna asked.

"No, and to this day still is not."

"Was Blackstone bitter?"

"He tried to conceal it, but I believe he was," Rowe went on. "And to make matters even worse, it was at this time that an old war wound acted up and required major surgery."

"What type of surgery?" my father asked at once.

"Apparently some sort of device that held his fractured thigh bone together had gone awry and needed to be replaced. The operation was quite expensive and depleted all of his savings."

My father and Joanna and I exchanged knowing glances, for this explanation solved the mystery of why the corpse of James Blackstone had an internal fixation plate that was inserted long after the Second Boer War had ended. There was now no question as to the identity of the corpse.

"He was fortunate enough, however, to gain employment at Hawke and Evans, but shortly thereafter a son was born with a clubfoot which did not respond to tight braces and would require a unique surgical procedure that was only being done at the Royal Children's Hospital in Melbourne, Australia. Poor Blackstone did not have the funds necessary for the travel and operation which would be considerable. And that is why he teamed up with Harry Edmunds to sell forgeries of French impressionists on the black market. It was all done so his son could have the needed surgery and not go through life with the burden of a clubfoot."

My father nodded unhappily. "So the little boy never had the necessary surgery."

"Oh, but he did," Rowe corrected. "His son and wife traveled to Australia where the surgery was successfully performed, using the money Blackstone had gleaned from the forgeries."

"Thus he planned to flee to Australia not only to avoid the authorities, but to rejoin his family," my father concluded.

"Exactly so, Watson," said Rowe. "Blackstone gave up everything for his small son. It is a very sad story."

"Sad in every way," my father concurred. "For it was the love for his son that brought about his wrongdoings."

"No doubt spurred on by the unprincipled Harry Edmunds." Rowe spat the name. His face hardened noticeably before he waved away his anger. "Let us put Edmunds aside for now and speak of a matter I believe will be of even more importance to you. I have news of the masterpiece on the black market."

The three of us, and Johnny as well, leaned forward to catch every word, for here was truly the key to the case of the art vandal.

"My source tells me that the bidding on this masterpiece is now approaching fifty thousand pounds, which is an extraordinary amount, particularly so on the black market," Rowe reported. "In the legitimate art world, that painting would easily bring two hundred thousand pounds."

"A fortune," I breathed.

"Enough to buy half of Kensington," my father added. "What could be worth that incredible sum?"

Joanna must have had the same thought, for she asked the consultant, "Were you able to attach a name to the masterpiece?"

"Not as yet, but the price alone tells us it has to be a painting done by one of the Great Masters," Rowe replied. "Only a Michelangelo or da Vinci or Raphael or perhaps a Rembrandt would give rise to such an enormous offer."

"Which of those would you favor?" asked Joanna.

"The masters of the High Renaissance," Rowe answered

without hesitation. "Either Michelangelo or da Vinci or Raphael."

"In that order?"

"In any order, but please keep in mind that the vast majority of Michelangelo's paintings were stunning frescos such as those on the ceiling of the Sistine Chapel, which obviously cannot be concealed under a canvas. There are very few of his works on canvas, and I can assure you all are accounted for."

"So we can exclude Michelangelo?" Joanna asked.

"Not necessarily, for it is possible someone discovered a painting by the Great Master in some long-ago deserted church," Rowe replied. "Just imagine if it was a portrait of his statue *David,* which the world acknowledges as one of the most magnificent works of art ever produced. Its value would be far beyond priceless."

Joanna nodded slowly. "I have heard the statue of *David* described as imposing perfection."

"And justly so," Rowe said, nodding back. "But there is a problem with this scenario, for such a find would have no proven provenance and would not require sale on the black market."

"Thus, the prospect that the hidden masterpiece is the work of Michelangelo seems unlikely, but nevertheless possible," Joanna concluded.

"That would be my opinion," Rowe went on. "And the same would hold true for Leonardo da Vinci. Although his paintings on canvas outnumber Michelangelo's, they are all accounted for. And if by chance any of da Vinci's famous works such as *The Last Supper* or *Mona Lisa* or *Salvator Mundi* were to go missing, the cry of theft would be heard around the world, yet not a whisper has been uttered."

"Which leaves us with Raphael," said Joanna.

"But there are problems here as well, for only Raphael's

most exquisite and adored works would attract this extraordinary sum of money. These include *Transfiguration, The Sistine Madonna,* and *The Triumph of Galatea,* all of which remain securely in place."

"So I take it you cannot narrow down the artist most likely to be responsible for the hidden masterpiece."

"Not with any degree of certainty."

Joanna gently tapped a finger against her chin before asking, "Who in all England would own the majority of works by these three Great Masters?"

"The Royal Art Collection at Windsor, with the National Gallery being a somewhat distant second."

"What if I included Caravaggio and Titian?"

Rowe shook his head vigorously. "Do not include them, for they would never attract that kind of money."

Joanna pondered the problem at length before she went over to the Persian slipper and extracted a Turkish cigarette which she carefully lighted. Then she began to pace the floor of our parlor, leaving a trail of dense cigarette smoke behind her. She ignored the rap on the door as well as Miss Hudson who entered with our tea setting and, having put it in place on our breakfast table, departed quietly. Joanna continued pacing and thinking.

"This can go on for a while," my father predicted.

"I am in no hurry," said Rowe.

"But I am, for our vandal will undoubtedly soon strike again and, if successful, he and the masterpiece will disappear and never be seen again," Joanna told our visitor. "But if we are to track and stop him, there is more information I require. First, I am assuming all works by these Great Masters are over three hundred years old."

"Correct," Rowe affirmed.

"And their masterpieces well known."

"Through the centuries."

"Then we can assume the hidden masterpiece was stolen."

"That is a certainty, for why else would they go to such far ends to conceal it, and why else would they have to place it for sale on the black market?"

"But if such a masterpiece was stolen from a museum or prominent collection, would not the art world know of it?" Joanna asked.

"We would indeed and be on a sharp lookout for it," Rowe replied.

"Yet there has not been a peep regarding a theft of this magnitude," Joanna pressed. "How could this be?"

"I can give you a number of reasons how a masterpiece can be stolen and not reported," Rowe expounded, then provided a prime example. "A few years back a wealthy royal was suffering from dementia and confined to her mansion, wherein hung some of the world's very best art. Her family rarely visited and simply waited for her to die so they could inherit the estate. While on her deathbed, a servant made off with a masterpiece by Vermeer which shortly appeared on the black market. Somehow a family member got wind of it and, knowing its rightful owner, reported the theft to Scotland Yard. The painting was recovered and returned to the family. Had a family member not had such a keen eye, the theft would have in all likelihood gone unnoticed. It would have slipped between the cracks, so to speak."

"Do you believe that is what happened in our case?"

"Yes, for there is no other explanation."

"Assuming you are correct, which of these would be the most likely origin of the painting?" Joanna asked. "A museum or an impressive private collection?"

"Either," Rowe replied at once. "Most of their works, even the masterpieces, are not always on display. Many of

them are kept in storage under carefully controlled conditions. One could be stolen from among the many and it
would require months to discover it was missing."

"How many paintings might be in storage at all the insti-
tutions you mentioned?"

"Thousands, and it would take months and months to
perform a thorough inventory, with no guarantees that the
origin of the masterpiece would be uncovered."

"Too long, too long," Joanna muttered to herself and
gave the matter further consideration before she flicked her
cigarette into the fireplace and began pacing again. The expression on her face told me that something in Rowe's answers had opened up another avenue worth pursuing but, for
reasons we were to learn later, she chose not to delve into it
at the moment. Turning to the consultant, she gestured to the
table settings and asked, "Would you care for tea?"

"If you would be so kind."

While Joanna poured and handed him a cup, she asked,
"Earlier you spoke of Harry Edmunds being unprincipled.
Did you know him well?"

"I knew him not at all, except by his reputation."

"As a criminal?"

"As a forger, for I was asked by Scotland Yard to examine
all the paintings in his home and determine which were forgeries and which were not."

"In his presence?"

"In his wife's presence, for by then Edmunds was locked
away in Wormwood Scrubs." Rowe carefully sipped his tea
before uttering a forced laugh. "And she was quite a piece of
work, I must say."

"How so?"

"She simply sat there, knitting away on a large afghan, while
I inspected the paintings that hung on the walls. I could have

just as well been the carpet cleaner. Nor was she concerned with the sergeant from Scotland Yard who accompanied me."

"Not upset in the least?"

"She did not bother to even look up, and seemed quite at ease while knitting the long afghan that went from her lap all the way to the floor before her."

"Do you believe she was attempting to project an air of innocence?"

"Perhaps, but my other findings in the house indicated she was aware, if not implicated, in her husband's criminal activities. For in a room off the kitchen was the ideal setup for either restoration or forgery. There were canvases and stands and paints and brushes and quite bright lighting that Edmunds used for his work."

"He would never do restorations at home," Joanna interjected.

"Of course not," Rowe agreed. "The room was for his forgeries. There was even an oversized oven so that the forgeries could be baked and thus give the paintings small wrinkles and cracks, which denotes considerable aging. When done by an expert forger, those changes can date a painting back hundreds of years."

"I take it his forgeries were quite good."

"But not exceptional except for the Renoirs. They were nearly perfect, but for the blue pigment which was just a bit off and never used by the French artist. It was a rather stupid mistake for a forger as talented as Harry Edmunds."

"Were the Renoirs in Edmunds's home signed?"

"He was too clever for that. Were they signed they could have been confiscated as being forgeries that would eventually be put up for sale. I suspect Edmunds considered himself to be an excellent artist and had the paintings hung to remind himself of his talents."

"Bit of an egotist, eh?" my father commented.

"All forgers worth their salt are, Watson."

"Yet I am surprised you did not find at least one signed forgery that was ready for sale," Joanna conjectured. "After all it was a most lucrative business and Edmunds had no idea he would soon be apprehended. There should have been another forgery or two on hand for the black market."

"Neither I nor Scotland Yard could find it despite a most diligent search."

"It was concealed by the wife," Johnny said in a matter-of-fact fashion.

Rowe looked at the lad quizzically. "On what do you base that conclusion, may I ask?"

"The afghan she was knitting that rested on her lap and dropped down to the floor," Johnny replied.

"I would have surely noticed the outline of a large canvas under that afghan, my good fellow," Rowe countered.

"It was not under the afghan, but under the chair which I am certain was quite large."

"It was a big, overstuffed chair," Rowe recalled.

"Then it all fits," said Johnny.

"Please explain," Joanna requested. "Tell us why the position of the afghan signifies it is hiding a painting."

"Did you read of the Dupont murder in Paris last year, Mother?"

"I must admit I did not."

"Then allow me to give you the details. A woman was stabbed to death and her body found in the drawing room beneath a large afghan she was knitting. The blood spatter seemed to indicate she was killed where she lay, but that was not the case. You see, the afghan was unfinished and hanging down, which the woman who was the knitter would never have permitted."

"And why not?"

"Because she would know that the downward weight would cause the new stitching to stretch and perhaps even disconnect. Thus, an experienced knitter would not allow the unfinished product to hang, but would place it on a table next to her. In the Dupont case, the hanging weight distorted the blood spatter in such a fashion that it seemed to show she was stabbed while under the afghan. The true splatter was later determined and revealed the victim was killed elsewhere in the house which provided an important clue that eventually led to the murderer. In your case, the woman who was obviously experienced would have never allowed the unfinished afghan to hang down, but she did so for a purpose. She wished to conceal something beneath the chair, which in this instance I would wager was a signed Renoir."

Rowe's jaw dropped at the lad's remarkable sense of deduction, then, after a brief pause, he nodded slowly to himself. "Now that I think back, she had the huge afghan covering the arms and sides of the overstuffed chair."

"Clever woman," Johnny remarked.

"I should return and search under that chair," Rowe said, more to himself than us.

"I think it best I do it," Joanna proposed.

"With all due respect, I very much doubt you would be able to distinguish a genuine Renoir from a well-forged one."

"I am not interested in that distinction, but rather in questioning the wife, for she may know the whereabouts of her husband and might even be aware of his next move."

"You are assuming they remain in contact."

"A reasonable assumption."

"But even if she has this knowledge, chances are she will clam up and do everything in her power to protect him."

"Clams can be opened when ample heat is applied," Joanna

retorted, and walked over to gather up Rowe's hat and top-coat. "Thank you ever so much for providing this important information."

"I can only hope it will bring down the savage who murdered my dear friend James Blackstone."

"We shall see," said Joanna, and upon opening the door asked a final question. "Does the name David Hughes have any meaning to you?"

"Not offhand," Rowe replied.

"Please be good enough to review the notes and articles in which Blackstone contributed and see if the name David Hughes appears."

"I shall at my earliest opportunity," Rowe assured. "Is he important?"

"Quite," Joanna said and left it at that.

21

A Near Miss

That evening we decided to celebrate Johnny's departure for Eton with a fine dinner at Gennaro's, a small restaurant just down the way on Baker Street. Although Christmas would soon be upon us, the lad wished to return to the school for the examinations he missed while sick with cholera in London. He would then return home to enjoy the merriest of holidays with us.

"What examinations are these?" Joanna asked, as we started on strawberry tiramisus after our most excellent veal dishes.

"German and Egyptian Hieroglyphics," Johnny replied.

"I was unaware that Egyptian hieroglyphics was actually a course at Eton."

"It is not, Mother, but rather an elective subject I chose out of interest."

"Then why must you take an examination and be graded?"

"Only because I wish to see how well I am performing in this most fascinating study."

"So you seem to be truly enjoying it."

"I am indeed, for it presents mysteries within itself. For example, there are no vowels and no punctuation marks, only pictures which can have several meanings depending on what comes before and after it."

"It sounds like a rather strange alphabet."

"It is quite strange, yet clearly decipherable. A picture of a vulture is an *A* and a foot is a *B,* and so on. Interestingly enough, a forearm responds to the letters *Ah.*"

"And how do you plan to use this knowledge of Egyptian hieroglyphics?" I asked.

"As a way to exercise my brain, of course," Johnny responded as he made short work of his tiramisu.

My father smiled at the lad and said, "I am not certain your grandfather would have approved of this exercise."

"Why not, may I ask?"

"Because Sherlock Holmes believed the brain was like a small, empty attic and you have to stock it with only important information that will serve you well in the future. To his way of thinking, this space is not elastic and once filled will accept no more. Therefore, you must be very selective in what you choose to store away."

Johnny dropped his fork and gave the matter considerable thought before asking, "Did my grandfather ever encounter a case that involved Egyptian hieroglyphics?"

"Not to my knowledge," my father answered.

"Had he, I am certain he would have approved of my current studies."

Joanna chuckled softly at the interchange. "I would pay a hefty sum to listen in on a conversation between Sherlock Holmes and his grandson."

"As would I," said my father.

I was about to signal our waiter for more coffee when my gaze went to the restaurant's front window that overlooked Baker Street. Peering in from the darkness was a hatted figure whose neck seemed to disappear into his chest. I gestured to the nearby waiter by pointing to my cup, and when I looked back at the window the man was gone. Probably some poor chap, I thought, who could never afford the delicious meal we had just enjoyed.

"Do you think Grandfather Holmes would have taken note of my deduction on the woman's afghan?" Johnny was asking his mother.

"He would have been delighted," Joanna replied. "And he would have been most interested to learn how the true blood splatter led to the arrest of the murderer in the Dupont case."

"You will recall that the hanging weight of the afghan distorted the original pattern," Johnny said and waited for us all to nod. "Good." He then went on, "Now, the altered pattern showed primarily pooled blood which was believed to have come from her severed jugular vein. Blood coming from a cut vein simply flows out, does it not, Dr. Watson?"

"Correct," my father answered.

"When the afghan was rearranged to its unstretched setting, the blood splatter resembled that made by intermittent spurts, which would occur if the bloodletting came from an artery. And the poor woman had her carotid artery severed, among her other stab wounds."

"But how did the apparent arterial exsanguination lead to the murderer?" my father asked.

"The husband's alibi was that he was asleep in the adjoining bedroom," Johnny explained. "When the bedroom was reexamined, the blood splatter on the walls had for the most part been washed off. But the splatter on the carpet could not be expunged and showed a pattern consistent with arterial spurting. Thus, she was obviously not murdered in the parlor, but in the bedroom, and her husband's alibi fell apart."

"Hmm," Joanna hummed to herself. "I find it remarkable that a French detective would be so familiar with afghans."

"He wasn't," said Johnny. "He was discussing the case with his wife who happened to be an experienced knitter. It was she who provided the clue that led to the case being solved."

"I do not believe we will be so fortunate when we look under the afghan of Harry Edmunds's wife," I surmised.

"One never knows," Joanna said. "Nonetheless, Lestrade seemed keen on the idea and will have a Scotland Yard detective accompany us to the wife's house which gives our visit an official flavor. He, by the way, also believes the wife is every bit aware of Edmunds's forgery activities."

"Does he have proof in that regard?" my father asked.

"In a manner of speaking," Joanna replied. "Lestrade apparently found her pantry stocked with very expensive items, such as an abundance of beluga caviar, which would cost as much as Edmunds's monthly salary at Hawke and Evans. In addition, there was a recently purchased dress in her closet that carried a label from Selfridges, which of course is a high-end department store. You should also know that Scotland Yard discovered two hundred pounds under a floorboard in that same closet. Thus, I think it is fair to say that the wife had to be aware of her husband's sudden abundance of money and from whence it was derived."

"Perhaps she was hiding money under the giant afghan as well," Johnny suggested.

"I think not," Joanna said. "A woman this clever would never hide such a small yet so valuable an item in the open, even if concealed by a afghan. She would find a more secure place for the stack of pounds."

"Where then?"

"Under her dress, where Scotland Yard would never bother to look."

"But you would."

"Of course."

My father inquired, "Is that the reason you seem so eager to investigate the wife further?"

"One of them," Joanna said evasively.

"Shall John and I accompany you on this hunt?"

"John will be at my side, but I have another task I will ask you to carry out. While we are on our way to the Edmundses' home, I would like you to travel to Number Three Pinchin Lane and fetch Toby Two, for I have work for her."

"To what purpose?"

"If you wish to outwit a fox, my dear Watson, you must use a hound."

On that note we departed Gennaro's and walked out into a cold, clear night. The lampposts suddenly lost their illumination and all the homes along Baker Street went dark, for the Great War was ongoing and intermittent blackouts were required in order to dim the lighted targets, which served as a beacon for the terrifying Zeppelin air raids. In the distance we could hear the siren telling us that such a raid could be imminent. We quickly picked up our pace.

"I have an early train to Eton in the morning and can make my own way to Paddington station," Johnny said to us. "There is no need to wake you."

"Nonsense," I insisted. "We shall be there to give you a proper send-off."

"And we shall be there for your return as well," Joanna promised.

"With a little good fortune, perhaps your case could be solved by then," said Johnny.

"Which would make for a most merry Christmas indeed," my father chimed in.

We paused to allow traffic to go by before crossing over to our rooms at 221b Baker Street. Our window was well lighted, for there was no alert for a blackout when we departed for dinner. We had left the lamp on and logs ablaze in the fireplace, awaiting our return. I was about to suggest we hurry to our rooms when my gaze went to the roof above our parlor. I saw a small, flickering light that seemed out of place. It was too small to be a torch.

I pointed to the light and asked, "Is that a candle or perhaps someone striking a match?"

As we hurried across the street, Joanna's eyes followed my line of vision. The small light now appeared to be moving to the very edge of the roof.

"What do you make of it?" I asked.

"Run!" Joanna cried out at the top of her voice. "Run for the vestibule!"

We sprinted for the entrance and managed to reach the door just as a lighted bottle hit the pavement and exploded into a wall of flames. I pushed Joanna, Johnny, and my father into the antechamber and slammed the door behind us, with only a moment to spare before the flames reached the entrance of the building. We waited anxiously to see if the door itself would catch fire, but it did not and remained surprisingly cool to the touch. Outside, we could hear brakes being applied so that the occupants of the passing automobiles might view the flames. Someone was shouting, "Stand clear! Stand clear!" We all took long, deep breaths to gather ourselves and allow our racing pulses to slow.

"Should we wait for the firemen?" I asked.

"Not if my assumption is correct," Joanna replied and cautiously cracked open the door. The fire was for the most part out, with only a few lingering flames remaining on the footpath. But the odor of solvent hung heavily in the air. "It was a bomb, which was thrown from the roof by Harry Edmunds."

"I may actually have seen him," I recollected and told of the man peering into the restaurant whose neck seemed to disappear into his chest. "It gave that appearance because he no doubt had a scarf wrapped around his neck. I thought he was a poor chap hungrily looking into the fine restaurant, but I was mistaken."

"It had to be Harry Edmunds, surveilling us prior to his bomb making," Joanna asserted.

"He no doubt used a lighted candle as a trigger mechanism," I noted. "And his timing was nearly perfect."

Joanna nodded and opened the door widely as neighbors looked out of their houses at the disturbance. "Exactly so, for Edmunds is an expert when it comes to making explosive devices from solvent, as his former cellmate Derrick Wilson could attest to were he still alive."

"Bravo to the junior Dr. Watson for spotting the flame on the roof," Johnny praised.

"Good show indeed!" my father lauded.

"It was happenstance," I said honestly. "It was simply a matter of me gazing up at a most opportune moment."

"Which sounded the alert and no doubt saved our lives," Joanna insisted. "This should be a warning to all of us, for a man who has killed once will have no hesitation to kill again."

"But why now?" I asked. "What suddenly goaded him into action?"

"The newspaper articles," Joanna replied. "They put a target on our backs, you might say. This was an attempt to kill us or at least frighten us off, but it failed in the former and it will fail in the latter as well."

"But all the same, I shall now carry my service revolver at all times," said my father.

"Better safe than sorry," Joanna agreed.

"Indeed," my father concurred, with a grim expression that told me he would have no hesitancy in dispatching Harry Edmunds should the occasion arise.

22

The Wife

Harry Edmunds's wife lived in a shabby, two-story brick house on the eastern edge of Brixton. Its shutters were in need of repair and a small shed in the back garden had not seen a coat of paint for years on end. After allowing us entrance, a stoic Charlotte Edmunds returned to her oversized chair and went back to knitting without saying a word. Within the parlor, there were no signs of newfound wealth other than the excellent copies of paintings by French impressionists that hung on every wall. Even as Joanna examined a Renoir with a magnifying glass, the wife showed no concern and continued to knit the giant afghan which covered her lap before dropping down to the floor. I had difficulty not gazing at the afghan in anticipation of Joanna searching beneath it.

"The Renoirs are of course unsigned," she reported.

"So they would not appear to be forgeries that would eventually be placed on the black market," I noted.

If Charlotte Edmunds was troubled by the term *black market,* she showed no hint of it as she effortlessly knitted a large loop.

"I wonder whether he planned to place Renoir's signature on them later," I said.

"Most unlikely, according to Edwin Alan Rowe," Joanna replied. "Apparently newly placed pigment is difficult to age and match the paint which has already been applied."

"So many Renoirs," I remarked.

"That is where his talent lay," said Joanna, while turning a painting to examine its backing. "Harry Edmunds was a master of details, which are the hallmarks of Auguste Renoir's works."

My gaze went from one painting to the next to the next. "Edmunds must have enjoyed viewing his own forgeries. I would agree that he is truly an egotist."

"Or perhaps hanging the copies was a convenient way to store the forgeries until he decided to dispose of them," Joanna surmised. "In all likelihood, these were copies which were not nearly as good as other finished products and were thus of no value to him."

"Yet, for all his cleverness, he still made a mistake in his forgeries," I recalled.

That comment caused the wife's eyelids to open just a fraction, but they quickly resumed their previous half-lidded position. Charlotte Edmunds was a rather attractive woman, in her midthirties I would guess, with catlike features and auburn hair that was severely drawn back into a tight bun. But there was a coldness about her that was unmistakable. For some reason she reminded me of the *tricoteuse,* the knitting women who sat around the guillotine waiting for heads to roll during the French Revolution.

Joanna examined and replaced the last of the Renoirs, then strolled over to Charlotte Edmunds and asked, "Would you be good enough to lift the unfinished afghan from your lap?"

Charlotte did so without hesitation. Her lap was empty.

"Now, if you would, please stand," Joanna requested.

Again Charlotte did so without hesitation. There was nothing beneath the chair's cushion or under the oversized chair itself.

"And now please allow me to frisk your clothing."

Charlotte raised her arms above her head instantly, as if she knew the routine for being searched. She had an ample bosom and broad waist, both of which showed through her tight-fitting sweater. The skirt of her dress was far more expansive, with multiple pleats and folds. Joanna gently ran her hands down the garment from collar to hem and found nothing of interest.

"Disappointed, are you?" Charlotte finally spoke.

"It was what I expected," Joanna replied. "Scotland Yard no doubt caught you unaware on their initial visit and you were forced to improvise. I suspect you learned from that experience."

"You are wasting your time," Charlotte said in a neutral tone.

"We shall see." Joanna gave the parlor a last, careful survey before requesting the wife follow us into the kitchen. The sergeant from Scotland Yard stayed at the door, his posture erect, his holstered revolver partially visible.

The kitchen itself was quite small, but had a surprisingly large pantry that was packed with expensive goods. There were jars of Fortnum & Mason marmalade and tins of beluga caviar from Harrods. On a top shelf were assorted spices from Asia and basmati rice from India.

"You live well," Joanna remarked. "These items are far beyond the reach of most people."

"These goodies bring me a bit of cheer," Charlotte said. "What with my husband facing jail time and all."

"I take it they were purchased by your husband well before he was apprehended for forgery," Joanna surmised.

"Oh, months before," Charlotte said. "Harry went to the fancy stores after work on numerous occasions. He once told me that the excess money came as a bonus for the restoration he did on a most important painting. I had no idea he was involved in anything illegal. Why, he even encouraged me to spend more and more, for there were yet additional bonuses coming his way."

"Was it also his suggestion that you purchase an expensive dress from Selfridges?"

"He insisted on it."

This Charlotte Edmunds was a most clever woman, I thought to myself, and certainly not one who could be easily outwitted. But then again the answers she was giving were in a way rehearsed, for they were no doubt asked earlier by Scotland Yard.

"He was most generous," said Joanna.

"To a fault," Charlotte agreed.

"Does he still tell you to continue your extravagant ways?" asked Joanna.

"Oh, no," Charlotte replied at once. "He has instructed me to—" She caught her first mistake and quickly backtracked. "Before his death he instructed me to be very careful with my spending, for I could no longer depend on his income or any surprise bonuses."

So, I deduced, Charlotte knows her husband is alive and that was obvious from her use of the present tense—"he *has* instructed me." Were she to have believed him dead, she would have spoken in the past tense—"he *had* instructed me." For the moment Joanna decided not to follow us and pursue Charlotte's miscue. I glanced over at Charlotte who was trying to keep her face expressionless, but a hint of concern showed itself for the first time.

Joanna peered into the adjoining room where Harry Edmunds produced his forgeries. It was well stocked with canvases and stands and various pigments. Off to the side was a chair and next to it a large oven that Edmunds used to bake his paintings and give them the tiny cracks and creases that are associated with considerable aging.

"We know there are additional forgeries hidden away in this house," Joanna cautioned. "For you to continue to conceal them makes you an accessory to the crime."

Charlotte shrugged, emotionless. "I know of no others."

"I wonder how a hard-nosed British jury would respond to that obviously false statement," Joanna pressed.

"But it is the truth," Charlotte said firmly.

"I can assure you that you will be singing a different tune before we leave here today, but by then your recanting will be of little value."

"And let me assure you, *Sherlock's daughter,*" Charlotte scoffed, "that I am not moved by your threats or those of Scotland Yard."

"The last person to utter those words was a rather charming woman who killed her two children for their insurance money," Joanna responded. "She is currently an inmate at Pentonville where she awaits a date with the hangman."

"Last I heard being the wife of a forger is not a hanging offense," said Charlotte.

"But being an accomplice to murder is," Joanna countered. "You see, we know your husband planned and executed the death of Derrick Wilson as a means of escaping from Wormwood Scrubs. And he did the same to James Blackstone, for his share of the masterpiece."

"I know of no such events," Charlotte refuted calmly.

"We shall see," Joanna said again.

The sergeant from Scotland Yard looked into the kitchen, saying, "Madam, Dr. Watson is here with the hound."

"Excellent!" Joanna gleefully rubbed her hands together

and turned back to the forger's wife. "You are about to be undone by a dog's nose."

Before she could utter another word, Toby Two dashed into the kitchen and, ignoring Joanna, went directly to the chair that stood between a canvas and the oven. She pointed at it motionlessly, with her tail held back straight as an arrow. This type of behavior was most unusual for Toby Two, for she had a particular liking for Joanna and always went to her first where she would await a delightful scratching of her head. But on this occasion, the hound continued to point and Joanna allowed her to do so.

Toby Two was the granddaughter of the original Toby, a dog made famous by Sherlock Holmes who worked so brilliantly with her in *The Sign of the Four*. The current Toby was the product of a second-generation Toby and an amorous bloodhound, which endowed her with the keenest sense of smell imaginable. The dog's mixed breed bestowed on her the features of a long-haired spaniel, but her floppy ears, sad eyes, and snout were those of a bloodhound.

Finally Joanna relented and came over to Toby Two to give the hound a pleasant scratch. "Picked up the scent of coal tar, have you?" she asked and reached in her purse for a lump of sugar which the dog eagerly accepted. Now that their bond was firmly reestablished, Joanna turned to my father. "I see you did exactly as I requested."

"On our journey over, I allowed her a brief whiff of diluted coal tar which I must say was not to her liking," my father reported. "Yet when I tossed the small vial out of the window, she became unhappy and simply laid about."

"Because you traveled away from the scent and it eventually disappeared," said Joanna.

"Precisely so," my father agreed. "For as we drew nearer

to the Brixton address the scent reappeared and, now understanding the game was afoot, Toby Two's tail began to wag."

"And she went directly to the chair because that is where Harry Edmunds sat to produce his forgeries and left the strong odor of coal tar behind," I chimed in. "But is it not surprising that the scent stayed for such a long period of time? After all, Edmunds has not set foot in this house for months."

"You must keep in mind that there are two noteworthy factors in play here," Joanna explained. "First, one finds windows in most of the house, but not the kitchen and certainly not in the enclosed, adjoining room. Thus, there is no aeration and the scents will linger on and on. Secondly, dogs have a nose that is a thousand times more sensitive than those on humans. I can assure you that, to Toby Two, the aroma of coal tar in this room is overwhelming. Yet you will note she has no interest whatsoever in the pantry."

"Is that of importance?" asked my father.

"Only that it proves Charlotte Edmunds is a liar," Joanna replied, walking into the pantry to fetch a jar of marmalade and a tin of caviar, which she presented to Toby Two. The hound remained disinterested. "Harry Edmunds never touched these expensive items, yet his wife insists he was the one who purchased them."

"I may have misspoken," Charlotte said defensively.

"Let us see where else your memory has failed." Joanna reached for Toby Two's leash and led the way to the staircase. "We will have a look in the bedroom which often provides the best of hiding places."

We all ascended the stairs and entered a cramped bedroom, with barely enough space for a bed and vanity chest. Toby Two sniffed about the bed and pillows, but appeared uninterested. However, when Joanna released Toby Two's leash, the hound quickly bounded over to the brick fireplace which seemed too large for the room. She ignored the cold ashes and stood on her hind legs, so that she could press her nose against the midlevel of the hearth. Then she excitedly pawed at the bricks and made a most unhappy sound.

"Hello!" Joanna exclaimed and, pulling Toby Two away, began to inspect the bricks which appeared to be mortared in place. She carefully pressed on them, one by one, until a few gave way, then did others, which allowed the stones to be removed. Joanna reached into a hidden space and extracted a thick stack of five-pound notes. Leaning down, she allowed Toby Two to smell the fresh banknotes. The dog's tail wagged furiously.

"How quaint," Joanna said, and looked over to the forger's wife. "Saving for a rainy day, were you?"

Charlotte Edmunds had no control over the noticeable hardening of her expression.

"All this money," Joanna went on, "and Harry Edmunds could not lay a finger on it. You see, Scotland Yard has had this house under surveillance since the moment Edmunds was arrested for dealing on the black market with his forgeries. Even when he was imprisoned, they continued watching the house and his wife, waiting for her to resume their shady business."

"Was Scotland Yard that obvious?" I asked.

"Not intentionally," Joanna answered. "But in this neighborhood, the presence of the police would be quickly noticed and the word would spread. You can rest assured that both the now freed Edmunds and his wife knew their house was being watched." She turned to Charlotte and asked with a thin smile, "Didn't you, dear?"

"They tried to be so clever," Charlotte said bitterly.

"Which worked to their advantage, for it kept your husband poor and forced him to go about his business on the cheap which led to mistakes. Like with his last Renoir, he is now making clumsy errors."

"You will never catch my Harry," Charlotte blurted out.

"To the contrary, he will spend his Christmas at Wormwood Scrubs," Joanna predicted, then pulled on Toby Two's leash. "Come on, girl. Let us see what other mischief you can stir up."

Down the stairs and out the back door we went, and entered a small, flowerless garden. To the rear was a wooden shed that had a thatched roof and a locked door. If there was anything of significance in the shed, Toby Two gave no indication of it. However, when the door was opened, the dog dashed in and sniffed at a wheelbarrow and tools with only a modicum of interest. I noticed there were no items that a restorer or forger would use, and no cabinets that might hold paints, brushes, or canvases. In a far corner was a dirty pine chest which Joanna opened and found empty. She tried to drag the chest aside, but she was met with resistance which required her to pull with even more force. As the chest finally moved, it produced the scraping sound of wood rubbing against wood. Toby Two instantly dashed over and began digging at the newly exposed ground. It took less than a minute for the hound to uncover a hidden, locked trapdoor that measured three-by-three feet and had atop it the carved initials HE. Charlotte was asked to open it, but refused, saying she had no key and did not know if one existed. Joanna gave her a look of disbelief, then gestured to a jimmy bar on a nearby shelf. Without permission, the sergeant from Scotland Yard grabbed the bar and used it to pry open the trapdoor. With care he extracted a large, square object that was wrapped in thick tarpaulin.

"Shall I open it, ma'am?" the sergeant asked.

"Please," said Joanna.

The sergeant slowly removed the double wrapping and held up the concealed item. It was a magnificent painting by Renoir, with his name clearly signed into it. The portrait showed two lovely girls, one a teenager, the other much younger, sitting on a terrace that was festooned with flowers. The red and blue colors were so stunning they literally dazzled the viewer.

"I wonder what Renoir called it?" I asked.

"*Two Sisters on the Terrace,*" the sergeant answered.

Joanna spun around to the Scotland Yard officer. "Are you a Renoir aficionado?"

"No, ma'am, but my wife is, and we have a reproduction of this very work hanging in our parlor."

"You may wish to mention this sighting to her, for it must so resemble the original."

"I shall, ma'am."

"And now, Sergeant," Joanna said, refocusing her attention, "please recheck the space beneath the trapdoor and see if anything remains."

The sergeant reached in to the length of his arm and retrieved a much smaller item that was wrapped in heavy sackcloth. Within were letters that had been well protected from the elements. The letters were addressed to Charlotte Edmunds and each carried a distinct postmark.

"You have no business reading my personal mail," Charlotte cried out.

"Then I shall make it my business," Joanna said as she carefully studied the postmarks. "Two of the letters were mailed weeks before your husband's escape from Wormwood Scrubs and the third following his departure. Let us see what they have to say."

I peered over Joanna's shoulder while she read from the first letter. The handwriting was neat and obviously masculine in nature.

My dearest wife,

I have become aware of an early release program which I plan to take advantage of. Once executed I shall be free in every regard and we can spend the rest of our days in great comfort which will be provided by the wealth to come.

Eternally yours,
Harry

"Ah!" Joanna exclaimed. "He writes in code which is quite easy to decipher. The letter was sent two weeks prior to Harry Edmunds's escape that he refers to as an early release program. Then he writes that once the plan is executed, he will be free in every regard. That is code for burning Derrick Wilson to an unrecognizable crisp so that dear Harry can take his place and be discharged from prison while everyone believes he lies dead cold in the ground. And finally he speaks of wealth to come which no doubt will be derived from the hidden masterpiece."

"So his wife knew of everything in advance," said I.

"She had to," Joanna agreed. "How else could she understand the code?"

"The information in outline could have been passed during her visits to the prison," the sergeant added. "They no doubt used imprecise wording that only they could understand."

"Clever pair, these two," Joanna noted, opening the second envelope after reading its postmark. "The next letter was mailed from Wormwood Scrubs a week before Edmunds's escape."

Again I peered over her shoulder as she read aloud from the neatly written letter.

My dearest wife,

The early release program I mentioned earlier looks more and more promising. As I go through the various steps, the

news may be upsetting to you, but rest assured all is not
what it seems. There will be no need for tears, for in the end
all will work out well.

Eternally yours,
Harry

"The upsetting news is the notice she will receive that her husband died in a fiery explosion," Joanna deciphered. "Then he writes that all is not what it seems, which translates that it was Derrick Wilson who died and not me. So she had no need for tears and thus did not provide a proper burial for him."

"She really should have," I thought aloud. "A grieving widow at graveside would have added a nice touch."

"Indeed," Joanna concurred, reaching for the third and final letter. "This is the one which should tell us the most, for it is dated after Harry Edmunds's escape. With a little luck, it will speak of his future plans."

This letter was not as neatly written as the others, but was still clearly legible.

My dearest wife,
    Please prepare for our future. As in your dreams, there
should be two tickets to Canada in hand for early January.
Be like an Angel and meet me on the Road to Paradise at a
time that is special to you.

Eternally yours,
Harry

"So," Joanna interpreted, "the loving couple plan to travel to Canada in early January, no doubt on a posh ocean liner. Those tickets will be quite expensive which indicates his wife knows where their hidden money is located. It also tells us that Edmunds has narrowed down the list of paintings that could conceal the masterpiece, for why else would he request tickets be scheduled for an early January departure. That is only two weeks from now, during which time he not only has to take possession of the masterpiece, but sell it as well."

"Which means Harry Edmunds will strike again very soon," I surmised.

"That is a certainty, but *where* is another matter," Joanna said, then reexamined the final letter. "And he wrote to meet his wife at a specific time and a place characterized by the words *angel, road,* and *paradise*. These three words all have their first letter capitalized, which indicates their importance."

The shed went silent as we attempted to decipher an address which somehow fit the three capitalized words. Could they represent a district, a street or neighborhood, or perhaps a restaurant they once frequented? The possibilities seemed endless, but we continued to seek an answer, for it represented the opportunity to capture Edmunds before or shortly after he struck again.

Joanna reached for a cigarette, but decided against it when she considered the straw on the floor and the thatched roof of the shed. Instead, she turned to Charlotte Edmunds and warned, "You would be wise to give it up, for you are clearly an accessory to these crimes which include murder. The court may be lenient if you cooperate."

Charlotte parted her lips as if she was about to speak, then firmly closed them.

"Your choice," said Joanna before returning to the problem at hand. "Is there a street or avenue that carries the name of Angel or Paradise?"

"There is an Old Paradise Street in Lambert," my father offered. "And a Paradise Street in southeast London."

"Are there any establishments of note on those streets?" Joanna asked at once.

"I believe there is a pub or two on the street in Lambert," my father recalled.

"Do their names come to you?" Joanna urged.

My father thought back, then slowly shook his head. "It was so long ago that they may no longer be standing."

The sergeant suddenly snapped his fingers. "I am familiar with the Paradise Street in south London. We made a counterfeit pinch there a few years back."

"Is there a pub or such nearby?"

The sergeant nodded quickly. "A pub called the Angel, for that is where the arrest took place."

Joanna stared at Charlotte. "You are involved neck-deep and it may work to your benefit to tell us when the meeting with your husband will take place."

"I know nothing," Charlotte insisted.

"To the contrary, you know everything and when you undergo a good and proper questioning at Scotland Yard, I believe all will be revealed." Joanna gestured to the sergeant who placed handcuffs on the wife. "You have one last chance, Mrs. Edmunds."

Charlotte smirked at Joanna. "I am smart enough to know that you cannot force a wife to testify against her husband."

"Your testimony will not be required," Joanna rebutted. "For the hidden money and Renoir and the letters from your husband will speak volumes."

"But it does not implicate me in murder."

"We shall let the court decide that."

As Charlotte was being led away, I asked, "Why in the world would she hold onto those incriminating letters?"

"It is a fatal flaw women have," Joanna replied. "We keep

all letters from a loved one, as if they are some sort of sacred document. Women are very sentimental, you see; men are not."

"But in a way those letters incriminate her husband as well," I noted.

Joanna smiled briefly and said, "There was a famous American lawyer who once warned—'Do *right* and fear no man, don't *write* and fear no woman.' These letters not only incriminate, but show that the crimes were premeditated."

"Edmunds will surely see the gallows, but I suspect his wife, assuming she has a good barrister, will receive a relatively light sentence."

"Female accessories usually do."

"But despite all the evidence, we are no closer to resolution," my father interjected. "It is quite clear from the last letter that Edmunds expects to have possession of the masterpiece in the very near future, whilst we have no idea which painting hides the treasure."

"I do not share that opinion, Watson, for resolution is now in sight."

"How so?"

"Because now I only require two additional pieces of evidence and I, too, will know where the masterpiece is hidden."

"May I ask where this information will come from?"

Joanna glanced out into the back garden to make certain the sergeant and Charlotte Edmunds were well out of hearing distance before saying, "From a very unseemly source, which Scotland Yard would not approve of."

"Does this source have a name?"

"In the underworld, they are known as the Morrison syndicate."

"Why call on this particular syndicate?"

"Because they specialize in stolen masterpieces."

23

An Unseemly Source

I had never worn a disguise and had no idea how truly effective one might be. But now, looking in our bedroom mirror, I did not recognize the person staring back at me. My silver gray wig and pasted-on, matching moustache, together with my gold-rimmed spectacles, added a good twenty years to my age. At my side, Joanna was likewise unrecognizable, with a wig whose brown-gray hair was drawn back severely into a bun that was held in place by a diamond-studded barrette. She had also applied lipstick in a fashion that gave her a pinched, stern expression. To add age, she had reading glasses on the end of her nose.

"These disguises are quite good," I said.

"Speak like an Afrikaner," Joanna reminded. "When you say *good*, pronounce it *goodt*."

"And raise my tongue to my palate when uttering words such as *great* or *greeting*, to give the *gr* a harsher sound."

"Precisely so, dear John, for the tone of our voices will be a most important part of our disguises," said Joanna. "They must have no doubts we are from South Africa."

Indeed, I thought to myself, with a bit of concentration, we should have no difficulty passing ourselves off as Malcolm and Olivia Vanderhorst, a very wealthy couple from Johannesburg, who had come to bid on the masterpiece. At least that was who the criminal syndicate was expecting on this cold, dreary London evening. The Vanderhorst name was well known throughout the Empire, for they had a substantial interest in the South African diamond industry. Their wealth could be counted in the millions.

My father came up behind me, saying, "I do wish you two would be careful, for this Morrison syndicate can be most dangerous."

"Not to worry, Watson," Joanna spoke the word *worry* in a distinct South African accent. "When it comes down to selling and making a huge profit, these people can be in every way businesslike and straightforward. Nevertheless, if one attempts to cross them, they will turn quite vicious and make that individual pay a terrible price."

"Like that poor blighter they hung from a lamppost for stupidly moving into their territory," my father remembered. "Allowed him to remain there all night."

"They know how to make a point," Joanna noted.

"So be double cautious," my father beseeched.

"We shall."

After checking our appearance in the mirror a final time, we put on our heavy coats and bade farewell to my father who continued to have a worried expression on his face. I believe he would have gladly accompanied us and waited outside our meeting place, with his service revolver at the ready. But Joanna would have never permitted it, for if he were discovered our very important plan would have gone dangerously awry.

As we departed through the front entrance, we encountered Miss Hudson hurrying in from the cold. She inspected us with a most careful eye, paying particular attention to Joanna's diamond-studded barrette.

"Here to see the Watsons, I would think," she inquired.

"Indeed, madam," I replied, enjoying the deception of our disguises. "Watson and I were classmates at Cambridge too many years ago."

"I am certain he took great pleasure in seeing you again."

"Quite so," I said and glanced at my timepiece. "But we must ask you to excuse us as we are already late for a previous engagement."

"Well then, I shall wish you a very pleasant good evening."

We climbed into a hired limousine and began our journey across London, all the while practicing our South African accents. Joanna spoke it with the ease of a true Afrikaner, so we decided she should do most of the talking to the syndicate. The stern appearance her disguise gave her suited Joanna well for that role. I still had questions about the London underworld and how Joanna expected our plan to play out. In detail she described the makeup of the syndicates which consisted of neighborhood crime families that had charismatic leaders with fearsome reputations. They were not petty thieves or smash-and-grab robbers, but were interested in far more profitable ventures, including extortion, drugs, prostitution, and contract killing. When highly priced and ill-gotten items, such as masterpieces, needed to be placed on the black market, the syndicates were more than willing to act as intermediaries for 20 percent of the selling price. Although this commission might seem extreme, it was well worth it, for it guaranteed the item would attract a select audience who were willing to pay extraordinary sums in cash and in total privacy. According to Edwin Alan Rowe, who had set up our meeting with the Morrison syndicate, a Raphael was recently sold by them to an Italian industrialist for twenty-five thousand pounds.

"I am surprised that a prominent and responsible art historian, like Rowe, would be involved with these people," I said.

"Only on the periphery," Joanna explained. "And I can assure you he is never involved with the actual theft or selling of the item."

"Then how was he able to set up our meeting with the Morrison crime family?"

"Through an underworld source."

"But why would this source be willing to serve as a conduit?"

"Because everybody benefits, on both sides of the fence," Joanna said and left it at that.

"Nonetheless, I would think that a distinguished historian would never want his name mentioned in such sordid dealings."

"It will not be mentioned, for both the source and Rowe no doubt used aliases to protect themselves."

"But we know Rowe is involved, at least to some degree," I argued. "And no alias was used."

"That is why I swore that our association with him and his source will remain absolutely confidential and never spoken of under any circumstances," Joanna went on. "Still, there is some small risk which Rowe is aware of, but he was driven to participate for revenge. You will recall that James Blackstone was a close friend, and the horrific picture of the man's tortured body keeps Rowe awake at night."

"May I ask how close?"

"Rowe is godfather to Blackstone's son."

As we rode south across London, I could not help but wonder what type of individuals we were about to encounter.

Would they be the rough gangsters depicted in novels or the dashing rogues written about in newspapers? Whatever the type, I was certain they had never encountered the likes of Joanna Blalock-Watson. If she had any worry or concern, it did not show in her face. My father once told me that Sherlock Holmes had the same response to approaching danger. His appearance took on the look of a man about to cast his fishing line.

Our driver opened the window to the rear compartment of the limousine and asked, "Please give me the exact address, madam."

"I do not have a number, but you should have no difficulty finding the Angel pub on Paradise Street," Joanna replied.

"Very good, madam."

My jaw must have dropped at the name of our destination. "The same pub where Charlotte Edmunds was to meet her husband!"

"The very same," said Joanna, "and now you can put all the points together. Harry Edmunds and his wife no doubt frequented the Angel pub which is surely connected to the Morrison crime family. Here is where their association began, dating back to Edmunds's forgeries and continuing up to the present. What better place for exchanging a masterpiece for untold thousands of pounds? Security and privacy in a back room would be assured and anyone who attempted to interfere would find themselves hanging from the lamppost that Watson so aptly described. I suspect the Morrisons might even supply an escort to make certain the money and masterpiece reached their final destinations. For an additional fee, of course."

I thought the matter through before saying, "But I see a problem. The sergeant from Scotland Yard was present when we discovered Harry Edmunds's connection to the Angel pub, which means it may now be under surveillance."

"I foresaw that problem as well and requested Lestrade not to surveil the pub for now," Joanna said. "You see, Harry Edmunds will not appear there until he has the masterpiece in hand. I assured Lestrade that the Morrisons would know they were under surveillance in the blink of an eye and that would surely result in the transaction being called off or moved to another location, either of which would place us at an unwanted disadvantage."

My brow went up. "And Lestrade agreed?"

"Reluctantly so, for he needs our assistance if he ever hopes to solve this case," Joanna replied. "And trust me when I tell you that Lestrade knows which side his bread is buttered on."

"I worry, for Lestrade would like nothing more than to apprehend Edmunds on his own and garner all the credit," I emphasized. "Recall how much he enjoyed basking in glory when the newspapers reported his discovery of the corpse in the chimney."

Joanna chuckled softly. "I am afraid that was my doing. You see, I asked Lestrade to leak the story to the press in an effort to flush out Harry Edmunds. The release was sure to reach Edmunds's eyes and alert him that we were closing in on his nasty little scheme, which might force him to act hastily and in an even more rash manner."

"Why did you not share this information with us?"

"An oversight," she lied easily.

"I think not," I argued mildly. "I suspect you wanted Lestrade to relish the limelight and take credit because you may wish to use him in a similar fashion on subsequent occasions. Had you told me of your plan, you assumed I would have included it when I chronicled this adventure and thus diminished Lestrade's role and glory, which would make him most unhappy and less cooperative in the future."

"You give me too much credit," she said with a mischievous smile.

"I think not," I said again. "But I must admit it was a good move on your part."

"I thought so as well," Joanna admitted. "Now please remember to put a *t* on the end of the word *good*."

When our limousine turned onto Paradise Street, I leaned over and asked in a quiet voice, "What do you expect to learn from the Morrisons?"

"The name of the masterpiece, of course," Joanna whispered back.

"But it has been kept a deep secret thus far," said I. "Why would they give it up now?"

"Because they will have no choice," Joanna replied. "No one will place fifty thousand pounds on the table for an unknown work of art."

"Perhaps a threat comes with the information."

"Undoubtedly."

"And you believe this knowledge will somehow lead us to the hidden masterpiece?"

"It is the first of two important clues which will do so."

As our limousine slowed and approached the Angel pub, the driver turned and asked, "Where shall I park, madam?"

"You will find an alleyway on the far side of the pub," Joanna instructed. "Stop there, and once we depart, wait for us on the opposite side of the street."

We left the limousine and walked down a dark alleyway which was dimly lighted by a lamppost on the street. From within the pub we could hear the raucous shouts and laughter of patrons having a jolly good time. Just ahead of us, a burly man wearing a leather jacket over a turtleneck sweater stood guard.

In a barely audible voice, Joanna said, "Say nothing and treat them as underlings, for that is what they expect."

"But they have the upper hand."

"And we have the money which is always the governing power."

The guard carefully measured us and, without a word, opened the door to a busy kitchen where a busy crew was preparing dishes of shepherd's pie and Welsh rarebit. Two slightly built Asians were washing and drying dishes while they smoked cigarettes and spoke in a totally incomprehensible language. We were ignored, with no one even bothering to glance our way. We passed through a crowded, noisy pub where we received a few curious stares, but little else. At the end of a long bar was a nicely decorated Christmas tree that was laden with circles of tinsel and gingerbread figures. Nearby, a happy working-class couple, with mugs of beer in hand, were embracing and kissing beneath mistletoe which hung from the ceiling. I could not help but wonder if they knew of the sordid and at times murderous dealings that emanated from the back rooms of the Morrison establishment. Of course they were aware, I decided, but one turns a blind eye to such activities when it is in one's best interest to do so. A door to our right opened and we were ushered into a rather plain office that was filled with cigar smoke. From behind an uncluttered desk, a heavyset man wearing a nicely tailored suit stood and motioned us to the two chairs in front of him. He was well groomed and could have passed for a businessman except for the deep scar that ran from his ear to his upper cheek.

Without introduction, he asked, "You have the bank's letter?"

"Yes," Joanna replied and handed him a letter obtained with the assistance of Scotland Yard, which carried a Bank of England letterhead and certified the Vanderhorsts could cover any purchase up to a hundred thousand pounds. "Your name, please."

"That is unimportant," said he.

"It is to me," Joanna said sharply. "You know our name and I must know yours, if you wish to do business."

"Roger Jones."

"That is not a very convincing alias."

"That is my name."

"Then we are not off to a very promising start, are we, Mr. Freddie Morrison?"

The mention of his true name did not seem to faze the man. "I see you do your homework, Mrs. Olivia Vanderhorst."

"That is how I do business," Joanna said, her South African accent spot-on. "I take it my letter of credit is satisfactory."

Morrison read the letter before holding it up to the light to ascertain its watermark. "It appears genuine."

"Then let us proceed," Joanna said, retrieving the document.

"First, I shall go over the rules you must agree to and follow. To begin, whether or not your bid is successful, neither this meeting nor the people involved are ever to be mentioned."

Joanna flicked her wrist at the demand.

"You must agree for us to continue. Please keep in mind that failure to follow the rules could end up being unpleasant for you. And we have friends in Johannesburg who owe us favors."

Joanna leaned forward and stared directly into Morrison's eyes. "We pledge to remain silent in all our dealings. But I would like you, Mr. Morrison, to keep in mind that I am not moved by your threats and, most importantly, that I have the power and money to wipe you and your family off the face of the earth."

Morrison smiled thinly. "Then we have an understanding."

"Go on with your rules."

"You can make one bid and only one bid, so I would advise you to make the very best bid possible. This is not an auction, nor will it become one. Each new bidder is told of the highest offer and can either increase it or withdraw. There are no second opportunities."

So very clever, I thought. Everything was straightforward and on top of the table, with no haggling or quibbling or messaging between the bidders. No time would be wasted and the masterpiece would still demand the highest price.

"If your bid is successful," Morrison went on, "you will be notified and a site agreed to where the transaction will occur. You alone will be present for the transfer, and no second parties will be allowed. How you transport the masterpiece and what you eventually do with it is your business and of no concern to us."

"We insist you guarantee it will reach the London address we give you," Joanna demanded.

"That can be arranged."

"And we will not be charged an additional fee for this service."

Again a thin smile crossed Freddie Morrison's face, but this time it was accompanied by a nod. "The transaction will of course be in cash."

"Of course."

"In hundred-pound notes."

"Done."

"We will have a man present to make certain the banknotes are not counterfeit."

"And I an expert to certify beyond any doubt that the item in question is a true masterpiece."

"We will require the name of the expert."

"That is none of your concern," Joanna snapped. "He has a reputation to protect and cannot risk his name being associated with the transaction."

Morrison considered the demand before giving the briefest of nods. "How do you propose your expert do the inspection?"

"You will deliver the masterpiece to a suite at a Knightsbridge hotel which we both will agree on," Joanna instructed. "The expert will take as long as necessary to certify that the painting is authentic. The room will have no terrace nor any exits to adjoining rooms. You can have one of your men stand guard outside the door, if you wish."

"I insist that I be in that suite," Morrison stipulated.

"You shall be, but you will be facing the door."

Morrison shook his head forcefully. "The masterpiece never leaves my sight until I have the money in hand."

Joanna pondered the quandary at length, obviously understanding Morrison's insistence. He wished to make certain that there was no possible way a switch could occur. Criminals at the level of Freddie Morrison were quite clever, particularly when it came to the various subterfuges of thievery.

"Then we shall have our expert masked," Joanna said, seeking middle ground.

"Agreed."

"And the money exchanged once the masterpiece is certified."

"Well and good," Morrison concurred. "Now let us move to the bidding. The highest bid thus far is sixty-five thousand—"

"Hold on," Joanna interrupted. "I need to know the details on this masterpiece I am about to buy."

"Such as?" Morrison asked tersely.

"I must know the name of the masterpiece."

"I cannot give you its name, for it has no official title."

"Then I cannot give you a bid of one hundred thousand pounds."

Freddie Morrison was taken aback by the unexpected, most extraordinary offer. It required a moment for him to regain his composure. "A hundred thousand, you say?"

"A hundred thousand," Joanna repeated.

Morrison dwelled on the spectacular bid, no doubt in large measure swayed by his greed. The syndicate's commission on a sale of a hundred thousand pounds would amount to twenty thousand pounds, or even more if additional services were required. He finally said, "Again, I cannot speak of an official title, for it has none according to the seller."

"Then this meeting is ended."

"But I can provide you with the name of the artist."

"Which is?"

"Leonardo da Vinci."

Joanna's eyes widened noticeably. "You have a da Vinci?"

"I have a da Vinci," said Morrison, enjoying Joanna's stunned expression. "A genuine Leonardo da Vinci."

"Please describe it," Joanna requested in a soft voice.

"I cannot, for I, too, have not seen it," said Morrison. "But I can assure you it has been authenticated. And most importantly, you will be able to openly display your da Vinci without fear of anyone ever claiming its ownership."

"How can that be?" Joanna asked at once. "It is stolen, is it not?"

"Of course it is stolen, madam," Morrison answered. "Why else would it be on the black market?"

"Could you please give me a clearer explanation?" Joanna queried. "To my way of thinking, if an item is stolen, its owner would surely demand its return."

"But what if the true owner never knew he possessed it?"

Joanna's brow went up. "Are you saying it was hidden from his sight, so he had no knowledge of its existence?"

"That is one way of putting it."

"And thus the owner will never know it was stolen from him."

"Exactly."

"So why then must it be sold on the black market?"

"Because at a proper art auction, people would demand to know how the seller gained possession of the masterpiece," Morrison explained. "This of course would reveal the true owner."

"And on the black market, no such revelation would be required," Joanna concluded.

"And we have a very happy ending for both the seller and buyer."

Joanna nodded, as if pleased with the cover-up. "When will the bidding come to a close?"

"In early January."

"Can you give me a specific date?"

"Not as yet."

"Perhaps the seller will consider bringing the bidding to an end when he learns of my offer."

"I shall inquire, madam."

"Perhaps it, too, would be to your advantage for the bidding to end," Joanna offered a subtle bribe.

"I shall inquire to that as well, madam."

Joanna pushed her chair back and rose. "We can find our way out."

We remained silent on our ride back to 221b Baker Street, but the name Leonardo da Vinci kept echoing through my mind. Da Vinci! Da Vinci! The famous da Vinci! The most gifted artist ever to walk on the face of this good earth. A man of such unimaginable talent that his name remains known and celebrated four hundred years after his death. Finally, I involuntarily uttered the words, "Leonardo da Vinci."

"Yes, da Vinci," Joanna said calmly.

"Oh, come now, Joanna. You must admit you, too, were stunned by the revelation."

"It was not the name that stunned me, but how well a most important piece of the puzzle suddenly fell into place."

"Shall we talk more of it?"

"Not until the final piece falls, then all will become clear."

"Do you still believe Harry Edmunds will spend his Christmas inside Wormwood Scrubs?"

"I am certain of it," said Joanna, closing her eyes and leaning back on the headrest as snow sprinkled down on our limousine.

As we approached 221b Baker Street, Joanna abruptly leaned forward and directed the driver not to stop at our residence, but rather to slowly circle the next block via Rossmore Road.

"I wish you to take at least five minutes before returning to our address," she instructed.

"Why the delay?" I asked quietly.

"To determine if we are being watched."

"By motor car?"

"By man."

I looked at my wife oddly. "With the heavy snow now falling?"

Joanna nodded. "That is what brought him to my attention."

We rode at a measured pace around the Marylebone area in which the roads and side streets were for the most part deserted. The moonless night was dark and the snowfall made it even darker, thus severely reducing one's visual acuity. I could barely discern the occasional figure on the footpath as we turned back for Baker Street.

"How can you be certain we are being surveilled?" I asked.

"Your question will be answered when we return to our address," Joanna replied. "If the man remains in place, we shall know."

"Where was the man standing?"

"Across the way in the shadow of a storefront," Joanna answered as our limousine gradually slowed to a halt. "Our headlights will briefly shine upon him, but do not gaze in that direction. We should simply keep our heads down and hurry inside."

After giving the driver a generous gratuity, we raced for the door and up the stairs to our rooms where we found my father enjoying the warmth of a three-log fire.

"Was your meeting a success?" he asked.

"Quite so, but more about that later," Joanna said hurriedly and switched off the lights in our drawing room. "Now I would like the two of you to stand in front of the fireplace and dampen the glow it gives off."

"For what purpose?"

"To darken the room, which will allow me to crack the drapes and not be noticed by the individual standing across the street watching our window."

My father and I positioned ourselves before the brightly burning logs, and the room darkened to the extent we could not see our shadows being cast upon the floor. Joanna crept over to our large window and parted the drapes ever so slightly. She stared through the falling snow for a full minute before speaking.

"He remains in place," Joanna reported as a transport

roared by on the street below. "He appears to be by himself, but the weather makes it impossible to describe him."

"Do you believe him to be Harry Edmunds?" my father asked.

"Perhaps."

"Or perhaps someone sent by the Morrisons," I speculated.

Joanna shook her head at the notion. "I am convinced that Freddie Morrison was persuaded by our disguises. Besides, that lot would never do business with us if they knew our true identity. They are far too clever to make that move."

"So it is most likely Harry Edmunds," I decided.

"That being the case, we should notify Scotland Yard immediately," my father proposed. "Let us be rid of him, once and for all."

"That would not serve our purpose at this juncture," said Joanna.

"But it would serve society's purpose to see him dangling from the end of a rope," my father argued.

"Based on what charge?"

"Murder, of course."

"Saying it is one matter, Watson; proving it is quite another," Joanna challenged.

"He was responsible for the death of his cellmate at Wormwood Scrubs," my father accused.

"It was a self-inflicted yet accidental explosion, which any worthwhile barrister would say."

"But then, the death of James Blackstone, which would be undeniable with Harry Edmunds's fingerprints on a brick that was stacked upon Blackstone's lap."

"One must be careful here," Joanna pointed out. "Remember, it was Edmunds who was paid to do the masonry at Hawke and Evans, and that might account for his fingerprints being on a loose brick. Thus, if Edmunds was captured now and represented by a clever barrister, the best we might hope for was that he be returned to Wormwood Scrubs for an extended stay. And let me assure you the masterpiece would remain hidden until his eventual release."

"So you believe it is in our best interest that he remain free," my father gathered.

Joanna nodded. "If we wish to bring this case to a successful conclusion, with the masterpiece in hand."

"But with this murderous villain surveilling us, does that not pose a danger?" my father warned. "Remember, it was no doubt he who threw the firebomb at us."

"You are correct, Watson, in that there is indeed danger," Joanna agreed. "For there can only be one purpose for his surveillance. He means to do us harm. For that very reason we must keep the drapes drawn at all times. And at night we should avoid walking in front of the drapes, for our shadows would be clearly visible from the street."

"He would not dare to toss a firebomb at our window," my father thought aloud. "It would be terribly difficult and too many things could go awry."

"Recall the rifle shot from the moving lorry, which nearly cost us our lives," Joanna reminded.

"Of course."

"A repeat performance should be our greatest concern."

24

A Violent Break-In

Early the next morning we were notified that Harry Edmunds had struck again, this time at the home of Sir Charles Cromwell, a member of the House of Lords and a key advisor to King Edward. Sadly, violence had occurred once more, with Sir Charles's young son grievously injured and the family dog stabbed to death. We could not help but wonder whether Harry Edmunds had been successful in his latest venture and now had the treasured masterpiece in hand.

"Was there any evidence to indicate that the masterpiece was hidden behind Lord Cromwell's painting?" I inquired.

"Such as?" Joanna asked.

"Was the portrait slashed wide open or was the entire frame disassembled to facilitate extraction of the ancient painting?"

"Excellent points, neither of which were mentioned by Lestrade," Joanna replied. "All we can deduct from the phone call is that our vandal has now become quite desperate."

"Because of the violence?" my father inquired.

Joanna shook her head. "Because of the dog that was stabbed to death."

"Pray tell what does the dog have to do with Edmunds's desperation?" I queried.

"A family dog will bark loudly at any intruder," Joanna explained. "Such barking will alert the family, which is the very last thing a burglar wants. In addition, a large hound can inflict serious wounds on an intruder, and one cannot always estimate the size of a dog by the quality of its bark. For these reasons, only a most foolish or desperate man would invade the house of a barking dog, and if anything Harry Edmunds is not foolish."

"And his lack of funds surely adds to his desperation," my father noted.

"Indeed it does, Watson, and his situation grows more dire by the day," Joanna went on. "Recall that he now has no source of income, for his home remains under surveillance by Scotland Yard and thus any remaining caches of money are unavailable to him. Therefore, he is forced to hire third-rate lockpicks who are greatly in need of work and will do so at a minimal wage. Lockpicks of any merit will not come within a mile of Harry Edmunds, for they are fully aware of Scotland Yard's keen interest in those who were associated with Edmunds in the past."

"Perhaps he could obtain an advance from the Morrisons at the Angel pub," I suggested.

"Only if he produces the masterpiece which he cannot," said Joanna.

"So we are all in agreement that Harry Edmunds is most desperate because of a lack of funds, and this no doubt accounts for his risky behavior," I stated.

"However, there is yet another reason for his latest perilous act," my father proposed. "He may have discovered that the painting in the home of Sir Charles Cromwell held the concealed masterpiece. Thus, he was willing to take one final, dicey chance and put this business to an end."

"That is a distinct possibility, and why we must hurry to the crime scene," said Joanna. "The evidence there may tell us whether that has occurred."

"Let us hope that Scotland Yard has not mucked up the telling evidence we require," my father remarked.

"Why, Watson, you sound much like Sherlock Holmes."

"It is an old habit of mine that shows up now and then."

On that note we departed 221b Baker Street and hurried in a four-wheeler to the Knightsbridge address of Sir Charles Cromwell. We remained silent until we passed along Hyde Park and approached Harrods department store where Charlotte Edmunds had purchased a variety of expensive goods, most notably tins of beluga caviar. Our conversation turned to the wife who we were certain was an accomplice. Lestrade had called to inform us that she had appeared before a magistrate and been granted bail since no specific charges had yet been made. She had hired a first-rate barrister which indicated she had more than sufficient funds at her disposal, which also indicated she had additional caches of cash hidden away in her home that we had not discovered. The possibility existed that she might secretively attempt to pass money to her husband, but this was deemed unlikely to occur since she remained under close surveillance by Scotland Yard. Nevertheless, Joanna cautioned that should Edmunds gain possession of the masterpiece, there existed the very real possibility that he and his wife might attempt to flee the country.

"And here is where the ocean liner tickets mentioned in Edmunds's last letter come into play," Joanna recalled.

"The well-thought-out escape," I noted.

"Exactly," Joanna agreed. "But they would in all likelihood

use aliases when booking passage, so not only should the ship's manifest be studied, but Scotland Yard should also have the passengers surveilled at the time of boarding."

"Of course they might be clever enough to don disguises and board separately," my father pointed out. "And that set of circumstances would make apprehension most difficult."

"Then we should convince Scotland Yard to question each passenger as they board," I proposed.

"That would be too time consuming and besides, if they are clever enough to wear disguises, they would be clever enough to have cover stories," said Joanna.

"So they might well slip through our fingers," I concluded.

"But not by Toby Two's nose that would accompany the police and sniff each passenger for the distinct aroma of coal tar," Joanna said, thinking two steps ahead of Harry and Charlotte Edmunds.

My father growled under his breath. "Scotland Yard did us no favor by releasing Charlotte Edmunds which complicates matters even further."

"They had no choice, Watson," said Joanna. "Unfortunately, she could not be charged because her involvement could not be proven. The magistrate would have to be convinced that Charlotte Edmunds either knew of or participated in the murders or break-ins. There is no evidence to back up these assertions. Furthermore, a hidden, forged Renoir and concealed caches of money are not crimes in and of themselves, nor are innocent letters which we decoded to our satisfaction. With this in mind, a good barrister would have her released in a matter of hours. I am afraid the best Scotland Yard could do was establish a police bail, in which a suspect is released without being charged but must return to the police station at a given date."

"During which time she and her husband could flee England."

"Sadly so."

Our carriage turned onto Sloane Square and pulled up in front of an impressive, three-story brick house, with window frames that were painted a sparkling white. Its door was solid mahogany, the brass fittings polished and gleaming. All of the drapes were drawn.

A uniformed constable was standing guard on the steps and recognized us from a previous investigation. With a tip of his hat, he moved aside and allowed us immediate entrance.

The crime had occurred in an eye-catching foyer that was richly appointed and spoke of refined wealth. It was done in white marble, with a broad mahogany staircase in its center. On the walls were paintings from the Italian Renaissance, one of which was slashed and smeared with blood. There were also blood splatters on the white marble floor and on the wall alongside the vandalized painting.

Lestrade hurried over to greet us, carefully avoiding the bloodstains on the floor. "Thank you for responding so quickly," said he. "I have tried to keep the crime scene intact, but unfortunately it has been marred by those who came to the aid of the gravely injured son."

"What is the nature of the lad's injury?" my father asked.

"I am afraid it is most serious, Dr. Watson," Lestrade replied. "As he was beaten down to the floor, his head hit hard marble, which resulted in a skull fracture. He is currently hospitalized at St. Bartholomew's where his very survival is in doubt."

"Do you know if it was an open fracture?"

"That I cannot answer, but the pool of dried blood you see to your right apparently came from the lad's head injury."

"Let us pray it is not an open fracture, for if it is, there is little chance he will survive."

Our conversation was interrupted by the approach of a tall, lean man, in his late middle years, with silver gray hair and sharp aristocratic features. His nose was aquiline, his face haggard and drawn, and there was caked blood on his hands.

"Ah, Sir Charles, allow me to introduce you to the Watsons," Lestrade greeted.

Sir Charles Cromwell gave us a brief nod and said, "I do hope you can bring this madness to an end."

"We shall do our best," Joanna responded. "But we must hear from you every detail of what transpired last night."

Sir Charles sighed wearily. "Again?"

"Again," Joanna implored. "For even the smallest clue may be important in bringing the man who perpetrated this vicious act to justice."

"Very well," Sir Charles said and sighed once more before beginning his sad story. "In the early morning hours, say about two, our dog Oliver started barking, which was not all that unusual, for he and the dog next door often exchange late-evening bouts of barking. But the noise continued and I soon became aware that there was no barking from the neighbor's dog. My son apparently did so as well and hurried downstairs to investigate, where he was savagely—" Sir Charles choked on his words for a moment before regaining his composure. "Where he was savagely attacked. Our dog had been released moments earlier and no doubt reached the intruder first, but was butchered by this most cruel man. I of course heard the sounds of a struggle and raced downstairs, but by then the burglar had departed, leaving my son gravely injured and the dog dead."

"What were the sounds you heard?" Joanna asked.

"The dog growling and a small table lamp being overturned." Lord Cromwell pointed to the small table on its side and a shattered lamp beside it. "I immediately dashed to a nearby den where I keep my hunting rifles and raced down the stairs, loading my weapon as I went. But I was too late. My son lay motionless, with a bleeding head wound and unable to utter even a single word. Our family doctor was summoned and, on examining the lad, rushed him to St. Bartholomew's where he now clings to life."

"I take it the dog was not allowed to freely roam the house."

"At night he is kept in a room adjoining the kitchen."

"So your son let him out just prior to encountering the intruder."

"As he was instructed in the event of a break-in, for some years ago we had a similar event and the dog responded in a likewise fashion."

"Thank you, Sir Charles, for that very excellent summary which I know was difficult for you," Joanna said sympathetically. "Now I have one more unpleasant task for you. Please describe everything you saw on reaching the foyer, including the position of your son and the dog. I also need to know the placement of the slashed painting, as well as the nature of all the blood smears and splatter you saw."

"You do realize the light in the foyer was quite dim," Sir Charles cautioned.

"I do, so please give us your description once the light was adequate."

Lord Cromwell motioned to the area directly beneath the dislodged painting. "My son lay there, bleeding from the back of his head. I could see a small pool of blood next to him. That pool was smeared by those of us who rushed to the lad's side. The same holds true for the dog beside my son. But the blood from the hound appeared to have come in squirts, some even reaching the wall surrounding the painting. There were bloodied footprints within the foyer, but those too have been smeared by people coming and going after the burglar departed. There was the overturned furniture as I mentioned earlier."

"That was most helpful," Joanna said and walked over to the slashed painting which now rested at an angle. She paid particular notice to the blood smears that stained it, then held the cut edges of the canvas apart to study its backing. I leaned in and could see bloodstains there as well. Finally, Joanna brought the edges together and studied the painting itself. "This work of art is quite lovely. May I ask its title and artist?"

"The painting is named *Saint Francis of Assisi with Angels* and was done by the well-known Italian artist Sandro Botticelli."

"From the Italian Renaissance, I gather."

"The Early Renaissance."

"May I ask where and when you obtained it?"

"I purchased it from an auction at Sotheby's earlier this year for a thousand pounds. Its owner was a small church in northern England, where it had been discovered covered with dust in the attic of the vicar's home. They were apparently most surprised at its value and were more than eager to sell it. Like most small churches, they were faith rich, money poor."

"When did you take it to Hawke and Evans?" Joanna asked.

Lord Cromwell raised his brow, obviously surprised that Joanna was aware of this information. "On the day of the purchase, for the canvas was covered with a yellowing varnish and the angels in the background were badly faded. The restoration took months to complete, but the result was near perfection." He glanced up at the damaged painting, shaking his head sadly. "And now look what this deranged man has done. I fear there is little hope it can be repaired."

Joanna restudied the painting at length, which showed a robed St. Francis holding a wooden cross, with colorful angels hovering above. "You say that Botticelli's angels were badly faded?"

"Quite so, but as you can see they had been beautifully restored," replied Sir Charles.

"Their overall texture seems so real," Joanna remarked. "They are reminiscent of the angel supposedly painted by Leonardo da Vinci in del Verrocchio's *The Baptism of Christ*."

"You have a keen eye, madam, for the very same comment was made by the appraiser at Sotheby's," Sir Charles said. "He also told me that it is believed that Botticelli and da Vinci were close friends and may have shared the same techniques early in their careers."

Joanna's eyes narrowed briefly. "Did they both train under del Verrocchio?"

"That I do not know, but surely Leonardo da Vinci did according to the appraiser." Sir Charles gazed up at the painting and gently touched the canvas. "So much damage," he said ruefully.

"Let us hope it can be restored."

"I have my doubts, madam."

"One never knows."

"Oh, rest assured I will look into possible restoration, for the painting is so lovely, and works by Sandro Botticelli are rapidly disappearing from the marketplace."

"Whatever the cost, I am certain it is worth restoring, for such works of art will increase in value manyfold as time passes."

Sir Charles nodded slowly. "If its value would go to a

million pounds, I would happily give it up, along with all of my other worldly possessions, just to see my boy return to his former self."

"Let us pray he does."

"And now, if you will excuse me, I must hurry to St. Bartholomew's to join my wife who sits at the lad's bedside."

As Lord Cromwell dashed away I felt true sympathy for the man, for I could think of nothing sadder than the sorrow experienced by parents who have lost a child. It was not supposed to happen in that fashion. The child was meant to grow and mature and age, and eventually bury his parents, not the other way around. For the child to die first seemed so out of order. I turned to my father and asked, "In your opinion, what are the lad's chances?"

"Nil if the fracture is open, far better if it is closed," my father prognosticated. "But in the latter much will depend on whether there is permanent damage to the brain."

"Let us hope for the best."

"A little prayer will not hurt," Joanna added, now carefully inspecting the blood splatter patterns on the floor and wall of the foyer. Her gaze went back and forth between the bloodstains and the door leading into a spacious parlor. "From the evidence at hand, the events went as follows. The lad releases the dog from its holding room, and the hound races in ahead of the boy, then attacks the intruder who was standing at Botticelli's painting. At that point, the—" Joanna interrupted herself and turned to Lestrade. "What breed of dog was it?"

"A rottweiler of considerable size," Lestrade replied.

"Where is its body?"

"It is covered in the garden."

"Please have it brought in."

Lestrade gestured to a nearby constable who hurried out. Joanna continued on as she envisioned the sequence of events. "So the rottweiler pounds on the intruder and a fierce struggle ensues, for this breed of dog is fearless and will go to any length to protect its master. The intruder has his knife in hand to slash open the painting, but instead uses it to defend himself."

"You keep referring to the vandal as an intruder, when we all know it was Harry Edmunds," Lestrade interjected.

"And where is the evidence for that which will hold up in a court of law?" asked Joanna.

Lestrade hesitated briefly before nodding. "You have a point, madam."

"It is best, Inspector, not to rush to an obvious conclusion, for in the process you may overlook clues that could prove to be significant later on," Joanna said, then returned to her summary of events. "The intruder uses his knife to stab the rottweiler, most likely in the neck where the carotid arteries lay. The severed artery then spurts blood against the wall beneath the painting, as evidenced by a pattern of intermittent splatterings. The rottweiler yelps and falls, and the lad rushes the intruder, only to be knocked to the floor where his head strikes hard marble which results in a skull fracture."

"That was my assessment as well," Lestrade concurred.

The constable hurried into the foyer carrying the dead rottweiler in his arms. "Shall I place him down, ma'am?"

"Please hold him in his current position," Joanna requested and removed the blanket covering the dead animal. There was a deep gash of at least three inches extending from its massive jaw to its heavily muscled chest. Dark, caked blood surrounded the wound and much of its neck. Joanna leaned over and sniffed at the rottweiler's mouth and snout. "Care to take a whiff, Inspector?"

Lestrade carefully approached the dog's massive head and inhaled. "Coal tar!" he announced.

"And now we know for a fact that it was Harry Edmunds," Joanna went on. "The rottweiler went for Edmunds's neck and in the process exposed its own neck where the blade of a knife was inserted."

"The dog was intent on ripping Harry's throat wide open," said I. "Do you believe he was able to inflict any damage?"

"The blood splatter says no," Joanna replied. "All of the bloodstains and pools can be attributed to either the rottweiler or the son. Nevertheless, to make certain, we should follow his footsteps out. I assume that he entered via a service door in the kitchen area."

"He did," Lestrade confirmed. "There were multiple scratch marks on the lock, indicating a rather clumsy lock-pick."

"After entering, Edmunds then crept through the kitchen and into the parlor to reach the marble foyer."

"Correct."

"And he would leave taking the same route."

"Correct once more."

"Were there any bloodstains on the carpet in the parlor or on the floor of the kitchen?"

"None."

"Then it is unlikely the dog inflicted any significant damage on Harry Edmunds."

"He is lucky as well as clever," Lestrade grumbled and gestured for the constable to remove the dead rottweiler. Once the foyer was clear, he came back to Joanna. "I do have one question for you, madam. You inquired of Sir Charles as to what sounds he heard downstairs at the time of the break-in. Did this have particular importance?"

"It did have some relevance," Joanna replied. "You will re-call that initially there was the sound of barking. Keep in mind that barking dogs bark, but do not attack. Harry Edmunds was aware of this, and when the barking remained distant and in place, he knew the hound was enclosed. Taking all this into consideration, he decided to make his move, hoping to be in and out before the hound was released. The growling sound came later, indicating that Edmunds had misjudged and the dog was on the attack."

"Most interesting and informative," Lestrade lauded. "But the most important question remains. Did Edmunds find the treasured masterpiece and make off with it?"

"He did not," said Joanna. "And there is evidence to clearly show that Harry Edmunds was unsuccessful."

"Please tell us how you reached that conclusion," Lestrade requested. "I see nothing, as you might say, that would stand up at an official inquiry."

"Allow me to walk you through the steps, Lestrade," Joanna proposed. "First, study the edges of the slash in the painting and describe what you see."

Lestrade inspected the edges before gently separating them for further examination. "There are abundant blood-stains present."

"Where did the blood come from?"

"Either from the dog or from an injury inflicted by the dog on Edmunds's hand."

"I believe we can exclude the latter because such a wound would have to bleed excessively, and this would have shown up on the floor around the painting and on the carpet of the parlor as he dashed out. This did not occur."

"Which indicates the blood came from the fatally stabbed rottweiler."

"Spot-on, Inspector. So now, the dog is dead or dying and the lad is lying on the marble floor unconscious. Edmunds must hurry, for he realizes the disturbance will bring forth others in the household. He next spreads the cut edges and peers in. Please do the same and tell us what you see on the backing of the canvas."

"A broad blood smear," Lestrade reported.

"From Edmunds's hand, no doubt," Joanna added.

"Which indicates he reached in and could not find the masterpiece, so he moved his hand around, searching, in the event the prized painting was hidden off to the side."

"*Masterpiece* is the key word here, Inspector. Harry Edmunds was an experienced restorer and knew all about ancient, fragile works of art. Even in his haste, he would never smear blood about the inner canvas in such a casual fashion. Thus, I think it fair to say he reached in and, finding nothing, left a large blood smear behind, which has a fingerprint or two embedded in it."

"And so he will strike yet again," Lestrade concluded.

Joanna nodded in agreement. "He is now truly desperate because of a lack of funds, and the only person he can turn to is his wife. You would be wise to keep a most careful eye on Charlotte Edmunds."

"We have her under surveillance day and night."

My father interjected, "It is unfortunate that you had to release her on bail."

"Actually I preferred it," Lestrade said. "Were she in jail, her husband would never dare to contact her. On the outside, he might well chance it. For that very reason, I have two of our best men surveilling her. If she chooses to sneeze, one of our watchers could hand her a handkerchief."

"Do you have female police officers at Scotland Yard?" Joanna asked.

"We do indeed," Lestrade replied. "Most are matrons, but we have several female officers who I must say are working out splendidly."

"Then I would assign one to the surveillance team, for Harry and Charlotte Edmunds are a most clever pair."

"But what purpose would the addition of a female surveillance officer serve?" Lestrade asked.

"If Charlotte wishes to transfer funds to her husband, she might accomplish the act in a public lavatory reserved for women. Harry of course would have entered wearing an appropriate disguise."

"Do you truly believe they are that clever?"

"A man who can burn his cellmate into an unrecognizable char and take his place for early discharge is beyond clever."

I had to smile to myself as I remembered one of Joanna's cardinal rules which was said to also be used by her father, Sherlock Holmes. In order to catch a cunning criminal, you must think like one.

"Are you not convinced that you discovered all of the cash caches that Charlotte Edmunds had hidden away?" asked Lestrade.

"We found only those tainted by the aroma of coal tar," Joanna answered. "There may be others."

"Indeed," Lestrade said and began to depart, then abruptly turned to us. "In all the turmoil and excitement, I neglected to give you a most important piece of information. We have uncovered the whereabouts of the mysterious David Hughes."

We moved in closer so as not to miss a word, for here was a missing link that could throw light on our most puzzling case.

"On further examination of the fireplace where the corpse was stored away, we found a hammer which was no doubt used to break bones and inflict torture. A fingerprint was gotten off the handle of the hammer and was shown to belong to one David Hughes, a nasty piece of work from Liverpool. His record revealed multiple arrests, with conviction for assault with a deadly weapon, for which he was imprisoned at Wormwood Scrubs. He was known to be friends with Harry Edmunds in that they served their time in adjoining cells. He was released a month prior to Edmunds's escape. What is equally as interesting is that Hughes was a jack-of-all-trades and worked as a stonemason before turning to crime."

"So it was he, along with Edmunds, who bricked in the fireplace," said I.

"And fingerprints on the bricks and tools revealed that both participated in the torture," Lestrade added. "We also have a third set of fingerprints on two bricks that are proving difficult to identify."

The third man! I thought to myself. Joanna had predicted that it would require a threesome to stuff the large corpse into the relatively small fireplace.

"In any event, all of England was searching for this man, for yet another brutal assault, but with little success," Lestrade continued on. "Then good fortune came our way. The Australian police, who were also on the lookout for David Hughes, reported that he was killed in a bar fight outside Adelaide."

"Thus he did in fact use James Blackstone's ticket to Australia after all," said Joanna. "And I suspect that the ticket was payment to Hughes for his participation in the torture of Blackstone."

Lestrade sighed resignedly. "All no doubt true, but I am afraid this brings us no closer to the apprehension of Harry Edmunds."

We bade Lestrade farewell and departed the elegant but sad home of Sir Charles Cromwell, where a most unhappy tragedy was unfolding. Our mood was somber, for despite an abundance of clues Harry Edmunds remained on the loose and was sure to strike again and perhaps bring even more violence with him. But as our four-wheeler approached Hyde Park, Joanna abruptly sat up in her seat.

"I almost missed it!" she proclaimed. "And it was right before my eyes!"

"What?" I asked quickly.

"The most important clue!"

"Which is?"

"Botticelli's painting with the faded angels that required restoration."

My father and I exchanged puzzled glances, for we had no idea of their significance. How could one relate Botticelli's angels to the vandalism incurred by Harry Edmunds?

"Think!" Joanna encouraged. "In addition to the faded angels, what was so curious about the painting?"

We had no answer.

"There was *no* female portrait," Joanna said, now gleefully rubbing her hands together. "It showed only Saint Francis and the angels."

"And what does that tell us?" my father asked.

"Everything," Joanna replied. "Now we only require one more piece of information to end Harry Edmunds's rampage through the west side of London."

"Who will provide this information, pray tell?"

"The Countess of Wessex," said Joanna and, using my father's walking stick, rapped impatiently on the roof of our four-wheeler. "Faster, driver!"

25

Setting a Trap

But alas, the Countess of Wessex was not at home to receive our phone call. She was away for the day visiting the Royal Art Collection at Windsor, and would not return until late afternoon. Joanna showed no disappointment in the delay. Quite to the contrary, she seemed quite pleased with it.

"For you see, Windsor holds the key to our mystery," she said.

"You will have to explain this connection to us, Joanna," my father implored. "For we do not see this key you continually refer to."

"First, it must be determined if my assumptions are correct," Joanna replied. "If the countess confirms my beliefs, then all will become clear. But for now, we should concern ourselves with what we know to be fact."

"Where should we begin?" I asked.

"With the discovery of the masterpiece, which beyond any doubt was found at Hawke and Evans by James Blackstone," said Joanna. "After uncovering the masterpiece,

Blackstone brought Edmunds in as a partner for unknown reasons."

"Perhaps because they were already partners from selling their forgeries on the black market," I suggested.

"Or perhaps because Edmunds was far more familiar with dealings on the black market," my father proposed.

"All distinct possibilities, but difficult to prove at this juncture," said Joanna. "In any event, once the masterpiece was uncovered, the restorers decided initially to keep it for themselves. Now here is where Harry Edmunds no doubt plays an important role, for he and his wife frequent the Angel pub which is owned and operated by the Morrison family who are key figures in London's underworld and will serve as middlemen for the sale of the masterpiece. But shortly thereafter, the picture becomes somewhat murky in that the partnership comes apart, and Blackstone decides to hide the da Vinci painting behind yet another undisclosed painting without informing Edmunds. I cannot help but wonder if Blackstone had a change of heart and wanted to return the masterpiece to its rightful owner for a substantial reward which they would all share in."

"Which would be a pittance when compared to what the da Vinci would fetch on the black market," I noted.

"Edmunds of course would have no part of this honorable act, and had Blackstone tortured in an effort to pry the location of the masterpiece from him," my father concluded.

"Which brings David Hughes onto the scene," Joanna went on. "From what we know, Harry Edmunds does not have this type of violent past, and thus needed someone with such a history to do the torturing for him."

"But there was a vicious side to Harry Edmunds," my

father remarked. "He stabbed a security guard at Hawke and Evans and brutally beat Sir Charles's son. In addition, he killed his cellmate to gain early release from prison."

"The latter was done out of desperation and did not require hands-on torturing that can only be done by the most cruel of men, which Edmunds is not," Joanna argued. "In the first two instances, I believe he was acting in self-defense. The lad's head struck the marble floor after he was shoved away or fell after he was hit by Edmunds. The security guard, like Cromwell's rottweiler, was stabbed only in the heat of battle. So, in all likelihood, Edmunds knew of Hughes's extreme viciousness from the time they spent together at Wormwood Scrubs, and wished to take advantage of it."

"Do you believe Hughes assisted Edmunds in the fiery death of Derrick Wilson?" I asked.

"An interesting possibility, and one I had not thought of," Joanna said, with a thin smile.

"Using your criminal instincts, how would Hughes lend a hand in burning Wilson to a char?" my father queried.

Joanna pondered the question for a few moments before answering. "He could participate in a number of ways, but the most likely scenario goes as follows. While Edmunds was concocting a batch of solvent, Hughes, who was some distance away, either handed or somewhat attached a lighted cigarette to Derrick Wilson who then unwittingly walked over to the open container of solvent which Edmunds had now deserted. And boom!"

"It would be interesting to determine if Hughes had a history of arson," my father wondered.

"We should ask Lestrade," Joanna said, then continued on. "So now Edmunds was free and contacted Hughes at some predetermined place. They plan and carry out the gruesome torture of Blackstone who, despite the agonizing pain, refused to disclose the location of the hidden masterpiece, which should surely fetch a fortune."

"Of which David Hughes would never see a farthing," I predicted.

"Of course not," Joanna concurred. "There was no need to inform Hughes of the masterpiece."

"So Hughes was paid with Blackstone's ticket to Australia and went on his way, never knowing of the fortune he was missing out on."

"Leaving Edmunds behind to search for the concealed masterpiece."

"Which accounts for him slashing all those wonderful works of art on the west side of London."

"But why did he initially slash only those paintings that featured a portrait of a woman?" I asked.

"Here I am guessing, but I think it is a quite good guess based on the clues we have uncovered," Joanna replied. "I believe Blackstone finally broke under the intolerable pain and gave them an incorrect answer to stop the pain."

"He told Edmunds the masterpiece was hidden behind a woman's portrait!" I exclaimed.

"My thought exactly," Joanna said. "Now that Edmunds had the information, he had Blackstone killed and went on his wild-goose chase. Edmunds only learned of this misinformation when he slashed open the last of the female portraits which had been restored at Hawke and Evans. Then he began with the other paintings on the list, the first of which was Botticelli's *Saint Francis of Assisi with Angels*."

"Was there a reason he began with the Botticelli?" my father asked.

"Of that I cannot be certain," Joanna replied. "But I suspect it was the first one Blackstone restored within the time period that the masterpiece was discovered."

"This Harry Edmunds is no fool by any measure."

"Indeed, for now he is thinking much as we do, which indicates we do not have a moment to lose."

The phone rang and Joanna hurried to answer it. She smiled to us upon learning who was calling.

"Ah, Countess, how good of you to call," Joanna greeted. "I trust your journey to Windsor was a success."

Joanna listened patiently and responded intermittently with, "Yes . . . Yes, of course . . . Not too tiring then . . . Well, I am delighted with your early return, for we have need of your expertise on the Royal Art Collection . . . I am interested in all their paintings that were restored by Hawke and Evans over the past year or so. . . . Yes, yes, all of them, please. . . . To what end? . . . The apprehension of the art vandal of course. . . . Should we visit you, then? . . . Oh, that would be quite excellent. We shall look forward to your arrival."

Joanna placed the phone down and quickly looked over to us. "Ha! Let us prepare for the countess. I will ask you two to fetch the blackboard and chalk that are gathering dust in our storage room. While you are away, I will collect all of our notes from Hawke and Evans."

My father and I hurried to the storage room which was situated down the hall just beyond the staircase. We opened the door and entered what appeared to be a museum dedicated to Sherlock Holmes. There were dust-covered boxes and files stacked up against the wall, some with the Great Detective's scribbled notes written upon them. On a rectangular table lay racks of test tubes and flasks and petri dishes whose contents had dried out long ago. Against the far wall was a blackboard, with several boxes of white chalk nearby. But what held my attention was the blackboard itself, for jotted upon it were the words *Moriarty, Lestrade, Gregson,* and *Mycroft at the Diogenes Club.* It was a journey into the past, and in my father's eyes I could see the memories flashing by.

"Who was Gregson?" I asked.

"An inspector at Scotland Yard who, along with Lestrade, Holmes thought was the best of the lot," my father replied.

"And this is Mycroft who was Sherlock Holmes's brother and long believed to be his only living relative."

"Before Joanna and young Johnny appeared."

"What price would you pay to overhear a conversation between Joanna and her father, Sherlock?"

"Any amount you name."

We moved the blackboard and boxes of chalk into the hall where we encountered Miss Hudson who gave us a somewhat disconcerting look.

"I would have gotten the blackboard for you, Dr. Watson," said she.

"We did not wish to bother you," my father offered as an excuse.

"It would have been no bother at all, Dr. Watson. None in the least."

"You are always more than helpful, and next time I will be sure to call upon your excellent service. But in the meantime I have one small task for you to attend to."

"Of course, sir."

"Shortly, we will be visited by the Countess of Wessex. Please show her up immediately."

Miss Hudson performed a slight curtsy, as if the countess was already in her presence. "I—I shall await her arrival."

"Thank you, Miss Hudson."

We wheeled the blackboard into our parlor and positioned it in the center of the room. Joanna briefly studied the names written upon it and, without showing even a hint of sentimentality, wiped it clean with a damp cloth.

"I have once again gone over the list of paintings restored at Hawke and Evans for the entire year prior to the forgers' arrest. A total of fifty-five were done, thirty by Edmunds, twenty-five by Blackstone. Obviously, we should concentrate on those restored by the latter. Of the twenty-five attributed to Blackstone, fifteen have already been vandalized. Thus, there are only ten remaining and one of those holds the concealed masterpiece. We must choose which."

"How do we go about making that selection?" asked I.

"By the process of elimination," Joanna replied. "Please write the names of the artists on the blackboard as I call them out."

"Should we list their paintings as well?" I queried.

"There is no need at this point." Joanna referred to her notes and began reciting the names of the artists. "Bellini—Tintoretto—Titian—del Verrocchio—Veronese—Renoir—Pissarro—Botticelli—Caravaggio—Degas."

She studied the list at length before turning to my father. "Now, Watson, I would like you to fetch our thick volume on Italian Renaissance painters and study their paintings as I call them out. In particular, I wish to know if the given work of art has angels in the background."

Joanna waited for my father to open the volume and began naming the artists and their paintings that were on the list.

"*Drunkenness of Noah* by Bellini," she called.

My father rapidly turned pages of the volume and, finding the correct painting, replied, "No angels."

"*Muse with Lute* by Tintoretto."

After thumbing through more pages, my father responded, "No angels."

"Botticelli's *Saint Francis of Assisi with Angels*."

"Multiple angels."

"Caravaggio's *The Entombment of Christ*."

"No angels."

"*Mars and Neptune* by Veronese."

"Multiple angels flying overhead and clearly visible."

Joanna again referred to her notes. "There is no mention of whether these angels required restoration."

"Is that important?" my father asked.

"Very, if my assumptions are correct," Joanna replied and requested I underline the artist Veronese. "Last on the list is del Verrocchio's *The Baptism of Christ* which we know had its angels beautifully restored, so underline his name as well. Thus, we have now narrowed it down to three."

My father inquired, "What of Renoir, Pissarro, and Degas?"

Joanna dismissed those artists with a flick of her wrist. "The French impressionists never once painted an angel, which allows us to concentrate on Veronese, del Verrocchio, and Botticelli."

"How can we possibly separate these three?" I asked.

"By their birthdays hopefully," answered Joanna. "Now, Watson, please recite for us the dates of their births and deaths. And if you will, John, write these dates next to the artist's name."

My father began his recitation and, after each name, waited for me to copy down the dates on the blackboard.

Veronese	1528–1588
del Verrocchio	1435–1488
Botticelli	1445–1510

"Excellent," said Joanna. "Please now do the same for Leonardo da Vinci."

I quickly jotted down the dates for the world's most famous artist.

Born 1452, died 1519.

Joanna studied the dates carefully before commenting, "The timelines do not work for Veronese, but they do for del Verrocchio and Botticelli."

"Which timelines are you referring to?" I asked.

"The ones that will show an association of some sort between Leonardo da Vinci and the three artists," Joanna replied. "Da Vinci died before Veronese was born, so they never came in contact, which leaves us with del Verrocchio and Botticelli as the artists who painted angels."

"Why all the emphasis on angels?" my father inquired.

"Because I firmly believe they will lead us to the hidden masterpiece," Joanna replied.

"Based on what evidence?"

"Three most important clues which have now come to light," Joanna disclosed. "These included the restored paintings of del Verrocchio and Botticelli, and the cryptic puzzle James Blackstone gave to Edwin Alan Rowe, which reads Angels to a Perfect Angel. When these three are aligned in the correct order, they will point to the masterpiece."

"And how do we establish the correct order?"

"With the assistance of the Countess of Wessex."

As if on cue, there was a soft rap on the door, and Miss Hudson, performing another half curtsy, showed the Countess of Wessex in and departed, quiet as a church mouse.

"Thank you for coming so promptly," Joanna greeted.

"I did not wish to miss the opportunity to meet the daughter of Sherlock Holmes," said the countess, giving my father and me cordial nods.

"And I, you," Joanna replied warmly.

"I take it the gathering has to do with the scoundrel who ruined my Veronese," said Lady Katherine.

"It does indeed, for I believe he is now within our grasp."

"I would not be displeased to see him hanged, particularly after what he did to the Cromwell lad."

"You have heard the unpleasant details, then."

"His mother and I are close friends," the countess informed. "And our sons are quite close as well."

"Then you should be most interested in bringing the perpetrator to justice."

"I would gladly do whatever is within my power," the countess vowed, as her eyes went to our chalked blackboard. "You have a very impressive list here."

"Are you familiar with them?"

"Quite so, particularly the Caravaggio, del Verrocchio, and Botticelli, for they are part of the Royal Collection at Windsor."

"And that is the reason I have asked you here, for one of these paintings holds a concealed masterpiece."

"Masterpiece?" Lady Katherine asked skeptically. "What sort of masterpiece?"

"One from the Italian Renaissance."

Lady Katherine's eyes widened. "How did you come by this information?"

"By deduction, which I shall clarify later," Joanna responded, then went on. "I believe this masterpiece is concealed beneath either the del Verrocchio or the Botticelli."

"And exactly what brings you to this conclusion, may I ask?"

"The presence of angels in their paintings."

"No, no," the countess objected at once. "There is a work by Caravaggio in the Royal Collection entitled *Saint Matthew and the Angel* which clearly depicts an angel."

"Was this painting ever restored by Hawke and Evans?"

"Never."

"Then we can discard its significance here." Joanna dismissed the Caravaggio. "So let us concentrate on the works by Botticelli and del Verrocchio. Please be so kind as to summarize your knowledge of these two artists."

"I shall start with Botticelli, for he was in a way connected to del Verrocchio," the countess began. "Sandro Botticelli was an esteemed Florentine artist whose paintings were revered during his lifetime, but his posthumous reputation suffered until the nineteenth century. His works are now seen to represent the linear grace of the Early Renaissance paintings. By far, *The Birth of Venus* is considered to be his greatest work, and by a few to be a masterpiece. Nonetheless, the glory of his works was pushed aside by the arrival of other Renaissance artists, such as Michelangelo and Leonardo da Vinci."

"So even Sandro Botticelli's *The Birth of Venus* was downgraded?"

"It was a fine work, but one that did not measure up to those painted by the Great Masters."

"You mentioned that Botticelli's works were pushed aside by Leonardo da Vinci," Joanna probed. "Were they competitive?"

"More like close friends, it is believed, for both studied under the tutelage of Andrea del Verrocchio," Lady Katherine replied. "There is an interesting story that involved all three men. Del Verrocchio admired both Botticelli and da Vinci, although he considered Leonardo to be the more talented. Yet he still wanted to compare the two side by side. So while del Verrocchio was painting *The Baptism of Christ,* he asked da Vinci to paint one angel and Botticelli the other. Both angels were quite good, but Leonardo da Vinci's was beyond magnificent. It was so very excellent that it is now referred to as the perfect angel."

Joanna smiled to herself. "Perfect angel, you say?"

"So it was called, and justifiably so."

"I have heard the term used before by Edwin Alan Rowe. Do you know him?"

"Quite well, for he is a fine art historian."

"Does his knowledge of Italian Renaissance art equal yours?"

"It would be a most interesting contest," replied the countess. "But pray tell, in what contact did he mention the perfect angel?"

"A riddle that was presented to him by his close friend, James Blackstone, just prior to Blackstone's death," Joanna responded. "It was a game they played in an effort to outwit one another. The riddle was Angels to a Perfect Angel."

The countess considered the brainteaser at length before saying, "No answer comes to mind immediately."

"What if I mentioned that there were angels in the most recently vandalized *Saint Francis of Assisi with Angels,* which required restoration at Hawke and Evans?"

"I trust you are not under the impression that they also were perfect angels."

"No, I am not," said Joanna before giving another hint. "They were the angels leading to the perfect angel. And of course the perfect angel can lead to only one man."

Lady Katherine's jaw dropped as the answer came to her. "Is there a da Vinci behind it?" she asked breathlessly.

"You are almost there," Joanna prompted. "Please keep in mind that over the past year James Blackstone restored only two paintings that contained angels. These were del Verrocchio's *The Baptism of Christ* and Botticelli's *Saint Francis of Assisi with Angels,* and both can fit into the equation we are attempting to solve."

The countess nodded quickly to the obvious solution. "That is why the vandal sliced open Cromwell's *Saint Francis of Assisi*. He believed the masterpiece was behind it."

"But it wasn't," said Joanna. "And that leaves us with which painting?"

"*The Baptism of Christ!*"

"Yes."

"But which of da Vinci's masterpieces is hidden away?"

"That is to be determined," Joanna replied. "But if one connects all the dots, it is a work of art done by Leonardo da Vinci during his early years while a student in del Verrocchio's workshop where he worked closely with Sandro Botticelli."

"It fits!" the countess said gleefully. "It fits perfectly!"

"Which brings forth yet another question, which is why did da Vinci feel the need to conceal it?" asked Joanna.

"I can think of a number of reasons," Lady Katherine replied, as a most serious expression crossed her face. "Most likely he hid it so that del Verrocchio could not see it and demand to participate in the work. Remember at this point the mentor may have recognized da Vinci's genius and sought to be part of it."

"Particularly after del Verrocchio had seen da Vinci's magnificent angel in *The Baptism of Christ,*" Joanna added.

"Precisely so," the countess said, then went on. "Another possibility is that the work was incomplete and one that da Vinci planned to finish once he left del Verrocchio and became independent."

"It must have been something very special to Leonardo da Vinci," Joanna remarked. "And one cannot even begin to imagine what that might be."

"Indeed," the countess agreed. "But, as fascinating as all this appears to be, there is no absolute proof for your conclusion which is based entirely on supposition."

"No, Countess, it is based on far more than supposition, for there is now word spreading through London's black market that a da Vinci masterpiece will soon be offered for sale."

Lady Katherine uttered a sigh of pure delight. "A hidden da Vinci masterpiece that has not seen the light of day for over five hundred years. It will be the Holy Grail of the art world."

"But I shall need your assistance to recover it, for the restored *The Baptism of Christ* has now been returned to Windsor," said Joanna.

Lady Katherine shook her head gently. "It is not currently at Windsor, but on display at the National Gallery, along with other works from the Royal Collection."

"Hmm," Joanna mused to herself while she pondered the situation.

"Does that present a problem?"

"No, Lady Katherine, it presents an opportunity."

"How so?"

"Do you have influence at the National Gallery?"

"I should think so, in that I sit on their Board of Trustees."

"Excellent!" Joanna cried out. "For it will require your influence to help set the trap to apprehend the scoundrel who ruined your Veronese."

"And who brought young Cromwell to the brink of death," the countess said bitterly.

"That, too."

"Tell me precisely what you want done."

26

The National Gallery

"I am afraid Harry Edmunds is on to us," whispered Lestrade.

"Why so?" Joanna whispered back.

"Because he has not shown," Lestrade replied. "And this was the very last day the paintings from the Royal Collection will be on display here at the National Gallery. Tomorrow all of them will be returned to the security of Windsor Castle."

"He is waiting," Joanna insisted.

"For what, pray tell?"

"For tomorrow to come."

Lestrade furrowed his forehead, making a show of thought. "Tomorrow is the day before Christmas. Other than it heralds Christmas Eve, no one places great significance on that date."

"You do if you are Harry Edmunds."

"Why so?"

"Because it is his wife's birthday," Joanna answered. "It is the special day Edmunds wrote about in the last letter to his wife."

"Are you predicting his actions on that basis alone?" asked Lestrade.

"That, together with everything else," Joanna replied.

"You will recall that Charlotte Edmunds was followed by your surveillance team to Trafalgar Square to join the tourists and feed the pigeons. Now, how many Londoners are you aware of that travel to the square to feed those annoying birds?"

"Virtually none," Lestrade had to admit.

"Which leads to the conclusion she was there on a reconnaissance mission for her husband."

"Quite possibly," Lestrade agreed. "But she entered the gallery and stayed for only a few minutes. She could not have obtained much information in such a brief visit."

"That depends on what her mission was."

"Which was?"

"To locate the exact location of the display, so that her dear Harry would not flounder around in the dark, searching for del Verrocchio's *The Baptism of Christ*."

"Very clever," Lestrade conceded.

"Then she strolled over to Leicester Square for a bit of lunch," Joanna continued.

"No law against that."

"It is if the restaurant is on Irving Street and overlooks the rear entrance to the National Gallery."

Lestrade nodded slowly. "Which would be Harry Edmunds's way in and out of the gallery. If, of course, all of your assumptions are correct."

"They are," Joanna asserted. "But the big *if* here, Lestrade, is whether the clever Charlotte Edmunds was able to detect your surveillance team. For if she did, Harry would not dare to attempt a break-in."

"So there is a distinct possibility that Edmunds will not show," Lestrade said sourly.

"Do not underestimate him, Inspector," Joanna cautioned. "For he is quite resourceful, and when the prize is great enough, greedy men will go to any lengths to obtain it."

So we continued to wait in a small room off the main gallery, with our ears pricked for any sound that came from the dead-silent museum. As the minutes ticked by, all of us, with the exception of Joanna, became less confident that Harry Edmunds would make his move on that cold, snowy December night. But then again, this would be his last, best chance to possess a prize beyond prizes. But what was this masterpiece by Leonardo da Vinci? The three of us had debated the possibilities over a bottle of Napoleon brandy the night before. I had no worthwhile idea, while Joanna and my father decided it was most likely a self-portrait of da Vinci as a young man which he had hidden to conceal his overwhelming hubris. It would also explain why he gave it no title, for self-portraits name themselves. But this possibility was discarded when Joanna referred to our volume of Italian Renaissance artists and discovered that Leonardo da Vinci had indeed painted a self-portrait in red chalk that was now held by a museum in Turin. Through the thick walls of the National Gallery we could hear the strains of "Silent Night" being played on the massive organ in nearby St. Martin-in-the-Field. It was the oddest of background music to accompany a trap for a murderous villain, I thought, for there was nothing holy in what was about to transpire.

Big Ben began to strike the midnight hour and our hopes faded further. Could it be that Edmunds had resisted the irresistible bait which Joanna had laid out? With the assistance of the Countess of Wessex, Joanna had articles placed in London's widely read newspapers that described the display at the National Gallery in detail, with emphasis on *The Baptism of Christ* by Andrea del Verrocchio, the mentor of Leonardo da Vinci. The articles urged readers to see the one and only display, for it would shortly be returned to the safekeeping of the Crown. Certainly, if Edmunds and his wife were made aware that the paintings were about to be removed from the gallery, they would be enticed to act quickly. Yet there were too many *ifs*, I thought to myself. *If this* and *if that*. And one did not catch a master criminal depending on *ifs*.

Big Ben struck the last number of the hour and the stone-cold silence returned to the gallery. Then we heard it. From a distance within the museum came a muffled sound. We pressed our ears against a large door and held our breaths, so as not to make any interfering noises. The sound reached us again, this time a little louder and then a little louder. It was approaching footsteps! As planned, we moved quickly back from the door on tiptoes, then waited in silence. The footsteps passed by us, heading in the direction of the display some thirty feet away. Quietly, my father and Lestrade checked their service revolvers.

"If you must return fire, please aim low," Joanna whispered to them. "We do not wish to ruin the del Verrocchio."

Lestrade noiselessly turned the doorknob and cracked open the door. The display area was every bit as dark as our observation room, yet we could still see a shadow moving in the dimness. The inspector had instructed us beforehand that no action should be undertaken until Edmunds was stationary, at which time he could be stunned and captured with greater ease. Lestrade held up his weaponless hand, signaling us to wait and remain silent. The footsteps had ceased now, and were replaced by a sound that resembled scratches which indicated Edmunds was in the process of dislodging del Verrocchio's *The Baptism of Christ* from the wall.

Lestrade flung the door open and directed his lightened torch at the intruder, temporarily blinding him.

"You are advised not to move, Mr. Harry Edmunds, for if you do, you will be shot!"

A shocked Edmunds dropped the painting that was in his outstretched hands and suddenly turned to bolt, but before he could take a step three Scotland Yard officers were upon him, pinning him to the floor and covering his mouth so he could not cry out.

We hurried over to the subdued Harry Edmunds who had been so very elusive. He was now being brought to his feet while handcuffs were tightly applied. As expected, he was quite thin from lack of adequate nourishment and still wore the beard he had grown to disguise himself as Derrick Wilson. By all appearances, he seemed to be rather timid, with a narrow, ferret-like face and darting, dark eyes that seemed to be searching for a way out. But his most remarkable feature was the intense aroma of coal tar that virtually engulfed him.

"How?" he asked in a monosyllabic tone.

"Toes," Joanna responded.

"What do you mean, *toes*?"

"You are missing one, the charred body had all ten, and thus the corpse could not be you."

"Toes," Edmunds groaned unhappily.

"And of course Derrick Wilson had a disfigured cheekbone which the corpse displayed, but you are lacking," Joanna went on. "You should have thought of these features before you murdered him."

"He died in an explosion due to his own carelessness," Edmunds said defensively.

"A court will decide otherwise, and you will soon have a date with the hangman." Joanna leaned down and picked up *The Baptism of Christ* by del Verrocchio. She held it close to Lestrade's torch and commented, "Look at how beautiful it is! Look at the perfect angel painted by Leonardo da Vinci."

"Magnificent indeed," Lestrade agreed, and reached for the painting. "Now let us return it to its proper place."

"Not quite yet, Inspector, for the del Verrocchio has one last service to perform," said Joanna. "Follow me, if you will, but remain a good ten feet behind."

"Shall I have the lights in the gallery turned on?" Lestrade offered.

"No, for now we need them off," Joanna replied. "Please direct your torch to the floor as we proceed."

In the dimness, we followed Joanna and walked past some of the world's greatest art including paintings by Raphael, Titian, and Tintoretto, and just beyond them the magnificent works of Rembrandt, Rubens, and Caravaggio. Finally, we turned sharply and hurried down a long corridor which led to the back entrance of the gallery.

"What lies ahead?" Lestrade asked.

"The mastermind," Joanna replied.

She opened the rear door and, after motioning us to stay behind, walked out into the cold night air and over to a waiting carriage.

In the darkness, she opened the carriage door and handed the painting to a shadowed individual.

"Ah, you have it!" said he.

"Yes, Mr. Simon Hawke, I have it and I have you," Joanna responded.

"I—I don't know what you are speaking of," Hawke stammered, stunned and caught completely off guard.

"Oh, to the contrary, you know everything, Simon Hawke, for you are the mastermind behind this entire criminal enterprise."

"You have no evidence."

"I have all the evidence, and it is more than enough to assure you have a slow walk to the gallows awaiting you."

"I shall call my barrister immediately, and he will point out you have neither the power nor authority to arrest me."

"But I can assure you Scotland Yard does," said Joanna and opened the carriage door farther, so Hawke could clearly see Lestrade and two of his officers approaching.

27

The Masterpiece

Rather than wait until later in the morning, our excitement was so great we decided to send for Giuseppe Delvecchio and allow him the honor of unveiling Leonardo da Vinci's masterpiece. Lestrade had earlier dispatched automobiles for the Countess of Wessex and Edwin Alan Rowe, to show his appreciation for their assistance in solving the mystery of the art vandal. As we awaited the arrival of the restorer, each of us took turns guessing what the masterpiece might be. Lestrade held no opinion, while Joanna, my father, and I stood by our prediction made late last night that da Vinci had decided to paint a greatly enlarged, perfect angel which he could take full credit for. This opinion would fit the riddle, Angels to a Perfect Angel. Rowe and the countess, however, had other ideas.

"I think it most likely is a self-portrait," said Rowe. "All of the Great Masters, including Michelangelo and Raphael, left behind paintings of themselves."

"But there is already a self-portrait of da Vinci in existence," Lady Katherine argued. "I saw it myself at a museum in Turin."

"True enough, Countess," said Rowe. "But that portrait was drawn in red chalk and depicts da Vinci as an old man since it was done in 1512, seven years before his death. I would propose the hidden masterpiece showed da Vinci as a young man while he was still a student in del Verrocchio's workshop."

"But why then would he conceal it?" asked the countess.

"Modesty perhaps, as this work would have been accomplished prior to his fame," Rowe replied. "I would suggest the portrait of the young da Vinci was painted in oil rather than chalk, which of course would make it even more valuable and more likely to last."

"A good choice, then," said the countess. "But I have yet another opinion. I believe it is a portrait of his mentor, Andrea del Verrocchio, with whom da Vinci was very close. Da Vinci may have felt he owed his mentor a great debt, for many believe he considered del Verrocchio a father figure."

"But again, why hide it?" asked Rowe.

Lady Katherine shrugged. "Perhaps it was to be a gift later on, or perhaps their relationship soured. Who is to know, for we are all guessing." The countess's face suddenly hardened. "But I will tell you what is not a guess, and that is Simon Hawke's role in this dastardly affair. To steal is one thing, to be involved in murder is quite another. I would have never suspected that. Never! But then again, maybe his overwhelming debts got the best of him."

"What debts in particular, madam?" Lestrade asked at once.

"There is a long list, including a young but very expensive mistress and large gambling debts which required him to borrow at high interest rates from some rather unseemly characters. You see, his credit at the banks had already been overextended," Lady Katherine reeled off. "Then there were the misguided purchases of various paintings, for which he greatly overpaid. His former partner, Andrew Evans, would have never done so."

Giuseppe Delvecchio overheard the latter portion of the conversation as he approached, and confirmed the countess's opinion. "Although he believed otherwise, Simon Hawke did not have a keen eye when it came to fine art, and for this reason he overpaid and later was forced to undersell. And I should say his integrity was not at the highest level. He did not hesitate to deal in works of questionable ownership."

"Did he have a hand in stolen paintings?" Lestrade asked quickly.

"I did not say that."

But all in the room knew he did, particularly Lestrade who gave the restorer a most skeptical look. At that moment I recalled Joanna once telling me that to Scotland Yard all art dealers were thought to be guilty of something.

"So I think it is fair to say that Simon Hawke was not the most honorable of purveyors," my father concluded.

"That description is more than charitable, Dr. Watson," Lady Katherine said, making no attempt to hide her contempt for the art dealer.

"Well, then," Lestrade said impatiently, "let us get down to the delicate task we face. Mr. Delvecchio, please proceed."

Delvecchio approached *The Baptism of Christ* by Andrea del Verrocchio with slow, deliberate steps, obviously in awe of the great mentor's work and even more in awe of what lay behind it. "If a da Vinci rests beneath the canvas, it is very, very old and in all likelihood very fragile. So we must be most careful."

"Perhaps it has been protected through all the years by the thick canvas that lies atop it," Lady Katherine hoped.

"No canvas, no matter how thick, can protect for five hundred years," Rowe said.

"We shall see." Delvecchio reached up for the painting and ever so gently placed it facedown on a nearby padded table. Opening a leather tool kit, he extracted a small, chisel-like instrument and a pair of thin pliers, and began to disassemble the frame which held the masterpiece. Once the outer frame was removed, we could see that the stretched canvas was firmly attached to its backing. Delvecchio stepped back and took a deep breath, as if gathering himself for the momentous event that was in his hands and about to occur. With the greatest of care, he slowly pulled out each fastener until the del Verrocchio was freed from its backing. He then stood the painting in a vertical position on the padded table and studied its top at length.

Taking another deep breath, he moved back and used his forearm to wipe the beads of perspiration from his brow. We had been forewarned by Rowe that the removal of the del Verrocchio's canvas to reveal whatever lay beneath it was by far the most dangerous aspect of the procedure. One wrong move could damage or even ruin the del Verrocchio as well as the masterpiece it covered. Of course we would all be responsible should such a tragic event occur, but the majority of the blame would fall on Delvecchio's shoulders.

With a slow, deliberate motion, Delvecchio began to peel back the top of the canvas. At first, we saw only a gray background, but then dark hair with a gentle part in it appeared.

"It is a da Vinci," Delvecchio said breathlessly. "The technique is his. He used metalpoint which involved drawing with a silver stylus and always with iron gall ink."

"Do you know what it is?" Lady Katherine asked anxiously.

"I think . . . I think . . ." It was as if Delvecchio couldn't find the words. Swallowing audibly, he returned to the task of gently and meticulously stripping away the del Verrocchio canvas.

Now we could see the broad forehead and dangling dark hair. Then came the beautiful eyes and the perfectly proportioned nose, and finally we saw the captivating, enigmatic smile.

It was an enchanting portrait of the woman who would later serve as the model for Leonardo da Vinci's most famous work of art.

It was the original *Mona Lisa*.

28

All the Evidence

After the unveiling, the ever-resourceful Countess of Wessex arranged for the National Gallery's cafeteria to be opened in the early morning hours and for deliciously brewed Earl Grey tea to be served all around. No one was anxious to leave, for the da Vinci masterpiece continued to captivate and mesmerize every one of us. Moreover, there were tantalizing questions remaining, which would only be answered by Joanna.

"What was your first inkling that revealed Simon Hawke was so deeply involved?" asked Lestrade.

"The bricks," Joanna said simply. "Were you not impressed by the high brick wall in the restoration area that nearly reached the ceiling? Was such a wall truly needed, only to enclose a central heating unit? And why were all the fireplaces bricked off?"

"To prevent heat loss," Lestrade replied.

"Pshaw! Here is a man deeply in debt, yet he spends money unnecessarily to block off fireplaces and builds an unneeded, high brick wall. The prevention of heat loss could have easily been accomplished by sealing off the chimney which was no longer in use. These measures were put in place to conceal something, not to keep in the heat."

"That something being the corpse of James Blackstone," my father added. "It was a convenient way to dispose of the body."

"Yes, but at the time we had no clues to tell us what was hidden behind those bricks," Joanna went on. "It was later we learned of Delvecchio's usually quiet dog barking and frantically pawing at the bricked-in fireplace. You see, dogs are greatly attracted to the scent of a carcass which was so powerful it eventually seeped through the bricks, as evidenced by the temporary foul odor in the restoration room."

"Which was attributed to a bird or squirrel that had become trapped and died in the chimney," Lestrade recalled.

"A convenient excuse, but no small carcass would ever generate a stench so lasting and intense that it required a fireplace be sealed off," Joanna countered. "That of course indicated we were dealing with a much larger carcass, such as a human corpse. Which brings us to how the corpse found its way into the fireplace."

"Why, it was stuffed in," said I.

"By whom?" asked Joanna.

"Harry Edmunds and David Hughes."

"A two-man effort, then?"

"I would think, although I know you favor a third individual being involved."

"You should as well, when you factor in we are dealing with a relatively small fireplace and a large, well-built corpse that measured nearly six feet."

Lestrade interjected, "The opening of the fireplace was just over three feet according to the crime report."

I gave the circumstances more thought and concluded, "It would have been a most difficult task for only two men to do the deed."

"If not impossible," said Joanna. "It requires three to properly stuff the corpse not only in, but up a small fireplace—one to guide in the head and shoulders, a second to support the heavy torso, and a third to hold the thick legs up and push forward. Now, who would that third person be?"

"Simon Hawke," I replied.

"Yes, Simon Hawke," Joanna repeated, with a firm nod. "And all this sordid activity, including the torturing of James Blackstone, was taking place in his art gallery, to which he held the only key, and yet he pretended to be unaware."

"He had to be aware," my father agreed.

"There were other clues as well to show he was deeply involved," Joanna continued on. "Recall that Hawke knew of Edmunds's skin condition, but we had to literally pry the information from him, for he did not want us to learn that Edmunds was responsible for the vandalism. Then there was the file box on his desk which contained all the restorations done at Hawke and Evans over the past year. He didn't seem to mind in the least for us to study the records, but attempted to prevent Delvecchio from doing so."

"He was frightened I might see the connections to the masterpiece," Delvecchio chimed in.

"*Esattamente.*" Joanna used the Italian word for *exactly*. "And of course we gave Harry Edmunds too much credit for being so clever. He was impressively clever because he had Simon Hawke guiding him every step of the way. Hawke knew many facets of the ongoing investigation and could alert Edmunds to possible risks and dangers. And the final clue was Simon Hawke waiting in his carriage behind the National Gallery in the dark of night for Harry Edmunds to hand over del Verrocchio's *The Baptism of Christ*."

"How did you predict that Hawke would be waiting behind the National Gallery?" Lestrade interrupted.

"There is no honor among thieves, Inspector," Joanna replied. "And now that both men knew of the exact location of the masterpiece, Hawke would be justifiably concerned that Edmunds would snatch the da Vinci and disappear."

"It was a stupid move on Hawke's part," said I.

"Greed often supersedes good sense," Joanna agreed. "In any event, when I handed him the del Verrocchio, he said and I quote, 'Ah, you have it!' With this in mind, I believe any hard-nosed British jury would find Hawke guilty and march him straight to the gallows."

"But they would have no evidence to merit capital punishment," Lestrade pointed out. "As a matter of fact, we have no proof that he was in any way involved or participated in the murder of James Blackstone."

"I believe you have that in your possession," said Joanna.

Lestrade's eyes narrowed. "Pray tell, madam, where can I find such evidence?"

"It will be found on the bricks that covered the lap of the corpse," Joanna directed. "You must restudy the fingerprints on their surfaces."

"But the only identifiable prints belonged to Harry Edmunds and David Hughes."

"But there was a third set which you have been unable to identify, is there not?"

"There is."

"I am confident you will discover they match nicely with those you obtain from Simon Hawke, for he is the sort of man who would find the torturing distasteful but would eagerly participate in hiding the corpse."

We spontaneously broke into applause at Joanna's remarkable deductions. She bowed with a cock of her head, much like a maestro acknowledging the adulation of his audience.

A brief blush came to her face before she returned to the business at hand.

"And the final piece of the puzzle is how the location of the hidden da Vinci was uncovered," Joanna recommenced. "Here, I cannot take full credit, for I required the assistance of Edwin Alan Rowe and Lady Katherine. Early on, Blackstone must have known that his life was in danger because of his insistence that the masterpiece be returned to the Crown. An honorable man, such as he, would devise a plan that could lead others to the da Vinci, should the worst befall him. He entrusted this scheme to his dear friend, Edwin Alan Rowe, in a riddle-game they often played. The message in the riddle was Angels to a Perfect Angel, which Rowe was unable to decipher. Then came the crucial clue, when Edmunds invaded the home of Sir Charles Cromwell and sliced open the painting by Botticelli, which showed angels that had been restored at Hawke and Evans. These were the leading angels Blackstone had mentioned in his riddle, for they had been painted by Sandro Botticelli who worked alongside Leonardo da Vinci in Andrea del Verrocchio's workshop. Now recall that Blackstone had restored both Botticelli's *Saint Francis of Assisi with Angels* and del Verrocchio's *The Baptism of Christ,* the latter containing the perfect angel, a subject upon which Mr. Rowe once wrote an enlightening monograph."

"The angel was so magnificent that del Verrocchio knew he could never match da Vinci's skill, and thus gave up painting and returned to sculpting," Rowe continued with the most interesting details. "Da Vinci's angel was said by all to be perfect in every way. This then was the perfect angel James Blackstone was referring to in his riddle."

"So very clever," Joanna noted. "He used Botticelli's

angels to lead us to da Vinci's, and da Vinci's angel led us to the masterpiece."

"Angels to a perfect angel," Lady Katherine repeated softly. "So it would seem in the end that James Blackstone outwitted his murderers after all. How remarkable!"

"And what is even more remarkable," said Joanna, pushing her chair back and reaching for her purse, "is that he did it from his grave."

CLOSURE

My father, young Johnny, and I sat around a cheery fire and sipped eggnog as we awaited Joanna, whom Lestrade had called and invited to witness a most pivotal and deciding clue. Thus, our four-wheeler had deposited Joanna at Scotland Yard while we continued on our way to Paddington station to fetch Johnny who had now completed his school activities at Eton. Of course the young lad asked question after question about the case of *The Art of Deception,* but was most interested in how his mother had tracked down the soon-to-be-famous original portrait of *Mona Lisa.* When told of the riddle left behind by James Blackstone, he gleefully rubbed his hands together and said, "There is truly nothing better than a mystery within a mystery!" My father and I exchanged delighted glances, for once again we were witnessing the genes of Sherlock Holmes residing at 221b Baker Street.

As more logs were being added to the fire, Joanna hurried in carrying two very gaily wrapped packages. After giving Johnny a warm embrace and tousling his hair affectionately, she came over and joined us at the fireside.

She accepted a brimming glass of eggnog with pleasure before explaining the ribboned packages. "They are gifts for Miss Hudson, who richly deserves them for her excellent attention to our needs."

"Hear! Hear!" I agreed heartily. "Might we know what they are?"

"A Harris tweed sweater from you, Watson, and me," Joanna replied. "And a beautifully stitched pair of leather gloves from Johnny, whom she cares about so deeply."

"Hear! Hear!" the three of us shouted approvingly.

"And now to Lestrade's pivotal clue, which will be a fine present for us all."

The three of us leaned in closer to catch every word.

"You will recall there was no definite evidence linking Simon Hawke to the murder of James Blackstone," Joanna went on. "Well, there is now. Mr. Hawke was good enough to leave his fingerprints on several bricks which sat upon the lap of the corpse."

"That may well merit a walk to the gallows," my father predicted.

"Or a very, very long stay at Pentonville, if the charge is accessory to murder," said Joanna.

"With all the misery he has caused to so many, I would not mind seeing his neck stretched," my father growled.

"And so it may be," said Joanna. "But now, let us turn to more joyful news. It appears that King Edward himself is mesmerized by the da Vinci portrait of the original *Mona Lisa* and has directed his treasury to issue a check for two hundred and fifty pounds as a reward to us for this most welcome discovery. But I instructed Lady Katherine to intercede on our behalf and see to it that the check is sent to James Blackstone's widow, for it was he who found the masterpiece and was instrumental in its return to the Crown."

"Well done, Joanna," I approved.

"You might also be interested to learn that Lestrade granted Giuseppe Delvecchio permission to return to Italy, for his testimony will not be required at the trial of Simon Hawke," Joanna reported. "Apparently, Delvecchio is being recognized throughout the art world as the restorer who uncovered the original *Mona Lisa* and has been offered a coveted position at the Uffizi in Florence."

"Well deserved," said my father.

"And now the very best present we could ever ask for," Joanna went on. "The Cromwell lad has regained consciousness and he is conversing with his overjoyed parents at this very moment. And when told of the reason for the home invasion, he immediately asked that he be allowed to see the da Vinci."

"I assume it can be arranged," said my father.

"It will be indeed," Joanna assured. "It is being seen to by the Countess of Wessex who we have learned never accepts the word *no* for an answer. Once the lad is up and about, he will be given a private showing."

"I should like so much to see it as well, Mother," Johnny requested earnestly.

"So you shall," Joanna promised. "And perhaps at the same time the da Vinci is shown to the Cromwells."

"The name da Vinci rings such a magical bell, does it not?" my father mused aloud.

"Indeed it does, Dr. Watson, for he was a true genius," Johnny said and reached for the volume of renowned Italian Renaissance painters, in which he had marked off a page. "Leonardo was not only a great artist, he was a scientist, anatomist, engineer, architect, and inventor. He was such a remarkably multitalented man that it makes one wonder why God did not create more like him."

"That is a question we should leave up to Watson, for wisdom is his forte, not mine," said Joanna.

Johnny turned to my father and asked, "Why did God not give us more Leonardo da Vincis, Dr. Watson?"

With a gentle smile, my father replied, "Because they were so difficult to make, I suspect."

"Hear! Hear!" we all shouted, and raised our glasses to toast the wisest of statements and the merriest of seasons.

ACKNOWLEDGMENTS

Special thanks to Peter Wolverton, for being an editor par excellence, and to Scott Mendel, for being such an extraordinary agent. And a tip of the hat to Danielle Prielipp and Hector DeJean, my superb publicists, and to David Rotstein, for his wonderful cover designs.

Steve Rosamilia

LEONARD GOLDBERG is the *USA Today* bestselling author of the Joanna Blalock medical thrillers. His novels have been translated into a dozen languages and were selections of Book of the Month, French and Czech book clubs, and Mystery Guild. They were featured as *People*'s "Page-Turner of the Week" and at the International Book Fair. After a long career affiliated with the UCLA Medical Center as a clinical professor of medicine, he now lives on an island off the coast of Charleston, South Carolina.